## WHAT PEOPLE ARE SAYING

Sarah Baughman manages to weave a warm and engaging tale of family and community life during an extremely tumultuous time in history while introducing the reader to fascinating characters and details of what we know as the Reformation. With a powerfully descriptive pen, Baughman will break your heart and mend it again with topics of loss, shame, honor, depression, and the challenges of family life. As an avid reader, as a wife and mom, and as a mental health professional, I found insight and application in every page of this meaningful work.

Heidi Goehmann
author of *Altogether Beautiful*

\*\*\*

Sarah Baughman is a gifted writer who not only brings detailed history back to life, but who also quietly weaves profoundly human stories of faith and love.

Colleen Oakes
author of the Queen of Hearts Saga

\*\*\*

Reading *A Flame in the Dark* is like stepping back into Reformation-era Wittenberg, Germany. Sarah Baughman carefully crafts a believable tale with a fresh perspective. Readers are treated to vivid and historically accurate descriptions of merchant-class life during this time period. The true delight of reading this book comes from seeing the ripple effect Martin Luther's teachings had on the faith of everyday people. Those who have wondered what it would have been like to live in Luther's Germany will thoroughly enjoy how Baughman's book skillfully portrays the rediscovery of the Gospel.

Sue Matzke
avid reader and pastor's wife

\*\*\*

Sarah's wonderful gift of storytelling exhilarates me. Her characters in this heart-stirring story each endure various trials and tribulations in their lives, and it isn't until they each assimilate God's teaching and His love do they find healing, peace, and joy. Even though this story takes place during the Reformation, the message in *A Flame in the Dark* is nevertheless prevalent today, tomorrow, and well into the future. I learned a lot about my own shortcomings reading Sarah's story, and I thank you, Sarah, for reminding me to seek God's words and His forgiveness.

Adriann Harris
book reviewer

\*\*\*

With historical detail and intrigue, Sarah Baughman will take you back to the days of Martin Luther and the turbulent time after Luther's Theses were nailed to the door in Wittenberg. If you enjoy historical fiction, be sure to add this one to your list!

Jamie Lapeyrolerie
*Musings of Jamie*

# A FLAME IN THE DARK

*A Novel about Luther's Reformation*

SARAH BAUGHMAN

CONCORDIA PUBLISHING HOUSE • SAINT LOUIS

Published by Concordia Publishing House
3558 S. Jefferson Avenue, St. Louis, MO 63118-3968
1-800-325-3040 · www.cph.org

Manufactured in the United States of America

---

Library of Congress Cataloging-in-Publication Data

Names: Baughman, Sarah (Sarah E.), author.

Title: A flame in the dark / Sarah Baughman.

Description: Saint Louis : Concordia Publishing House, [2018]

Identifiers: LCCN 2017048954 (print) | LCCN 2018013051 (ebook) | ISBN
        9780758660091 | ISBN 9780758660039

Subjects: LCSH: Brothers and sisters--Fiction. | Scandals--Fiction. |

        Vocation--Lutheran Church--Fiction. | Families--Germany--Fiction. |

        Religious fiction. | GSAFD: Christian fiction.

Classification: LCC PS3602.A9446 (ebook) | LCC PS3602.A9446 F53 2018 (print)

        | DDC 813/.6--dc23

LC record available at https://lccn.loc.gov/2017048954

---

1 2 3 4 5 6 7 8 9 10          27 26 25 24 23 22 21 20 19 18

*In memory of*

*Mary, my grandma who taught me to look for beauty in the simple and to serve others in Jesus' name;*

*Frieda, my grandma who taught me perseverance and patience in the face of hardship, and to always cling to Christ;*

*and Adele, my godmother who taught me to cherish life and the Word.*

*All three were women of grace, faith, and light.*

N

NW · NE

W · E

SW · SE

S

EMNELDA'S
COTTAGE

Friedrichstr

Elsterstrasse

Grosse

DIEFENBACH
HOUSE

MONASTERY
UNIVERSITY

Sedanstrasse

Elbe River

# PROLOGUE

## OCTOBER 1517

Autumn's morning fog swirled with each step he took, feet spurred on by the hope surging in his heart. Surely this would open the door for discussion, for debate. There were goings-on that he felt in his gut were not right and, further, that he found no support for in the Holy Scriptures. There must be a way to mend it, to repent and turn back to what was presented in the Word of God.

The more he read of that Word, the more certain he became. But years of training and thinking and *believing* did not simply dissipate like the mist about his feet. Steps forward were hindered by the mire of the past, of *his* past. Of the past of the church and the pasts of its people.

But he'd had a taste of mercy, and like the psalmist, he now saw that the Lord was good. And not only perfectly, condemningly good, but *graciously* good. Surely the bishops would see that too.

If he could but speak with them.

He'd reached the door of the *Schlosskirche*, just over an arm's length before him, and stopped. Seeing few other notices posted, and those old and weather-worn, he knew his theses would be seen. That is, if people took the time to stand there and read all ninety-five of them. Either way, posting them should open the way for debate and discussion, which may pave the way for change.

Spurred on by what he was convinced to be the Spirit's urging, he opened the roll of paper in his hand and stepped determinedly to the door.

CHAPTER

# 1

Heinrich marched down *Kollegienstrasse* toward the University of Wittenberg, the scrap of paper crinkling in his hand and absorbing perspiration from his palm. The ink on it would soon begin to run from the moisture. His hands were cold and clammy in the crisp, autumn air, even as his ears burned, slowly spreading first to his face and up to his sandy hair, then seeping down his neck to the rest of his body. The missive, obnoxious in its brevity, could not even be termed a letter, as it held only one sentence.

> *The Alscher family says I must leave by autumn, and unless I hear otherwise from you, I will proceed in my current plan to join a convent. —Brigita*

She must have had someone write it for her, with her name scrawled in her own hand at the end. Perhaps one of Alscher's sons or the man's wife. Brigita was only seventeen, much too young to be traveling alone to another city.

Crossing the courtyard of the university, Heinrich all but ignored the other young men around him, dressed similarly to his own black doublet and *Hosen,* his knee-length black cape billowing behind him as he moved. He was known to be a studious young man, with midnight blue eyes set in a serious face, and it seemed few of his peers noticed anything odd in his silence. He was cognizant enough of that small blessing despite his inner turmoil.

Long strides carried him swiftly to the lecture hall. The large room was nearly empty, excepting the professor and a scattering of students. Doctor Luther, known to the parishioners of the *Stadtkirche* as Father Martin, was bent over his book, scalp glistening in the middle of his tonsure. He scribbled furiously in the margins, stopping only to dip the tip of his quill in ink. Heinrich absently wondered how the good doctor could write with such a badly trimmed pen.

Turning toward his place, Heinrich suddenly realized that he had only a folio of loose papers and had left his bound copy of the Letter to the Hebrews in his room. Could the day grow any dimmer? The autumn rainclouds threatening the area were nothing compared to his mood. Forcing his thoughts away from his growing melancholy, he shoved the crinkled paper into the bottom of his satchel and waited for the lecture to begin. With every breath he took, he felt the tension seeping from his shoulders as his mind began to focus.

This room was comfortably familiar, with its shiny wood panels and tidy arrangement of rows of slanted desks. He'd spent so many hours in it over the past several years as he worked toward earning his doctorate in law, and the familiarity of the place was a much-needed balm to his troubled spirit.

Before long, other students began filtering into the room. Luther's lectures were wildly popular, and while punctuality at class was expected, students seldom showed such eagerness to arrive at other lectures as they did to this professor's. Heinrich had studied the Letter to the Galatians with Luther last year and there witnessed firsthand the friar's legendary skills in rhetoric and philosophy. His mind was astonishing and his humility even more so. When it was made known that Doctor Luther would be leading the students through the Letter to the Hebrews, Heinrich looked forward to it. If attending this lecture was not required for his course of study, Heinrich reasoned to himself, then further exposure to Luther's skills in rhetoric could only aid his own; never mind that when Luther read the Holy Scriptures to them, it seemed as though God Himself had delivered the messages they were hearing.

With a startling *screech*, Luther scooted back his stool and the assembly stilled; all sound in the room fell like leaves from a tree. His face appeared pale against the dark wood of the room and the brown of his habit as he gazed at his students, his eyes open, honest, and sparking with eagerness. Heinrich reached for the quill resting in the inkpot at his side of the bench-like desk, ready to write and forget about the trouble with his sister.

"A few of you, who have been here an extraordinary length of time, will recall," began Luther without preamble, "that when I lectured on the Psalms several years ago, we explored throughout the idea of God's righteousness. Here, in the Letter to the Hebrews, we see a further exploration of the implications of His righteousness as well as our righteousness, in the way the author describes Christ as the great High Priest and the manner in which His all-sufficient sacrifice atones for our unrighteousness, our sins. Some would argue that a person can act rightly and somehow do what is in him to placate the righteous God. But here we see that the opposite is true. All the sacrifices of the Israelites were merely pointing to Christ, for it is He alone who saves. Listen to me repeat myself, for this is of great importance: Christ alone can save."

Heinrich wrote as fast as he could. Thankfully, the lectures followed the book sentence-by-sentence, sometimes word-by-word, so he simply titled his notes "On Righteousness and Salvation." He would need to take some time later to look over them again and transfer them from his loose papers to his book's margins.

The lecture flew past, and before Heinrich knew it, Luther had dismissed them. With the dismissal, reality came crashing back on him. Heinrich stood numbly and began shuffling his papers into the folio. He almost didn't hear when someone spoke to him.

"Heinrich, will you come to the tavern with us?" asked Romauld, who had sat beside him. "Karl has a copy of Doctor Luther's Theses; we're going to discuss them over a tankard and bowl of stew."

"Not tonight," Heinrich declined. Any other day he'd have gladly accompanied them, but he was in no mood to fraternize at the moment. "I forgot my book and need to copy my notes while the lecture is still fresh in my mind."

Romauld nudged him with a good-natured grin upon his ruddy face. "The most studious Heinrich has forgotten his book! What will become of us average students?"

Heinrich managed a small smile and watched his classmate's energetic exit. With a shake of his head, he placed the borrowed quill into its inkpot and closed his folio, embossed with his family name. His father had commissioned it from a *Lederer* near their home in Braunschweig only months before his death last year. The death that caused Brigita, eight years his junior, to be sent to live with neighbors while he finished earning his doctorate in law. Neighbors whose protection she had left weeks ago. To an unknown convent.

Heinrich swallowed frantically against the knot in his throat, suddenly finding it nearly impossible to breathe.

"Young Ritter, are you well?" asked Luther, who was also gathering his books and papers.

"Yes, Doctor Luther. I've just received some news from home is all." He debated confiding in his professor.

The concern on the man's face was sincere, but it twisted something in Heinrich's gut and suddenly he could not give voice to his fears. "I must hurry, or there may not be any supper left for me," he joked half-heartedly. "Good evening, sir."

While it would have been quicker to avoid *Kollegienstrasse* and walk directly to Johann Diefenbach's shop, Heinrich instead walked westward along the bustling street until he came to the *Marktplatz*. He needed time to compose himself before meeting with the others.

The *Marktplatz* felt more like home to Heinrich than nearly any other place in Wittenberg. Located just across from the City Church, *Stadtkirche Sankt Marien*, the *Marktplatz* teemed with activity as the craftsmen sold their wares. Several of Heinrich's friends found the place to be too noisy and busy for their liking, but it put him in mind of Braunschweig, the much larger city where he had spent his formative years. Not every memory of his life with his father and sister was pleasant, but it was still his home.

Swallowed up by the *Markt*, Heinrich allowed the activity of the waning day to soothe his nerves. Some of the craftsmen had already packed up, but many of the small wooden booths were still filled with various goods made from fabrics, metals, wood, and foodstuff. The feelings of home that washed over him, the sounds and smells, calmed him and allowed his mind to focus clearly on his situation. Brigita's situation.

The note was not dated, but if she was to have left the Alscher family by autumn, she had left weeks, possibly even a couple of months, ago. He might be able to make a search for her, but that was only if he happened upon the correct convent. It had been his business, his burden, to care for his sister since their mother's death shortly after Brigita's birth and their father's subsequent melancholy. Hanz Ritter had saved carefully over the years, but for an education for his son rather than a respectable dowry for his daughter. It was the reason for Heinrich attending the University of Wittenberg, that he would take up law, earn a good living, and provide for his father in his old age, as well as contribute a sizable dowry for Brigita. Thankfully, if she truly did desire to enter a convent, her lovely voice would make her an asset to the choir, and they would likely overlook that he could not provide an endowment for the convent with her entry. But he didn't want her entering one because she saw no other options for herself.

By the time he emerged from the booths of the *Markt* and turned right on *Jüdenstrasse*, Heinrich felt ready to face Diefenbach's apprentices. Then, a left turn onto *Bürgermeisterstrasse* and he was there in a matter of minutes. This street, too, put him in mind of home; the narrow structures, packed tightly together, housed many of the town's master crafters. He greeted a metalsmith and a weaver before reaching the shop of Johann Diefenbach, the candlemaker. As he neared the building, unremarkable among a dozen others just like it, two men stepped from the door, locking it behind them.

Matthäus and Sïfrit were two very different men. While Matthäus was tall and broad, Sïfrit was of average height and slender. Matthäus's hair was dark, his beard a shade lighter, and his eyes were a kind, pale brown. Sïfrit's red-blond hair was shoulder length and wavy, his eyes a cold hazel, and his face clean-shaven, if he had anything to shave. Matthäus wore practical clothing that was sturdy, if a bit worn, in browns and grays. Sïfrit wore *Hosen* and a doublet with slashing, made from a fine green wool with yellow showing through the slashes. Matthäus wore an older style felt hat—a wide, circular thing with a stuffed band wrapped with cording and a single plume being the only decorations. Sïfrit wore a fine woolen hat with a tall crown and no brim that allowed his shoulder-length hair to hang free. The style had become popular throughout Germany recently, but just scarcely reached the small city of Wittenberg.

"Good evening, Matthäus, Sïfrit." Heinrich offered a strained smile to the younger of the two. He did not enjoy Sïfrit's company as much as Matthäus's, but tried to behave civilly toward him. "Did you sell well today?"

It had been Sïfrit's first day in the booth, and he had been speaking all week of how he would sell more than Matthäus, who had been manning the booth for more than two years and had served nearly his entire apprenticeship to the candlemaker. Sïfrit, barely more than a lad at nineteen years old, nodded his head. When he did not expound upon his excellent take for the day, Heinrich supposed he did not do so well as he'd boasted he would. Sïfrit moved ahead of the other two, so Heinrich offered to carry one of the crates Matthäus was hefting, and they fell into step behind Sïfrit.

"Think he's hurrying to go bother Marlein?" asked Matthäus quietly, an undercurrent of humor running through his words.

Heinrich forced a chuckle, though he found little amusement in the younger man sniffing around the Diefenbachs' eldest daughter. Besides being young, he was also entirely too full of himself. "She knows better than to listen to his self-absorbed overtures." The two watched as Sïfrit turned off onto a different street. "I suppose he plans to stop at the tavern on his way to the Diefenbach house."

Heinrich and Matthäus continued on their way, passing the monastery and university as they headed east on *Kollegienstrasse*, then along the road that led to Elster. In no mood for idle chatter, Heinrich was grateful for his companion's quiet and steady presence; Matthäus was never one to fill silence merely for the sake of filling it. Moving through the city gate, they turned northward, their booted feet taking them from the gravel road of the city to the dirt road outside of it. The ground had dried since the last rain, so rather than circumnavigating puddles, they walked easily on their way. As they went, Heinrich's thoughts swirled in a pattern of note, sister, convent.

Note, sister, convent.

Note.

Sister.

Convent.

Heinrich was so lost in his thoughts that the Diefenbach home was in sight before he knew it. The house stood about a twenty-minute walk from the edge of Wittenberg. The longer sides of the rectangular structure were lined with windows and squat to the ground, the steeply sloping roof meeting the walls at about the height of a man's head. The front and back walls were taller, angling up with the slope of the roof. As the men drew nearer, the contrast between the stone facing of the walls and the wattle and daub of the upper portion of the walls sharpened until the individual stones were discernible.

To the right of the house spread the stubbly field, barren until spring. The corner of the garden was visible from the side of the house, between the building and the field. Every so often, a small figure of some size or shape, a child, would dart out from the garden to the edge of the field, only to be chased back by another of the children. Despite his worry, a smile pulled at Heinrich's lips as he thought of Marlein out there with the children. She was likely in the garden to fetch some last-minute addition to the meal.

At the thought, though, his smile slipped downward until it was a frown. Marlein shouldn't be preparing the meal with four or five children, none of whom were hers, clinging to her skirts. Not without anyone to help. With a huff, he scraped his boots against the pebbles spread along the path near the house in an attempt to knock off most of the mud before entering the house. He knew Marlein had more than enough to occupy her time without the added nuisance of dirt from the road. Not that she would ever say such a thing.

The two men stepped onto the flagstone floor that served as a base for the entire house, even in the entrance alcove at the front of the house. The double doors nestled into the recessed space, sheltered from the elements. Wide enough for even the horses and cows to walk through when both were opened, the doors were made of thick, strong wood.

"Here," Matthäus said as Heinrich struggled to grasp the right door's carved handle with a few fingers extending from his hold on the crate. "Give it to me, then you can manage the door."

Heinrich nodded silently. He stacked his crate on top of the one Matthäus held and yanked on one of the doors, probably harder than necessary, if the way it swung violently open was any indication.

"Thanks," he managed gruffly.

"Of course," Matthäus responded, stepping past him into the house. Heinrich followed, closing the door more gently than he'd opened it. A black horse nickered and stuck his head over the half door of his stall, greeting his master with a whinny and a shake of his glossy mane.

"Hello, Jäger," Heinrich said to the animal, patting the white star in the center of the horse's face. "I promise I'll ride you tomorrow."

He hurried to catch up to Matthäus, who was already halfway across the *Diele* between the stalls that housed the family's animals. Chickens were opposite the stalls of Jäger and one of the Diefenbachs' horses. After the chickens came the cow, then the storage stall for their cart and saddles, and last, closest to the living area, was the more enclosed stall where the servant, Steffan, slept. Horses and the room storing winter feed took up the stalls along the left side of the house. The *Diele* was wide enough to tie a horse in while grooming or saddling, which they did on occasion, or to bring in the wagon the family owned when the weather turned bad.

"The air is almost cool enough to make me appreciate the heat of this hearth," Matthäus commented as he and Heinrich approached the living area of the house. Matthäus set both crates against the wall of Steffan's stall, and Heinrich realized he'd forgotten to take his crate back from the other man.

As Matthäus stood from his task, he turned and extended a hand to shake Johann Diefenbach's. The older man sat in his usual chair, a sturdy thing draped in several furs and soft wools, situated near the fire. "The shop is secured and prepared for the morning," Matthäus said to Diefenbach.

"Very good. And how are you fellows this evening?" he asked.

Heinrich allowed Matthäus to answer, not really listening to the conversation, but attempting to contrive an excuse to absent himself from the family that evening; he wasn't up to pretending all was well and did not feel equal to the task of explaining what was upsetting him. It would not be easy, unless he kept in his room; the house offered little privacy. The *Diele* opened up to the living area, which boasted a large, freestanding hearth at the place where the *Diele* and the *Flett* met. The hearth separated an area for sitting and talking near the side door that led to the garden from the other side, where the large table used for preparing food and eating sat. A window sat squarely on the far left wall, larger than those in the bedchambers or stalls, and was outfitted with glass as opposed to the simple shutters on the other windows. It provided a point of anchor for the table on the left side of the *Flett*, illuminating it with sunlight until day's end. Besides the window and the doors along the back wall leading to each of the four bedchambers, every place on the walls was hung with useful items: a metal tub; shelves with dried foodstuff, dishes, and mugs; tools and utensils hanging from pegs. Large candleholders suspended from the ceiling lit the area after the sun set. Crocks and barrels lined the walls between the four doors to the bedchambers, except for the few places occupied by seats. A bench sat between the two doors to the right of the hearth, and several chairs, including Johann Diefenbach's, sat opposite the bench that abutted the wall shared by Steffan's stall.

"I see you are still trying to become my apprentice," Diefenbach teased Heinrich. Heinrich had no answer, and so simply shrugged and attempted a grin. "I suppose your attention wandered and you didn't hear Matthäus admit that you helped to carry the crates of candles." Diefenbach shook his head, concern deepening the furrows in his brow. "Sïfrit will need to carry his own weight when you graduate."

Diefenbach was both kind and honest and treated guests, apprentices, and servants with respect and dignity. He had earned the status of master candlemaker some years ago and become a guildsman after he established himself as a man with an eye for the business of selling his candles and a leading resident of the small town. His unassuming appearance reminded Heinrich of a quiet, calm, cloudy day—bushy gray beard, soft gray eyes, and modest but quality gray clothes surrounding a round, open face—and reflected the quiet honor with which Diefenbach lived his life. In his wooden chair, covered with plush animal pelts, he scribbled in a small book with a nubby quill that Heinrich would have stopped using ages ago.

He clasped the older man's gnarled hand before going to store his satchel in his room, the farthest to the right and closest to the side door. The space was small, but cozy. The bed was built into the left wall, and a window opposite the door lit the space with sunlight, helping to warm the room in the winter. A small, oft-used desk allowed a place for Heinrich to attend his studies, and a chest occupied the right corner of the room and held his belongings. The room was lately occupied by the younger Johann, Diefenbach's son and firstborn, who was away serving an apprenticeship with a candlemaker in Magdeburg. Despite it being only a two-day walk northwest, the younger Johann Diefenbach was not able to leave his apprenticeship for even holy days, and so he had little use of the room while he was away. It served Heinrich well while he attended the University of Wittenberg.

Upon his arrival in the city, Heinrich had not been at all acquainted with the family, but his father was apprenticed to Diefenbach's father years ago. When Hanz Ritter wrote to his old master's son, applying to him to host Heinrich, Diefenbach's affirmative reply arrived with expediency. Hanz insisted upon forwarding payment for his son's keep, though he was told it was unnecessary. Due to his stringent mode of living, it was easily afforded and sent. Now, though, it all seemed to Heinrich such a waste of resources in the wake of his father's death and the possible loss of his sister.

Heinrich emerged from his room and found himself nearly knocked over by the four young girls scampering into the house from the side door, a blur of varying shades of pale hair, dark dresses, and undyed woolen aprons. Their chatter and giggles coaxed a small smile from him as he quickly closed his door behind him before any other people came through the side door that sometimes blocked his.

"*Vati!*" squealed four-year-old Maria, clapping her hands and sending up a puff of dust and dirt. She ran to Matthäus and wrapped her grimy arms around his legs, smudging the hem of his knee-length tunic.

"*Meine Tochter*. How has your day gone?" Matthäus lifted her in his arms, smiling broadly.

While the little girl chattered on, her dark-blonde head contrasting with her father's brown mop of hair, Heinrich heard someone close the side door behind him. He knew it was Marlein, but didn't turn around. Instead, he adjusted his stance subtly to stand a little more in her way, watching as Matthäus carefully set his little Maria on the ground.

"*Vati,*" she said as she reached for the hand of five-year-old Aldessa Diefenbach, "we want to pet the horses. May we, please?" They moved off toward the horses as he began a story about what mischief the horses might have gotten into that day.

"Ahem," said a firm voice behind Heinrich.

Heinrich turned to raise his eyebrows expectantly at her. "Yes, Marlein?"

"May I get through?" she asked after a moment of returning his expectant smile. "Or are you determined to behave like Sïfrit?"

Heinrich grunted, knowing she had put him in his place for attempting to tease her; he stepped back. Trying to keep the mood light—lighter than he felt—he followed her and asked, "Rough day?"

"Hm?" She was already headed to the table, the seven-year-old Leonetta trailing her closely. "What do you mean?"

"Your head is uncovered. Did you lose your *Steuchlein* somewhere?"

She looked upward, as though she'd be able to see the top of her light-brown hair to determine whether he was telling the truth. After reaching up to lightly touch the top of her head, she shrugged. "It appears I did. Oh! I remember. Herlinde," she explained, referring to the youngest of the Diefenbach girls, a chubby little child of three years, "threw a fit at the end of the midday meal, and I had to wrestle her into bed for a short sleep; it must be on the floor in the girls' room."

Marlein's smile was broad, causing her hazel eyes to sparkle before she turned to help Leonetta chop the herbs they had brought in, nearly the last of the garden's offerings. "Keep your fingers curved and pointing down, or you'll cut off the tips."

"And I don't want that!" answered Leonetta, shaking her head and grinning up at the young woman who was almost more mother than sister to her. Leonetta, carefully curving her fingers, finished chopping the herbs under her sister's watchful eye.

Marlein lifted her head, grinning in Heinrich's direction before she shooed her sister away. "You can go listen to Matthäus's stories, if you wish. I will clean up today."

"Really?" Leonetta didn't wait for her sister to answer before she pulled off her apron, tossed it haphazardly onto its peg, and took off for the front room.

The relief on Marlein's face once the girl was gone was almost comical.

"Has she been helping much today?" Heinrich asked, hiding his laughter.

"Yes. And she spilled barley. All over the floor." Marlein pushed some strands that had escaped her braided hair away from her face before turning to step through the door farthest to the left, near the table. She returned shortly with her *Steuchlein* dangling from her fingers. "She wants so badly to help with everything, but she is still so young. The barley bag was too heavy for her, the table too high for her to easily control the knife while chopping, and I won't even try to understand how she thought of trying to get to the pot that had been hanging out of her reach this morning."

Taking the seamed center of the fabric and settling it over the middle of her head, Marlein pulled it snug over the braided crown of her hair before beginning to slowly twist the ends of the cloth, wrapping them about her head as she went. "Needless to say, it's been a long day."

"She will grow," Heinrich attempted to comfort her, as the slight crease between her dark eyebrows remained. "I remember when Brigita started trying to help with things . . ." but he stopped himself, suddenly remembering the note, the uncertainty, the fear. His stomach lurched and twisted, his breath stuttered, and his heart felt like a stone sinking in the depths of his gut. He gritted his teeth and swallowed again. "How is your mother today?"

Heinrich held back a grimace as the easy smile on Marlein's face dissolved and her hands stilled, hovering over the *Steuchlein* she'd just wrapped. He'd escaped his pain by mentioning hers and despised himself for it.

"She is as she always is." Marlein's voice was hushed, as her father sat ten paces away by the fire. She lowered her hands and briskly stepped up to the table to chop some of the larger pieces of herb that Leonetta had left behind. "This morning she was working so intently in the garden that I hoped it would be a good day. After lunch, though, she grew lethargic and has been in bed since."

He nodded, unsure what to say. Since before his arrival almost four years ago, Keterlyn Diefenbach had struggled. Lately, though, it seemed to be worsening. Marlein looked remarkably like her mother, with similar height and features. But where Marlein was hearty and hale, Keterlyn was sickly and wan. Where Marlein's hazel eyes sparked with light and life, Keterlyn's were dull and listless. Where Marlein's hair was shiny and healthy—the few times he had seen it unbound—Keterlyn's frequently hung limp and thin just past her frail shoulders.

"Tell me, though," Marlein spoke up, changing the subject, "where is Sïfrit? He made a point of telling me he would be at supper when I brought Emnelda's beeswax to the shop earlier today."

"I can't say; he should have arrived before us," he replied. Undesirous of discussing Sïfrit and realizing he oughtn't eat supper in his school clothes, Heinrich murmured, "Excuse me, I should go change."

Focusing on the task of undressing, of performing another part of his usual routine, helped keep his worries at bay for a brief time. The students' garb was not necessarily uniform, but it did distinguish them from the people of the town. His cape he hung on its peg on the wall, beside the door to his room. Then he removed his doublet and the shirt under it. The collar, the trim, the stockings—all indicated his status as a student. While the demarcation did not bother him most days, today he found himself frustrated with the reminder that he was not free to simply pack his things and go search for his sister. He *could* leave his studies to find Brigita, of course. But at what cost?

Quickly re-dressing in a simple shirt and jerkin and pulling on brown breeches over his stockings, he tied the laces in the front of the jerkin, adjusted the billowing sleeves of his shirt, and stepped back into his shoes. He was almost completely resolved; he would not leave now. But as soon as lectures recessed after this term, he would take his horse, Jäger, and head for Braunschweig, searching every convent along the way.

When he opened his door, he saw that the children had migrated from Matthäus and were now gathered around Diefenbach. As he passed them, he heard the man describe a knight's dangerous journey in a foreign land. On the other side of the hearth, Sïfrit was trying to corner Marlein behind the table. Relief smoothed the features of her face when she glanced in Heinrich's direction and saw him approaching.

"There you are, Sïfrit!" he called. "We were just wondering where you'd got off to." He strode over and clapped the younger, slightly shorter man on his shoulder.

"Heinrich." He stepped back, allowing Marlein to move out from behind the table with the roughly carved wooden bowls she had gone there to retrieve. "Well, if there's nothing I can do to help," Sïfrit said, "I'll go and visit with your father, Marlein. Someone's got to keep those rascals from bothering him."

Heinrich felt a smirk tilt his lips as he met Marlein's eyes. They both knew how her father adored the children and cherished his time with them.

"Heinrich, would you pull the chicken pies from the oven?" she asked as she picked up a knife. "I made bread earlier—when Netta spilled the barley—and need to cut it now; I'd ask you to, but you nearly destroyed the last loaf you cut."

"Of course," Heinrich laughed. He helped her on occasion, when she couldn't quite manage the children and the food at the same time. He was mildly heartened by the knowledge that she had grown comfortable asking him for help when she needed it; she so seldom did. With little difficulty, he managed to pull the golden pastries enveloping pieces of chicken onto the paddle and remove them from the low oven. Two years ago, Marlein had been so excited when the stone mason completed the small, dome-shaped structure. It now felt as much a part of the rectangular fireplace as he felt of the family.

Marlein had just finished cutting the hearty bread into chunky slices when he carried the paddle with the chicken pies over to the table. Heinrich learned upon moving to Wittenberg that while the Diefenbach household indulged more than his spendthrift father had, the finer, more costly wheat flour was still reserved for special occasions. Barley and oat breads were most commonly found on Marlein's table.

Everyone sat at the table, listened to Diefenbach recite the obligatory blessing, and began eating. Several of the family's wooden bowls had been broken or lost over the years, so the children shared two to a bowl, and the servant, Steffan, ate balancing his food on a piece of the hearty bread. Keterlyn still did not come out. Instead, Marlein carried a bowl into her parents' room and returned with little Fridolin on her hip. She sat and began to eat too, handing her brother, who'd turned a year old in the summer, pieces of food from her bowl. The toddler chortled happily with each bite, clapping chubby hands and bobbing his white-blond head merrily. Lively conversation swirled around Heinrich, the food warming and filling him until he felt mostly content with his decision to wait for word from Brigita—for the time being. Wishing he could pray as Luther encouraged them to—as children to their dear father—he instead merely hoped. He felt that he could bear any circumstance so long as his sister had not taken any lasting vows; he did not wish to be alone in a world where his only relative was cloistered far away from him.

After supper, Marlein rounded up the older children to help her tidy the kitchen. Fridolin played on the flagstone floor near the men, who kept him from the fire. Marlein could not help but wish for the days when she sat upon the knee of her *Vati* and watched as he trimmed the candles. He'd even begun allowing her to help trim, until the time came that she was needed to help with the cooking or cleaning or sewing . . . all the little chores to keep the household functioning.

But she still knew the process. Each man had a small knife; she'd seen Heinrich several times withdraw his from inside his boot after he'd settled on the bench. Using their knives, each man drew a candle from the crates brought from the shop and cut off the irregularly shaped bulge at the base of the candle. The bulge had formed as the wick, tied at its base to a round metal weight, was dipped repeatedly in the melted wax. As wax built up on the wick, forming the candle, excess wax dripped and collected on the weight. The weight had to be removed from the candle and used the next day. Time after time she'd watched her father's large, knotty hands perform the task. Starting from the cut side, he'd work his knife along the small length of wick until he dug out the weight. After scraping off as much of the hardened wax as possible, the circular piece of metal, with the braided cord of the wick's end tied to it, was ready for the next candle.

"Here, Aldessa. Wrap the last of the bread in this cloth. It should be enough to thicken the stew for tomorrow." Her little sister, hair the color of a ripened wheat field, scooted along the bench, away from the window she'd been peering through. The kitchen window was a series of glass triangles and somewhat larger than many windows of even the wealthier people of Wittenberg; her father wanted to have light in his house in the daylight hours to lessen the need for candles during the day. He reasoned that even if they had plenty of candles, the fewer they used, the more they could sell.

Marlein handed the rag to seven-year-old Leonetta and the short, stubby broom to Maria, Matthäus's daughter. Though only four, Maria was always eager to help.

"Be sure to gather all the crumbs, girls," she admonished them. "It won't do to attract rats."

"Eww!" they cried together before they settled in to their tasks, their exclamations dissolving into giggles.

Smiling at their friendship, Marlein took a cask of wine from its place on a shelf near the table and turned to the hearth. As she poured the wine into the pot hanging over the fire, the men's conversation drifted to her ears.

"Have you read Father Martin's Theses? Someone translated them into German; I saw it today. He posted them just days ago, and already people are bandying about his irreverent ideals. I can hardly imagine a silly friar having such gall as to question the church," groused Sïfrit.

"Hush, boy," said Diefenbach before Heinrich could even formulate a response. "Saints know, Prince Frederick prizes him. And he is a priest; you should have more respect for his office. Besides, you know that Heinrich attends his lectures on the Letter to the Galatians and thinks well of him."

"Actually, we are studying Hebrews now."

Through the open hearth, Marlein could see that Heinrich was studying the candle in his hands, perhaps as a means of avoiding eye contact with the others. He'd been quiet at supper, bordering on taciturn. It was unusual for him.

She turned to place the cask back on the shelf and then retrieved some spices—cinnamon and nutmeg—from beside it. When she returned to add the spices to the wine, she heard that someone had coerced Heinrich to speak again.

"Likely we will finish soon. I wonder what he will lecture on next?"

"If he's so constantly studying, when does he have time to write these Theses and stir up trouble?" asked Sïfrit.

Marlein knew from previous discussion with Heinrich that he enjoyed Luther's lectures, but he remained quiet. She supposed that whatever had sent him into this fit of melancholy suppressed any desire he had to engage in a debate over what the professor was saying or writing. She crouched a bit, pretending to stoke the fire beneath the now-simmering pot, to hear whether he'd respond. She glanced at him. He set the knife between his teeth while using his fingers to smooth out the raw edge of the candle's base.

When no one said anything, Matthäus offered, "I suppose we find time for what is important to us."

As Marlein turned to shoo the girls from the table into their shared room, the men settled into a quiet rhythm of trimming candles. She followed the girls, pausing to glance at her parents' room, hoping that Keterlyn might emerge to kiss her children goodnight. The door remained closed, with no sound coming from within. Pushing down a sigh, Marlein entered the girls' room and set down the sweet-smelling beeswax candle she'd taken from the *Flett*. She set to the task of untying the kirtles of the four girls, helping them slip the overdresses over their heads. Left in just their shifts, they all took turns using the pot before piling into the one bed built into the wall, Leonetta being the only exception. Marlein smiled at their giggles. It was rare for Herlinde not to cry for her *Mutter*, and Marlein was grateful for the reprieve this night.

"Now settle down. I'll say a prayer over you and ask the Blessed Mother to keep you well in your sleep."

"Ask Christ our Lord too, Marlein!" Leonetta's voice was very serious. "Father Martin said in his sermon last week that He cares for us too."

Marlein nodded, thinking of the prayers she knew, and whether any met both criteria, or if she would need to recite two. She felt that prayers were good, though they seemed to help very little. She prayed nightly for her mother, but nothing seemed to change.

After the three youngest had been tucked beneath the covers, Maria on the edge for Matthäus to more easily retrieve her when he returned to his room above her father's shop, Marlein guided Leonetta from the girls' *Stube* and into their own. She placed the candle on the shelf on the wall.

"Why do most of our priests say in their sermons that praying to saints is good, but Father Martin does not?"

Marlein started at Leonetta's question. She set the pot, covered with a cloth, on the floor beside the door before helping Leonetta climb into the bed they shared.

"What do you mean, Leonetta? I hadn't noticed."

"Well, do you remember when that very tall, very thin priest gave the sermon?" Marlein nodded. "He spoke nearly the entire sermon about praying to the saints and how their treasure of merit will help us. Father Martin never says that. Or, if he used to, I can't remember."

"I'm not sure, dear." Marlein was often bouncing young Fridolin on her hip in recent days, to keep him quiet during the service, but Father Martin's sermons were spoken with such fervor that she remembered most of them, and Leonetta was correct; she could recall very few instances of his praising prayers to saints. Of the other priest, she remembered only his sallow face and sunken eyes, rather than the words he'd spoken. "I know that Father Martin has taken pains to teach us during his sermons that God loves His children, and that we are those children."

"Do you suppose that he thinks the saints are bad?"

Marlein shook her head. "No, he still tells us to follow their example. I think, though, that perhaps he wants us to think more of God than we do of them."

"Because He is our Father! I remember he said that once. No, more than once. Twice?"

"I think he says it every Mass." Marlein tucked Leonetta into their bed. "Remember when we pray 'Our Father, who art in heaven,' we ourselves call Him our Father."

Leonetta nodded, her blonde hair looking almost brown in the dim light. "Yes."

"Good night, sweet sister."

Marlein blew out the candle and took up the pot before returning to the *Flett*. She slipped over to scoop up Fridolin, who had a chubby fist in his mouth. Her father smiled at her, his eyes tired and more wrinkled of late, as she took the toddler over to the table to prepare him for bed.

Marlein cleaned up his face, which had bits of supper smeared across his chubby cheeks.

"Let's go to bed." She carried him into her parents' room, cringing when the door creaked a bit on its hinges. "Quiet now."

Still cradling Fridolin in her arms, Marlein knelt to place him on his small mat in the corner beside the wall near the hearth when a tired voice reached her ears.

"Please bring him to me," it croaked.

Marlein swallowed her feelings—conflicted and uncertain as they were—and approached the lump in the bedclothes of her parents' bed. It was the only bed in the house that was not built into the wall, but rather stood in the center of the slightly larger room beneath a canopy that hung from the ceiling to trap in warmth during the cold months.

"He ate well at supper and used the pot just now."

She could scarcely make out the contours of Keterlyn's face as the woman nodded, reaching her hands for the small tot. She took him and clutched him to her bosom, silent sobs racking her body.

"Do you need anything, *Mutter*?" Marlein asked as she glanced at the side table, where she'd left the bowl. The food was still in it, cold by now. Still, she wouldn't take it up until morning. On occasion, Keterlyn had roused herself to eat in the middle of the night.

"No, *Tochter*," she croaked. "My milk's long dried up, but I still ache for the baby to drink."

Marlein wasn't certain how best to respond, so she simply laid a gentle hand on her mother's frail shoulder. At one time, it had been as strong as her own.

"Sleep well, *Mutti*," Marlein whispered, bending to leave a light kiss on Keterlyn's head.

Back in the main part of the house, the men's conversation had drifted to the number of candles produced with the last batch of wax from Emnelda Steuben's bees and whether they had enough tallow candles in stock for deliveries scheduled in three days' time. Marlein allowed the mundane nature of it to comfort her, breathing deeply of the aroma of the wine and spices as she stirred it with her wooden spoon. She thought perhaps it was the one Matthäus carved for them after one of the children broke an older one trying to swat at a fly.

"If we weren't so free with candles for those who can't afford to pay, we would not be in danger of failing to meet orders." Sïfrit seemed set on complaining this evening, and Marlein found a slight smile tugging at her lips when Heinrich coughed over what sounded suspiciously like a grunt, though he said nothing.

"Perhaps," her father answered. "But we have been blessed with land to grow food and graze our animals, and with full bellies every day. How can I then withhold caring for another? It would be selfish in every way to pursue only my own gain." He spoke slowly and with great patience.

Marlein had just returned from fetching four tankards from a shelf near the table when there was a quiet but startling clatter near Heinrich. She poured the wine, ducking to see through the hearth as the other three men's eyes looked at him.

"Ow!" she whispered as some of the wine spilled over her hands. She hurried to wipe the offending hot liquid onto her apron. When she looked back to the men, Heinrich was stooping from his seat to reach for his knife on the flagstone floor, which had caused the clatter. Marlein grasped two tankard handles in each hand and walked around the hearth just as Sïfrit scoffed, preparing to say something.

"Forgive me for interrupting," she interjected, "but I've warm, spiced wine. Would anyone care for some?"

Sïfrit was sitting closest to her, so she handed him a stein first, and then moved on to her father. After Matthäus took one from her, she stepped over to Heinrich, handing him the wine as she took the candle from his hand. Sitting beside him on the bench, she inspected his work. She hoped her presence offered support against whatever was troubling him.

"You do this very well," she murmured as her fingertips tested the smoothness of the candle's base. "Even, and expertly cut. Your father taught you well."

Heinrich nodded, taking a sip from his stein. He did not speak of his family often, and she hoped she hadn't overstepped with her words. His face was neutral, but his voice a bit strangled as he replied, "He did well in his trade, but when he saw my aptitude for learning, he began saving to send me to Latin school."

"And now you have nearly finished earning your doctorate in law."

"Yes." Heinrich reached for another candle as he set his stein upon the floor beside the bench. "It's a shame he won't see it, but at least he knew it would happen."

"He would be proud of you, without question." After a moment, she asked, "How is your sister? Have you heard from her lately?"

Heinrich shook his head, fiddled listlessly with the candle in his hands, and stared blankly into the fire. It seemed their conversation was over. Feeling the familiar sense of her own insufficiency to help, Marlein rose from her place on the bench. It was time to prepare for bed.

Brigita carried her shame like a torch in her heart. It scorched and charred her, but by now, she had almost grown accustomed to the pain. It had burned away so much of her, too much for her to still be the same person she once was. Even so, she had to push it deeper still, for she had just reached Coswig, mere hours from Wittenberg—and her brother. She wasn't certain she could make it, despite how close she had come to him. She was on foot, and her pursuers likely had horses at their disposal and must know where she was going; they would surely overtake her soon. If, however, she could reach Wittenberg before they reached her, she was certain that Heinrich would protect her.

Very few souls were out in the streets of the small village that evening. As the sun disappeared below the horizon, it ripped apart the gray-blue sky with streaks of red and purple and finally a deep blue so like her brother's eyes that Brigita's heart ached to look at it. She hovered near the edge of the cluster of buildings, hoping to find some source of food. She would not work for it or beg for it, for she could not risk being seen.

They would be here soon. She knew it without a doubt.

So instead of knocking on the door to her right that a kind-looking woman had just closed, Brigita ducked behind the building to her left, finding a small shack built onto its rear stone wall. The shack had a collection of rough-hewn boards passing for a door that matched the boards of the walls. Inside, she was assaulted by the heady aroma of hay and manure. A goat bleated at her from its place tied to the far wall.

"Well, hello there, girl," Brigita murmured, picking up a handful of the sweet-smelling hay and holding it out for the goat. "Hungry, are you? So am I."

But she couldn't eat the hay, and the bag Sister Margreth had given her was now empty. Perhaps it was foolish to try to throw her pursuers off her trail, but she had done just that, at least so far. And now, due to the backtracking and hiding that had slowed her journey, she had not eaten in a day and a half. Nausea assailed her, and she ran from the building, retching just outside the rickety door. Her stomach heaved violently, unproductively. After several moments, she was finally able to stand upright, belching several times. Stumbling back into the building, Brigita offered the goat another handful of hay before she collapsed into the rest of the pile. She wiggled and burrowed until she was covered.

"Achoo!"

The sneeze caught her off guard, but it did not seem to bother the goat who made no sound. Exhaustion swept over her again, as it had several times during the past several days of her journey. Eyes closed, she started to drift toward sleep.

"Are you certain she hasn't been through here?" Brigita's eyes popped open and the familiar voice set her stomach to roiling again. Nikolaus. She buried her mouth in her arm, trying to calm her revulsion; though she could not see him, she easily called up an image in her mind of his fair hair and icy eyes, the sneer nearly always on his thin lips, the almost-hook of his nose. She suppressed a shudder. "She's a tiny little thing, hair the color of unbleached linen and eyes pale blue. Likely dressed as a peasant."

"No strangers came through here," said an unfamiliar voice,

though Brigita could imagine it belonging to the old woman she saw.

"You say her trail ran cold in Magdeburg?" questioned another man, whose voice she recognized as belonging to Bartolomäus. "Perhaps she is still there." Hearing that he was helping search for her settled into her heart like a heavy rock. She'd imagined the whole family would be glad never to see her again.

"I was sure she'd have run to her brother. Maybe she's already there." A pause. "Or maybe you're right and we should return to Magdeburg and make a more careful search there. If she's with Heinrich, she will stay with him. And if she isn't, there's no sense alerting him that she's left."

"Either way, I can spare little more time away from the shop. For what purpose did you say you need to find her?"

Footsteps and the fading voices hinted that the people were moving off, and Brigita slowly lifted her head, straining to hear. Did they already know of her hiding place and were trying to frighten her into running so they could catch her? The hay scratched and poked, but she didn't dare shift anything to make herself more comfortable. She heard heavy footsteps move farther away and a door close. The goat bleated, a horse whinnied in the distance, and all was still.

Her heart raced, her lungs burned, and her eyes welled with scalding tears. As she lay on her side in the hay, the tears spilled, leaving hot tracks as they trailed from her eyes, dripping across her nose into her other eye and down her temple to land in the hay beneath her head. It would be a miserable, sleepless night, she was sure, but at least it seemed she would be safe for a brief time, until light from the sun once again demanded that she return to her journey.

\*\*\*

Nikolaus Alscher could have kicked himself, if he wasn't so angry with *her* for running. Sure, he'd told her that he lied when he said he loved her, and that it was a good thing she was heading to a convent, as no one would want such a scrawny slip of a woman, but he hadn't counted on her leaving so quickly. She'd disappeared weeks before she was appointed to go.

*Women.*

Now, though, he wished he'd pretended to her a little more, let her keep believing that he loved her. He would surely have benefited from an arrangement with her. After all, her brother still owned the shop next to his family's. As the second Alscher son, he would have to either serve his older brother or find his own way. A shop given to him in place of a dowry—he truly doubted that the girl had much of one—would not be a bad start to a life of independence for him. True, it was a chandler's shop and not a smithy's, but several modifications would see to that. Perhaps he would work in another metal than did his father and brother. If only he'd known a couple of months earlier that Heinrich didn't plan to keep the shop, he would not have waited so long to go after her. It wasn't until he received a letter, filled with a great deal of regret and shame on her part, that he finally realized how advantageous a marriage to her could be.

"Come on, Bartolomäus." He mounted his horse and turned the beast westward. "Let's not continue to Wittenberg. If we alert her brother, he'll know she fled. As it is, he won't expect to see her until spring, when he'd planned on visiting her after the school term, so we have time to find her before he grows suspicious."

"Did she not send a message to him?" Bartolomäus asked. "You hired the courier yourself."

Nikolaus shook his head. "I told her I would hire a courier to deliver her note, but I hid it in the bottom of Mother's sewing basket. She clears it out so rarely that I knew it would be at least a month before it was sent. At first, I simply didn't want Heinrich to hear that I'd been bothering her. Now, though, it's allowing me the time to find her and marry her before he gets involved."

They rode through the shadowy village until they found the tavern, as the sky had grown dark and they could not leave Coswig until morning. He might not be above a bit of thievery to gain what he wanted, but he would not risk being assaulted by a robber himself. Nikolaus and Bartolomäus enjoyed several tankards of strong beer, along with plates of thick stew and a wedge of coarse bread. Tomorrow, they would return the way they'd come, and with enough prayers to the right saints, he would find his runaway nun-to-be and conscript her into his own service, rather than the Lord's.

# 5

Matthäus Falk, carrying an earthen crock, easily kept stride with Marlein as they walked to a small cottage just east of Wittenberg. They were delivering candles and bread to the family dwelling there. The father, an unskilled laborer, had been struck down by an injury. Matthäus was unclear on the nature of it, but he knew that without Marlein's kindness, the family would have starved.

He stood back as Marlein knocked gently upon the door.

"Yes?" asked the woman who answered the door. Her head was uncovered, her thin hair in disarray and a small girl clinging to her skirts.

"Good morning, Jonatha. I have here some candles and bread to trade for your fats. My father needs more tallow."

The woman's wan face lit up a bit, her eyes brightening and her thin lips curving slightly. "Yes, let me fetch them."

She turned, leaving the door open. The little girl stayed behind and stared up at Matthäus with wide eyes. She reminded him of his Maria when she was just beginning to walk. He smiled at her, and her bow-shaped lips curled upward.

"I have just a little," the woman said apologetically as she returned, carrying a small crock. "We don't have much meat most days."

"Well, we are collecting from several families," Matthäus spoke up, "so between yours and theirs, I think we will have enough."

She nodded awkwardly and tilted her crock into the larger one he held. The fats fell into the crock with a *plop.*

"*Danke,*" he said.

"I've two loaves of barley bread and several candles," Marlein said quietly, pulling back the fabric covering her basket. "I should be able to bring some fish and maybe a small roast later this month, as we'll be slaughtering several of our stock soon."

The woman's pale face suddenly reddened, but she nodded and said, "Thank you. I've asked the owner of this land to allow our Fritz to trap some hares; he has in the past, so long as Fritz brings some to him. I hope to have more fat next time you come."

Matthäus noticed she didn't quite meet Marlein's eyes as she accepted the bread and candles.

"That sounds good. Little Fritz is quite good at trapping, is he not?"

Pride raised the woman's eyes for the first time; she smiled as she said, "Yes, he's clever with a snare. Just about as old as your sister Leonetta, I'd say, and has been trapping since he was four."

"Well, I'm glad to have your fats. I'll be back next week, if that suits you?"

"Yes, Marlein." Her voice grew hoarse. "*Danke,*" she said as she handed the bread to her daughter to accept the candles from Marlein's outstretched hand.

"Think nothing of it." Marlein began to turn around, but stopped. "Oh, and I think I saw some wild carrots growing in the woods near our house. You and your girl are welcome to come and dig up as many as you can carry."

The woman nodded, murmuring another "*Danke.*"

After they had bid the woman goodbye, Matthäus looked sideways at Marlein as they walked toward the city wall surrounding Wittenberg. The tallow candles and bread she'd given the woman more than compensated for the meager amount of fats. He knew this. Marlein knew this. Jonatha Eilerts knew this. But he said nothing about it, hoping that someday he could be as generous as the Diefenbach family.

Before long, they arrived at *Kollegienstrasse* and began following it toward the town center. As they walked, he reflected not for the first time that Marlein was a kind and gracious woman. He could do worse in finding someone to be a mother for his daughter. Marlein would have no grand ideals of love, as she was much too pragmatic for such fancies.

Yet he hesitated.

Certainly, there was the question of whether the guild would allow him to marry before achieving status as a master chandler. But that was not the primary difficulty for Matthäus in seeking a wife. Just as he had been bound—heart and soul—to his deceased wife, Petrissa, in her life, he was now bound to his guilt in her death. It haunted him, followed him. He stumbled over it often and felt its icy grip upon his heart throughout the day and the night.

Besides, even if he found a way to be free, he had nothing with which to provide for a wife. Marlein's father was no nobleman, but he provided a better life than Matthäus could ever hope to offer. After making that mistake once, he did not plan to do so again.

No, a wife was out of the question until he had established himself as a master chandler in some town somewhere. Perhaps away from Saxony, away from anyone who knew him. Only then might he be free to entertain such thoughts. Perhaps. If he ever found a way to forgive himself for Petrissa's death.

***

Brigita had awakened hours before to the insistent bleating of the goat, confused at the noise and the straw in her hair. Instantly, the previous evening had come back to her, and she jumped up from her hiding place. With a steadying breath, she'd shaken out her dress and hair as best she could, startling the goat into kicking nervously against the wall.

"Sorry, little friend," she had whispered before picking up her empty sack and peeking through the door of the small structure. Seeing no one, she'd slipped out, sighing in relief when the door made no sound closing on its leather hinges.

But that had been hours ago. Her journey from the space she'd occupied with the she-goat had been uneventful, but tense. She ducked into the hedges along the roadside every time she saw a traveler. Her journey thus far had taken most of the day rather than the half day it should have been. She knew the risk of encountering a wild animal was greater off the road, but she'd much rather take her chances with that than be seen by her pursuers if they'd decided to go ahead to Wittenberg after all.

Now, she saw Wittenberg ahead of her. It was so close.

Legs trembling and burning from so much walking with no nourishment for nearly three days, Brigita stumbled forward. She must keep going. To think of something besides the cold of the air and the pain in her legs, she grasped the rosary hanging from her belt and began reciting the *Pater Noster* again. She suddenly lurched forward, catching herself on her hands and knees. Her foot had caught in a rut. Her prayer interrupted, she instead began to pray to St. Christopher, asking for protection and mercy. She knew she deserved no mercy, but hoped that the prayers she recited would allow her some measure of protection.

She was so close. If only she could reach her brother, all would be well. She dreaded confiding to him the reason for her flight, why the convent did not work for her, but she knew it was better than any alternative. Fear coursed through her, lending strength to her body. And she ran.

She ran as fast as she could, the torch in her heart burning brighter than ever, urging her forward, threatening to consume her.

# 6

Marlein walked with Matthäus to her father's shop. She did not enter with him when he carried the earthen crock through the door, but waved from the threshold. The men were melting down the fats, and the whole place stank. It was their livelihood, but she was thankful that her responsibilities fell more in the realm of keeping the house than keeping the shop. She was also thankful that the shop, where her father's family had lived ever since they secured the building some few generations before, was not their living place.

Her father met her at the door with several short, stocky candles formed around sturdy wicks. They would burn brightly and, in the safety of a lantern, would even withstand windy weather.

"Here, *Vater*. I've bread and cheese for your meal," she said, reaching into her large basket. She'd been forced to push down rising guilt at not sharing the cheese with the Eilerts. Her first responsibility, as she was often compelled to remind herself, was to her family. "Oh, and some apples."

"Thank you, Marlein," he answered. "How is your *Mutter*?"

Marlein paused, wishing she could give a better report. "She was working in her garden when I left, the children with her."

"Ah." He nodded, and she imagined he was not surprised by her answer, but disappointed nonetheless. It seemed the only thing that could stir the woman to action anymore was her garden. "It is good she finds occupation for her time."

Marlein pressed her lips together, hiding a sigh, before answering. "*Ja*. It is." She smiled a goodbye to her father and turned to walk southward down *Bürgermeisterstrasse* before heading through the city, the *Stadtkirche Marien* to her left and the *Marktplatz* to her right.

The streets were rather busy, it being midday. As she arrived at the *Markt*, she passed a group of students, likely enjoying a brief break before they needed to be at their next lecture. She would be buying nothing, but paused at several of the wooden booths to visit with the people she knew.

"Good morning, Marlein Diefenbach!" said Albrecht Klaus, a widower of middle age with two children. The towheaded girl and boy were stacking the baskets their father made, sorting them by size. "Are you ready to marry me yet?"

Marlein laughed good-naturedly, but shook her head. "You know my family needs me still." It was a longstanding joke that Klaus never seemed to find dull.

"Soon then?"

"I cannot say," she returned, rather than outright deny him. She doubted he was serious in his weekly question, but she had no wish to be unkind on the chance that he was. Truthfully, she intended never to marry. Her family needed her too much, for if she did not bake bread and cook food, who would do it? The other children were too young. Even if, in ten years, Leonetta and the other girls could do all the cooking and mending, she would be past marrying age. If the time came that her family did not need her, she planned to live the rest of her days as a nun in one of the convents dotting the country.

Marlein continued through the bustling collection of merchants and craftsmen. When she passed a weaver, though, a lovely blue wool caught her attention. Leonetta desperately needed a new dress, and while Marlein could make over some of her old ones, the girl never complained and helped more than many seven-year-olds did. It seemed to Marlein that Leonetta deserved something all her own.

"How much for the blue?" she asked the man at the booth. Ercken Klein looked up from his small loom, which he used for smaller pieces than the one that had caught her eye. His pale eyes reflected the gray sky, turning them the same color as his hair.

The price he named seemed fair, and with winter coming, Marlein knew that the warm fabric would make a good dress for Leonetta. She withdrew several coins from the pocket hidden beneath her wide apron and purchased the material.

"It will look lovely with your coloring," Klein said, the wrinkles around his eyes growing deeper as he smiled kindly at her.

"Oh, it's for Leonetta," she said, smiling back.

"And what a fortunate girl to have such a kind sister."

Marlein felt her face heat as she quickly excused herself and turned to go. She forced her feet to carry her sedately away despite the discomfort that rose with the praise. She knew how unequal she was for the task of caring for the household and her family. Rather than feeling flattered, she wanted to run.

After reaching the edge of the *Marktplatz*, Marlein stopped to wrap the blue wool in her apron, tying the ends about her waist. The fabric secure, she began making her way along the streets that would lead her to the river. Her feet carried her where she needed to go out of a long-familiar habit, so her mind was free to wander this way and that. Unusually, Klaus's words lodged in her mind, and she contemplated marriage.

Several years had passed since she had any notion of marrying and having a family of her own. The church taught that marriage was not as honorable as remaining a virgin and serving the Lord, but for those who felt compelled, marriage was nevertheless an honorable estate.

Whether or not she thought she'd like it, marriage simply could not be in her future. Today the children were with Keterlyn while Marlein made several calls about town, but she knew it was just as likely—perhaps more so—that instead little Fridolin would have been wrapped up and carried upon her back, the girls trailing along behind her, while Keterlyn lay abed. Her spells of melancholy came with as little warning as did her good days. Marlein picked up her pace, knowing she should hurry along with her errands and return home.

Still, an image of a young man floated across her mind, his sandy hair never staying where he haphazardly pushed it back and deep blue eyes sparkling with mirth. Were circumstances different, she would not mind living in marriage with him.

As she approached the edge of the city and headed toward the shore of the river where the fishermen were working on their boats, she heard a cry and turned her head. A woman with dirty, blonde hair stumbled into the arms of the man who had just appeared in Marlein's mind, his eyes wide and confused. The woman was unkempt in appearance, her dress a light brown, though from dirt or dye, Marlein couldn't say. A threadbare cape covered her shoulders, and straw clung to the hair that had escaped the ratty piece of fabric wound about her head. Even with her untidy appearance, her features were even and beautiful. It was evident she was a very lovely young woman.

It made no rational sense that Marlein's heart would clench and her stomach drop at the sight of Heinrich standing so close to the woman. He could very well have an understanding with someone. Never mentioning such an understanding to her did not exclude the possibility; besides, it really was no concern of hers. Even if they were . . . fond of each other, Marlein knew she could never marry him. And yet, a small part of her thought back to his smiling image, and the sadness seeped into her heart without permission. She took off nearly running to the river.

Marlein could easily have gotten two more fish for the candles she offered for trade with two of the fishermen, but her heart was not in the haggling. The men had broad smiles when she turned away, heading eastward along the Elbe to avoid passing by Wittenberg. It would be a longer walk, but at least she would not run the risk of seeing Heinrich along the way. She was relieved in spite of herself; her heart seemed oddly ignorant of the fact that she could never marry, for it squeezed painfully every time she thought of Heinrich and the lovely girl standing so close together.

***

Heinrich's mind was still reeling. He could scarcely believe Brigita had made the journey from the convent by herself. As he embraced his sister—caught her really—he glimpsed Marlein from the corner of his eye, but she was already turning away before he could call to her. Certain she had seen him, he could not imagine why on earth she would rush away as she did. Marlein was the very picture of gracious kindness, and it baffled him that she would not come to meet his sister.

Brigita did not offer much in the way of an explanation for either the state of her dress or her sudden appearance in Wittenberg, aside from assuring him that she had broken no vows in leaving the convent. He thought to question her further, but for now it was enough that she was safe and well.

"I've a lecture to attend this afternoon, but here are some coins, if there is anything you need from the *Markt*."

"I don't need anything, Heinrich. Is there a quiet place I can wait for you, though? I think—" but she stopped talking and clutched at her head and stomach, swaying slightly on her feet.

"Brigita!" Alarm raced through him, tensing his muscles and furrowing his brow. She couldn't be sick with fever, just a year after it took their father. "What is wrong?"

She swallowed several times, shaking her head and finally opening her eyes. "Nothing. Nothing's the matter. I just . . . I haven't eaten in a few days, and I think . . ."

"A few days?" He picked up her sack where she'd dropped it on the ground and took her arm in his other hand. She was frail and weak, which alarmed him further. "Come, I'll buy some food."

She made no objection, meekly following him toward the *Markt*. She faltered a few times as they made their way down *Kollegienstrasse*, but his hand on her arm kept her upright. The farther they went, the more heavily she leaned on him and the more his concern grew.

"Did they not feed you at the convent?" he asked.

"Of course they did."

"Did the Alscher family feed you?"

Her silence could have been from the sight of the *Marktplatz*, filled with people and goods, but he suspected not. Still, he did not force an answer. Instead, he moved to the first booth with food and purchased two small meat pies. A booth farther into the square had weak beer, so he purchased a small tankard of that. He thanked the man, promising to return the tankard when they had finished. Brigita ate quickly while they walked, finishing her pie before they reached the far side of the square.

"Do you want to wait here?" he asked, wondering where he could leave her, though it was clear that the simple meal and drink had refreshed and strengthened her. "If Marlein had not hurried off, she could have taken you to the house."

"Marlein?" Brigita asked, not concealing the way her eyes strayed to his half-eaten pie.

"Yes, Diefenbach's daughter." He took one more bite of his food before offering it to his sister. "They are the family I am boarding with."

"Oh yes," she said around a mouthful of food. "I just couldn't recall you mentioning her name during any of your visits. It's always been

'Diefenbach's eldest daughter.'"

It seemed that Heinrich's relief at seeing his sister and worry over her well-being had made him unguarded with his words.

"Well, if you think no one will mind, I will wait here." Brigita finished the last bit of his pie. "Perhaps someone needs some sweeping done for a small wage or bit of bread?"

Heinrich nodded. "The *Stadtkirche* is there, just on the other side of the *Marktplatz*." He pointed, though the twin steeples were obvious to anyone who looked in that direction. "Can you meet me in front of it in about two hours?"

Brigita nodded, glancing about her, her eyes much too anxious to be merely taking stock of her surroundings. Heinrich itched to ask, but held his tongue. "Very well, then. If you have trouble finding it, any of the craftsmen can direct you to it."

She nodded, something shimmering in her eyes. When she said nothing more, Heinrich nodded awkwardly, patted her arm, and said, "I am glad you are here, sister."

He saw her smile before he turned around and headed toward the university's lecture hall, and the ghost of a whisper followed him.

"Me too."

# 7

By the afternoon, Johann Diefenbach was ready to leave his shop. Matthäus and Sïfrit would close up in the evening and bring home any work that could not wait until the next day. Despite the rainy fall weather, the roads were in good shape and Diefenbach made his way easily, even with the increasing cold and rising wind. His day had been unremarkable, save for the fact that his wife had roused herself from her room. It allowed Marlein time to see to some things away from the house without having to bring the children with her. It pained him to see his lovely *Ehefrau* feeling poorly so much of the time, but he knew the pain was worse for her.

And Marlein. The girl could have been married and expecting his first grandchild, but she stayed because she was needed. He sometimes felt he ought to encourage her to seek a husband and move on, but he could not bring himself to begin the conversation. The thought of her leaving, with Keterlyn as she was . . .

He was selfish.

Diefenbach forced a smile to his lips as he opened the front door, a more strenuous task than usual due to the wind's attempt to steal the door from his grip and its hinges. Passing through to the living quarters of their house, he was surprised to find the space occupied.

"Good evening, Diefenbach," said Heinrich from where he sat on his usual bench, beside a slip of a young woman. As he spoke, Diefenbach noticed that Heinrich had slipped into his Braunschweig dialect more than he had since coming to them. "May I introduce my sister, Brigita, to you?"

"It is good to meet you, Brigita," Diefenbach returned after he removed his cape and hung it on a peg beside the side door. "What brings you to Wittenberg?"

The girl blushed and looked down, pinching folds of her skirt between her fingers. She opened her mouth to speak, but Heinrich spoke first.

"As you know, our father passed away almost a year ago. Brigita had been staying with some friends"—Diefenbach saw the girl flinch at that—"but they were no longer able to keep her. We'd hoped her situation with them would last until I was finished with my studies, but as you see . . ."

"Yes." Diefenbach moved to his chair and sat, holding his hands out to the blazing fire. "Because you had not mentioned her impending arrival, I assume that this is a surprise?"

Heinrich nodded in answer, a muscle twitching near his jaw. Diefenbach wondered if the young man was angry or anxious. Perhaps both. The conversation was interrupted when the side door opened and in walked Marlein. She had a basket under her arm, likely empty if its awkward angle against her hip was any indication. Her hair was windblown and her cheeks a rosy pink.

"And here I thought you would not be back until supper, *meine Tochter*. Have you been away all day?"

"No, *Vater*. I came back midday to prepare the fish and check on *Mutter* and the children."

"And where are they?"

Marlein's eyes widened for a moment, glancing about the room.

"*Mutter* said she was well today, so I left them with her while I called on Emnelda. Are they not here?"

Her movements were jerky and abrupt as she dropped her basket beneath the pegs and tugged at the strings holding her cloak about her shoulders. She scooped up the basket and crossed to her parents' room without speaking further. Heinrich followed hastily, leaving his sister to stare apprehensively after him.

"My daughter worries too much over her family," he chuckled lightly to Brigita in a fumbling version of her Braunschweiger dialect, hoping to ease her alarm. She sat on the bench, wide-eyed and still.

The girl nodded her head at length, looking to where Heinrich hovered near the doorway to the room. Her answer was whispered. "As does my brother for me. They seem very much alike."

Diefenbach barked a short laugh, then sent a sly grin her way. "I like you, Fraulein Ritter."

She shook her head. "Please, call me Brigita, Herr Diefenbach. I am no noblewoman."

"Then you must call me Diefenbach, for neither am I."

From across the large fireplace, he heard Marlein and Heinrich's voices.

"Are they in there?" asked Heinrich.

"Yes. Mother was napping with Fridolin, and the girls are playing."

"That is good."

"Yes." There was some shuffling, a quiet "Excuse me" from his daughter. Diefenbach turned slightly toward the fireplace to hear better as Marlein asked, "Did you start the fire?"

For a moment, he thought she was asking him, but then Heinrich answered her question.

"Yes. It had been banked and covered with the grate when Brigita and I arrived, so I stoked it and added some logs; I presumed you'd need it hotter for supper when you arrived home."

"Oh! How rude of me!" The sound of something being set down. "I should go and meet your . . . um . . ."

"*Schwester.*" There was a knowing tone in Heinrich's answer to her unasked question that tickled Diefenbach more than maybe it should have.

"*Schwester?*" His daughter's voice was weak; it seemed she was unaware that Brigita was Heinrich's sister.

Diefenbach shot Brigita a mischievous smile.

"*Ja.* I've been eager to introduce the two of you. I saw that you saw me, you know." There was a pause, and Diefenbach nearly couldn't hear because Heinrich's voice was lower, gruffer, when he asked, "Why did you run off?"

"I, uh . . ." Marlein cleared her throat, and Diefenbach could hear his daughter's hesitation as she answered. "I needed to be somewhere."

The following silence was telling; even though he was careful to keep his back to them, pretending not to listen, Diefenbach could sense the tension between the two young people. A glance at Brigita confirmed his impression of the interaction. The girl's eyes were wide with mirth, and her lips scarcely kept laughter from bursting forth.

"But I would love to meet her now!" Marlein's words were firm and perhaps a bit too eager. The two returned as Diefenbach hurried to straighten in his chair, observing Brigita raise her hand to hide laughter as she caught his eye.

"Marlein," announced Heinrich. He led Marlein over to the younger woman, hand ghosting the small of her back. "May I introduce my sister, Brigita Ritter?"

"My eldest daughter, Marlein," Diefenbach added unnecessarily, barely concealing his amusement. While he still refused to encourage his daughter to marry, he was enjoying himself at his daughter's expense too much to resist teasing her a bit.

"I am pleased to meet you," murmured Brigita, rising to her feet.

Marlein grinned broadly. "And I you. Your *Bruder* did not tell me you were nearly grown; he always spoke of you as a little girl. It is a little difficult to understand you, like Heinrich was when he first arrived. But I imagine we will do well enough."

Brigita's smile grew, though the brief wave of sadness in her eyes betrayed . . . something. Diefenbach could not entirely decipher what, but he had a clear sense that something was troubling the girl, and not even formality or shared laughter could chase it away entirely. "Even so, he is the best of brothers."

"Would you mind helping me prepare supper? Most days, I struggle with teaching Leonetta, the eldest of my sisters, about what I am making. She is occupying the younger ones now, though, and I would rather not bother her."

Brigita nodded and hopped up from her seat, following the other girl to the kitchen. Their quiet voices drifted across the room and the men glanced at each other, understanding dawning on Heinrich's face.

"You heard us."

Diefenbach nodded, not bothering to conceal the grin that stretched across his face.

"I always underestimate the volume of my voice."

Diefenbach nodded again.

"By your grin, I can only assume you did not find me too forward?"

He shook his head. "Young man, you will have to pursue her a great deal more earnestly before you could be considered even a tiny bit *forward*. Even appropriately so." Diefenbach allowed Heinrich time to flush and scowl a bit before changing the subject to a more serious one, his smile fading as his face matched his tone. "What will your sister do until you have completed your studies?"

Heinrich shifted in his seat, avoiding his gaze. "I, uh, I hope to find her a situation in town. Perhaps one of the craftsmen needs a girl to cook and clean?"

"Well, given that many have already taken on a servant or two, and our own household has expanded quite a bit . . ." Diefenbach glanced up at the young man seated across from him. "What would you think of your sister helping here? I'm sure we could find a place for her to sleep, somewhere or other. And goodness knows, Marlein could use the help."

Heinrich's eyes lit up, his face positively glowing. "That seems too easy a solution. Would Marlein mind another person under her care? Though I would hope that with very little instruction, Brigita would be more of a helper than a dependent. She helped with basic chores at the Alscher house back in Braunschweig, and kept house for my father before his death."

Diefenbach stood and said, "There is only one way to answer that question. Come."

The men stood and stepped around the hearth and into the kitchen, Johann eager to settle the arrangement. He had just been contemplating the difficulty of his daughter's life and now here was a means of lessening her burden.

"*Meine Tochter,* it has come to my attention—"

"Forgive my interruption, Diefenbach," interjected Heinrich, "but I just noticed that the wood for the fire is low. Marlein, let Brigita and me bring some in for you."

Marlein's eyes were wide, and understandably so, for Heinrich never interrupted his host. For his part, Heinrich's face showed alarm and discomfort. With a wave of self-deprecation, Diefenbach suddenly realized what he was doing. Thankful for Heinrich's intervention, he answered for Marlein, "Excellent idea. You know where it is?"

Heinrich nodded, then walked to the side door, gesturing for Brigita to follow. Diefenbach waited for the door to close before turning to his daughter.

"What was that about?" she asked, confusion on her face as she turned back to her supper preparations.

"It was an intelligent and thoughtful young man saving me from an untimely blunder. I wanted to ask you whether you would like Brigita to help here in the house. She needs a position until Heinrich is conferred with his degree and can begin practicing law, and earning their keep. If this is agreeable to you, she would likely need to stay in your room, as your brother Johann's is already occupied by Heinrich. It wouldn't do for her to stay in the servant's room with Steffan. All things considered, though, it might ease some of your burden to have another set of hands. And I believe it would relieve the Ritter siblings of a burden of their own."

His daughter smiled as she moved the uncooked food she'd been preparing for the oven and said, "I was about to ask you, *Vater*, whether she might stay here with us. Already I can tell that she is a sweet girl and seems to know her way about the kitchen. And I could easily teach her what she doesn't know. Besides, she is about the age that Niesenn would be, had she lived."

The mention of his third child was painful. She had been the first taken from him and his wife, but not the last. Niesenn had been a happy baby, for the two years she was with them. Even surrounded by his melancholic thoughts, Diefenbach was struck by Marlein's generous spirit. Life had been difficult for his wife, and consequentially for him and their eldest daughter, who had made it her life's work to support her family as best she could. Despite how she labored—and some would say suffered—she constantly searched for ways to ease the burdens others carried.

"You are a good girl, Marlein," he said, voice gruff with emotion.

He laid a hand for just a moment on her back between her shoulders—so much stronger than they looked—before he turned back to the chair waiting for him on the other side of the fireplace. He felt he should stay, spend some time with his daughter, but his mind was already filled with thoughts of his guild meeting next week and the crates he needed to order from the woodworker. His work needed his time more than his strong, capable daughter did.

# 8

For as long as she could remember, Brigita had marked her life by the rare happy moments it yielded for her. An early memory of laughing with her mother, father, and brother, all carrying candles for a Christmas procession. Her brother teaching her the letters of her name by candlelight while their father slept. Nikolaus telling her she was pretty, in the light of the hearth's fire.

But that memory was now tainted and no longer brought the happiness it once did.

Brigita shook herself from her thoughts and returned to sweeping out the *Diele*. The morning following her arrival at Wittenberg, Brigita had risen feeling refreshed and safer than she had in a long time. She helped Marlein prepare breakfast and asked how she could help. When Marlein suggested she sweep out the *Diele*, she eagerly set to her task. The older servant, Steffan, was out harvesting rye from the field next to the Diefenbach house, and they needed to have the floor cleared for threshing. As she cleared the flagstone floor of the hall, starting just a few paces from the hearth and working toward the front gate, she began to hum quietly.

"That's lovely," Marlein called from where she was kneading dough in the *Flett*. "What is it?"

"Just a chant we used to recite at the convent." Brigita hadn't realized she was loud enough for Marlein to hear her.

"Don't stop," Marlein said with a gentle smile when she didn't go back to humming.

"I actually can't remember the rest," Brigita returned. It was partially true; she could have hummed a few more phrases, but the rest was lost in the memory of other songs and chants.

"Was it terribly difficult, living in the convent?" asked Marlein as she covered the dough with a cloth and picked up a second broom to join Brigita.

"No. We rose early and worked all day, but that's no different from life outside its walls."

"True!" They giggled a little at that.

"The rhythm of the days comforted me. We had prayers throughout, and tasks between them. Spending so much time in prayer and exercises was calming to the soul."

"I can imagine."

They had reached the front of the *Diele*, where one of the Diefenbachs' horses, a pretty gray named Berte, was stabled with Heinrich's horse, Jäger. As Marlein went to unlatch the front gate, Brigita stepped up to the stall and reached out her hand while making soft clucking noises. Heinrich's large black animal ambled over to the stall door, stuck his head over it, and nuzzled Brigita's stomach.

"He is a good horse," Marlein said.

"Have you ridden him?"

"Heavens no. But I held him once when Heinrich forgot something in his room, and Jäger didn't pull against the reins once."

Brigita smiled, remembering the couple of times she had convinced Heinrich to take her for a ride. "He's got a very smooth stride. Perhaps one day, Heinrich will take you out for a ride."

"Oh! That would be . . . um, I really don't think . . ." Marlein trailed off awkwardly, and Brigita was forced to hide her laugh behind a cough.

"I suppose the dust is getting to me," she said when Marlein's eyes turned concerned.

"I can sweep everything out into the yard," Marlein offered, "if the dust bothers you."

"Oh, no. I'm feeling better now."

Wordless, they both returned to sweeping. Brigita couldn't wait until she could speak to her brother.

This was a moment of happiness for her. Here in the same house with her brother after years apart, possibly making a friend, and watching sweet, tender feelings unfold between her brother and her new friend. She dearly hoped that she would still be here to see the fruition of those feelings.

***

For days, the house had been filled with the crisp scent of apples, cut in slices and strung about the house to dry. Having Brigita around had been an unexpected blessing for Marlein; she could see this after only a few days. Rather than having to put up the food for winter while also keeping the little ones out of trouble and teaching them to help, she had Brigita to share the tasks. It was pleasant working alongside another woman.

Rye had been harvested and threshed on Wednesday, the grain separated from the chaff and stored, and the chaff thrown into a stall for winter fodder. On Thursday, cabbage had been chopped and packed with salt to begin the fermentation process that would produce sauerkraut. A small store of meat that Marlein had traded for candles on Friday was hanging from the rafters. Along with the apples that were drying, some fresh apples were packed in straw in a crate and stored under the bench near the side door.

On the following Monday, Marlein took down the now-dried apple slices and packed them in cloth bags to be stored in another crate. She had just closed the crate when Heinrich emerged from his room.

"Marlein, I don't know where Brigita is this morning. Do you think you would have time to fix this seam for me?" he asked, wearing his billowy shirt and puffed-out *Hosen*, snug stockings, and sturdy shoes and carrying his doublet. Marlein suddenly felt very awkward. Why on earth would the lack of one simple article of clothing unsettle her so? She'd seen him in his nightdress just last summer when there came a loud banging on the family's door—the Kunze place had caught fire just north of the city—and everyone was called from their beds to help put out the fire without time to dress properly.

Careful to avoid looking at him, she took the doublet and examined it. The garment's dark wool was good quality, but the seam holding the puff of the sleeve to the bodice had come loose, leaving a gap wide enough for her to fit three of her fingers through.

"What happened?"

Heinrich grinned sheepishly, and it helped to put her at ease. "I noticed it was loosening a week or so ago, before Brigita had even arrived. You've been busy, and I didn't think it would come apart this soon. It ripped when I was taking it off the hook this morning."

"I see." After a brief pause, she quipped, "Putting off until tomorrow what could have reasonably been done yesterday?"

"Always."

Shaking her head at him, she said, "It should take but a few moments. I'll stitch this for you right now. In the meantime, would you mind taking these two crates to the loft for me?"

"If I must," he sighed.

Hiding her laughter behind a scowl, she made as if to throw the garment at him, before turning on her heel. It was nice to feel something of their earlier camaraderie; she wasn't sure what to make of herself lately. Glad of occupation for her hands and her mind, she stooped to gather mending supplies from a basket sitting beneath the bench. Marlein turned around in time to observe Heinrich heft the first crate as though it was filled with stones rather than dried apples. Quickly, though, she bowed her head to her work. About twenty stitches later, she tied off the knot of her thread and raised her head to see him returning for the second crate. When he again hefted it with exaggerated difficulty, she pulled a face at him, saying, "I could carry that without difficulty, Heinrich. No need for such dramatics."

He laughed, but said nothing as he easily transferred the crate to his left shoulder. The muscles in his arms were rather hidden by the wide sleeve, but the fabric pulled taught to reveal the expanse of his shoulders as he twisted to look back at her with a teasing quirk of his lips. She rolled her eyes and shook out his doublet in his direction, and he laughed before strolling down the long hall toward the stalls, crate on his shoulder.

"Thank you, Marlein," he called over his shoulder, "for rescuing me despite my procrastination!"

Marlein carefully laid out his doublet on her father's chair, knowing it wouldn't be disturbed or dirtied there, studiously avoiding watching as Heinrich reached the ladder near the front gate and began climbing. One of her ancestors had placed ten or so planks across the rafters near the front of the house, creating a cool storage area in the winter for some items. A trunk of outgrown clothing to be later remade for the younger children, an old candle-dipping frame of her father's that he couldn't bear to part with, and now the crates of dried apples occupied the space. As Heinrich disappeared into the rafters, she turned to scrape the last of the porridge into a bowl for him.

She waited a moment to be sure Heinrich did not call down to ask for clarification as to where she wanted the dried apples to be stored. Hearing nothing, she set his bowl on the table and plucked her cloak from its peg by the side door; before he could see that she was leaving, she stepped outside.

Recently, Keterlyn seemed to be having an unusually lengthy spell of good spirits and was working in the garden, about ten paces from the side door. She was showing Brigita, Leonetta, Aldessa, and Herlinde how to pull the dying stalks and vines of parsnips and gourds while keeping watch for leftover vegetables and herbs that had not yet succumbed to the cooler weather. When something was pulled from the wreckage of the autumn garden, little Fridolin was called to carry it to the basket harboring the last of the year's produce.

In the morning light, the beauty of their home warmed Marlein despite the crisp quality of the air. There had been frost on the roof of the woodshed this morning, but the rising sun had melted it and begun to marginally warm the earth. The sun shone pale on the distant horizon while earth and leaves scented the air. Golden leaves supported by the dark undergrowth of trunks and branches hung in the near distance, across the small field beyond the garden. The slight tang of burning wood in the air drew Marlein's eyes to the very edge of the field, where a small cottage sat; its faint trail of smoke up into the sky told Marlein that Emnelda was hard at work with her herbs.

Once upon a time, the field between the house and the cottage had supported sheep, which Keterlyn's family kept. Her father had been a weaver, and they used the land owned by their family to raise sheep for their wool. He worked the loom and his wife and daughter tended the sheep. Now, though, the field grew barley and oats in turn, feeding the modest collection of livestock kept by the Diefenbach family.

A sharp breeze sliced through Marlein's thoughts, bringing her back to the activities of the women and children in the garden. The weather was certainly turning cooler. She fastened her cape about her shoulders, relishing the extra warmth as she sank to her knees beside the garden. It consisted of three large beds, raised and supported with interwoven sticks, allowing the soil to drain when heavy rains came.

The land around Wittenberg was sandy and ill-suited to most crops, but Marlein had been taught years ago by her mother that they could use waste from both plants and animals to improve the quality of the soil. As she sorted through the decaying plants before her, she could see that the soil in their gardens was still in good shape.

Marlein finished her corner and gathered up the dead stalks, leaves, and vines. She deposited them in the pile with the rest and was about to turn to help Aldessa with her section of garden when a hand to her elbow stilled her.

"Marlein, I am off to the university now." His grin was infectious.

"Did you eat your porridge?" she asked.

"Yes, *Mutti,*" he teased lightly. She scoffed, but before she could reply, he asked, "Would you mind terribly checking to see if that seam is still holding?"

She almost wanted to deny his request, as he flipped the cape over his shoulder to expose the seam. What could he mean asking her to come so close to him? But then another thought occurred to her. "Are you questioning the quality of my stitches?"

He jerked his head back to look her in the face. "What? No, not at all!"

"Humph. I should hope not." She peered at the seam. "I can't even see where it was. Though it seems to be getting a bit small on you."

Confusion wrinkled his face. "I'm twenty-five. How could it be getting small on me?"

"Well, I suppose you are unused to hard labor," she returned. Marlein was so very relieved to feel none of her earlier awkwardness that she added smartly, "Studious and sickly fellow that you were when you came to us."

"I was not!" he cried with pretend indignation, barely able to hide his grin.

"I am teasing." She allowed herself to laugh with him before continuing. "Truly, though, did your other schools afford time to do the work you do here?"

He paused, considering. "Well, no."

"See, then? I think you're simply growing stronger. And part of that includes actual growing."

Heinrich adjusted his satchel's strap on his shoulder before a grin quirked his lips. "Hm. Are you certain you aren't simply flattering me?"

"When have you ever known me to do that?" she huffed.

"Never." He grinned broadly at her and stepped away. She hadn't realized they were standing so close. It was a good thing only her family was about; anyone else might misconstrue their proximity for something more intimate than what they shared. "Well, I should be off if I don't want to incite the wrath of my professor."

He was far enough away from her now that the full effect of his school clothing struck her: dark cape hiding all but the front of his doublet, *Hosen*, and a bit of the ruff of his collar. She thought he was quite arresting in his simple working clothes—the blue jerkin especially. But whenever he wore his student's clothing, she felt frumpy and plain in comparison. Not that he ever acted in a way to encourage such feelings, but the puffs on his doublet made his shoulders look broader than they had recently grown, the stockings showed the strength in his calves, and the dark material of his cape made him seem so very serious.

"N-no, but thank you," she managed to say, even as she wondered why it was she he had greeted first, instead of his sister or even her mother. And suddenly, the awkwardness rushed over her again. "I . . . hope you enjoy the lecture."

"It is with Father Martin. I always enjoy his." His grin was so carefree, even playful, that Marlein found herself fumbling for words. Embarrassed, she merely smiled and returned to her work.

"I'll see you later, then," he said before turning to speak to his sister who was several paces away.

The garden beds were cleared easily. They would take some of the plants, chop them, and work the smaller pieces back into the soil. While her mother and the others started on that, Marlein retrieved the sack of small seed potatoes from near the house. The potatoes would be planted and would grow before the first hard freeze, God willing. She glanced toward her mother, who occasionally would stop her work and gaze off into the woods beyond the house. At least there had been no episodes recently.

"Leonetta, come here, please." Marlein handed her sister a small knife. "Cut the potatoes in half while I turn the soil."

Marlein took up a shovel and set to work. The rich aroma soon filled her nostrils as she made her way down the row, upturning soil and decaying vegetation together. The edge of her shovel was useful in chopping away at the hard clumps until the soil was soft and ready to welcome the potatoes.

"Ow!" cried Leonetta. Marlein dropped the handle of her shovel and sprinted to her sister's side. Their mother arrived a moment later, gasping when Leonetta raised her hand, split open with a gash, blood oozing from it onto her palm.

"Here, darling, give me your hand," Marlein said. She held her sister's wrist, using the corner of her apron to press on the wound before the blood began to drip. "Mother, can you—" but she did not continue, for the woman was staring, wide-eyed, at Leonetta's hand, wrapped in the corner of Marlein's apron. "Brigita! Please get some clean cloth from my sewing basket in the kitchen. Maria and Herlinde, will you help Leonetta press this onto her hand?" She hurried to untie her apron, leaving it with her sisters. "Aldessa, stay with Fridolin; be sure he doesn't wander off."

Leaving her apron with the girls, she put an arm about her mother's shoulders and guided her toward the house. Brigita met them at the door to the kitchen, rags and a small tub of salve in her hands.

"Do you know how to care for her hand?"

"Yes. I helped at the infirmary at the convent."

"Good. Thank you, Brigita. If you have trouble, take her to Emnelda's cottage. I'll get *meine Mutter* settled in her room and then find you."

Marlein led her mother through the house to her bedchamber. Once there, she urged Keterlyn to slip off her dress to just her shift beneath it for sleeping. Trying to avoid meeting her mother's vacant eyes, Marlein used her own skirt to wipe away the worst of the dirt from Keterlyn's hands.

"I suppose I should have thought to clean you up before we came to your room. I'm sorry about that, *Mutter*." She pressed her lips together, the trembling in her mother's hands causing her worry. "If I'd known it was such a bad cut, I'd have made sure you didn't see."

Keterlyn said nothing, and Marlein could see that her mother's eyes were blind to the room, instead seeing horrors brought back by the cut on her young child's hand. She helped the older woman climb into bed, where sleep claimed her almost immediately. Marlein's heart ached for her mother. Grief had turned her skin pale, cares had streaked her honey-colored hair with silver, and sorrow had shrunken her once ample figure. And while Marlein did all she could to ease her mother's burden, she knew it would never be enough.

She could not restore the woman's losses.

# 9

Heinrich's thoughts on the way to the university were consumed, once again, by Brigita; only this time, he did not feel so frantic and uncertain. Things seemed to be going very well with her living at the house. The sharp angles of her face were already beginning to fade in the week since her arrival, due to Marlein's generous meals. Brigita clearly looked up to the eldest Diefenbach daughter, though only a few years separated them. Marlein, too, seemed to benefit from the arrangement; she was humming more, like she did before her mother's decline, and her smiles were more frequent.

But Brigita's eyes betrayed her. She looked over her shoulder whenever he took her to the *Marktplatz*, and though she smiled and even occasionally laughed, it seemed to him that sometimes she was merely playing a part. He doubted she knew how often her eyes darkened with fear.

But perhaps he was imagining things. Ever since the moment he realized that her security at the Alscher family's home had dissolved, worry for her had been eating away at him. It clawed its way into his mind and heart, disrupting his thoughts and concentration. But she was here now. Nothing should be upsetting her, now that she was near him and under the kind protection of the Diefenbachs, until he finished his schooling and began to practice law. Nothing should be upsetting her, but something was.

He needed to find out what troubled his sister. Each time he attempted to broach the subject, she deflected every question. And so the worry continued to burrow, making itself quite at home in his anxious thoughts.

Heinrich enjoyed the lecture given by Luther, as he'd told Marlein he would. Each time that he sat in the lecture hall, listening to the dry wit of his professor, all else faded. On his way back to the Diefenbach house after the lecture, his professor's words rang in his head, clamoring with the worries over his sister, until he decided he needed to talk it all over with Marlein. Perhaps she could offer some insight where his sister was concerned, so that he could finally give full attention to the words of his professors and his study at home.

He entered the house, finding it quiet and the fire banked. The women were still out in the garden. He hurried to his room and changed into his working clothes, choosing his blue jerkin this time. Moments later, emerging into the garden from the side door, he was surprised to find only Marlein there. In the distance, he could see Brigita's tiny form leading the four smaller girls and toddling little Fridolin across the field toward Emnelda's cottage.

Marlein still hadn't seen him, intent on her work. Her apron ends were tied about her waist, creating a pouch where something was stored. She reached periodically for whatever she had in her apron, tossing it into the holes she dug with her shovel. After, she used the shovel to push dirt back over the hole. Heinrich strode over to her and removed the shovel from her hands.

"Oh!" Marlein spun around, eyes wide. "You startled me!"

The flush on her face was so pretty, and a few strands of her light-brown hair had escaped her hood; his fingers itched to push them back where they belonged. Or at least to touch them and see if they were as soft as they looked.

Instead, he grinned jauntily at her. "Forgive me, but you really should learn to be more alert to your surroundings. What if I had been Sïfrit?"

A slight scowl furrowed her brow, and he burst out laughing. It only took a moment for her to join him. "I can hardly imagine Sïfrit coming to the garden and taking the shovel from me."

Heinrich chuckled, then used his foot to push the shovel into the next patch of ground. "How about I dig, and you plant?"

She nodded and bent to place a piece of potato into the soil, then gently covered it with dirt.

"Marlein," Heinrich began, gazing down at the top of the young woman's head and thinking of his sister. "I wanted to know—"

Marlein suddenly looked up at him. He was shocked to see that tears shone brightly in her eyes, reflecting the grayish light that the cloudy sky allowed through. His breath caught in his throat; in all the years he'd lived with this family, never had he seen their eldest daughter cry. She was the strong one. Whatever brought tears to her eyes made his concern for Brigita seem trivial. His sister did seem to be improving, and she was here with him. Safe.

Rather than ask for her help with his sister and because he did not suppose Marlein would share what was bothering her, he instead started to talk of other things.

"My lecture today was interesting. Would you like to know why?"

She did not answer right away, but placed another potato slice into the hole he'd just dug. She swiped at her face with the back of her dirtied hand before smoothing soil over the potato. "I would, Heinrich. I find Father Martin's sermons during Mass to be intriguing, but I truly cannot imagine spending a lecture listening to him. He has a brilliant mind, does he not?"

"He does." Heinrich hurried to dig several holes for potatoes, then leaned the shovel against the garden's fence and squatted beside

Marlein, holding out his hands. She questioningly met his eyes for a moment, and he looked down at her apron, silently asking for some of the potatoes. She scooped some out, and he closed his hands over the potatoes and her hands. He held his breath while she withdrew her hands, leaving the potatoes in his grasp. He had to clear his throat before continuing. "Today he mentioned some of his Theses. In the week since he posted them on the door of the Castle Church, he has been going on with our lectures as though nothing has changed. And perhaps for him, it hasn't. His change has begun already, as his understanding of Scriptures began to grow some time ago. But for the rest of us, we are just beginning to see what he has seen . . ."

Marlein looked up from her work, tears gone and interest lighting her eyes. "Have you read them?"

"His Theses?"

She nodded eagerly.

"Yes. Have you?"

She shook her head. "Father suggests that it remains a matter for the scholarly and we should leave it alone." A brief grin quirked her pink lips. "But we do listen to his sermons, and perhaps that is worse."

An unexpectedly loud laugh burst from Heinrich's throat, and his enjoyment in her company washed over him. "You may be right about that. They—the Theses, that is—were translated from Latin into German, though." He stood and reached for the shovel.

"They were? Oh, that's right. Sïfrit mentioned them after supper the other evening, didn't he?" She paused, waiting for him to finish digging more holes. "Did Father Martin translate them?"

"I doubt it. He intended them as a call for discussion, for debate. They are being printed, though, and distributed throughout the area. I . . . I can bring you a copy, if you'd like."

Her eyes met his again, and he felt his stomach dip and churn. She was an intelligent girl and would likely have done well in a convent's school. But then, had she been afforded that opportunity for learning, she would not be here, with her family. With him.

After an eternity that stretched through three agonizingly long breaths, she looked away again, shaking her head. "I cannot. My father said we should wait, so wait I will." Heinrich was vaguely disappointed, though he did not think it was for good reasons. "But you may, my good man, discuss any of the illustrious Father Martin's ideas with me that you wish. *Vater* has said nothing against that."

Her conspiratorial smile met his grin.

"In that case," he said, pushing the shovel into the soil, "do you recall what he mentioned during Mass yesterday?"

"The passage where Jesus teaches the disciples to pray, and gives us the *Pater Noster*?"

"Yes!" He watched as she dropped a potato into the hole he'd dug and covered it with soil. "Today he spoke to us of God's love for us— love as a dear Father loves His dear children. The last part of the fourth chapter tells us to draw near to God's throne with confidence."

"'With confidence'?" she asked as he dug another hole. "I'm not sure I could ever do that."

"He invites us," he said as he straightened to look at her. "He invites you."

"How does . . . one . . . do this?" Her voice was quiet and uncertain—so unlike her.

"In prayer. With the Sacraments. With the Word of God." Heinrich dug a few more holes as Marlein's face scrunched in thought. At length, he continued, "Father Martin seldom mentions his Theses in class, but today, he gave indulgences as an example of where some people move away from the throne of grace, rather than toward it. That grace and mercy are found there alone, and no other place. The chief 'other place' being Tetzel's indulgence sales."

Marlein was quiet for a moment, continuing with her planting after his digging. After they had planted five or so potatoes, she asked, "So he is calling for change in the church?"

"It would seem so. I believe that is to what purpose he wrote his Theses. He has become convinced by Scripture that grace is found nowhere but in Christ."

"We have long been told that we are to do what is in us, and God's grace in Christ and the saints will fill what we lack," Marlein countered.

"His grace in Christ does fill what we lack, but I think that what Father Martin says is that we have nothing in us that can contribute. We are entirely empty, unable to do anything at all for our salvation."

"I . . . I have been convinced in these last months of my utter insufficiency to meet the needs of my family." Her voice was quiet. "I'd not given voice to it, but the truth would just as easily apply to my soul as well."

"Father Martin would say that's the mercy of it." Heinrich dared to reach a comforting hand to rest on her shoulder. "Christ took care of it because we can't."

"So, my insufficiency doesn't really matter?"

"He makes us sufficient. He makes us enough." He stared into her hazel eyes a moment, unsure why it felt as though the rest of the world was fading away. Remembering, though, that she was his host's daughter, and that she had expressed several times the impossibility of marriage as an option for herself, he shook his head a bit and chuckled half-heartedly. "Or so Father Martin says. His ideas are fascinating, but to speak against what the church has taught for hundreds of years?"

"He is a brave man," she murmured.

"Or at the least, convinced of what he says."

The pair continued with the work, their conversation charging the air around them even as the clouds thickened and the air grew heavy with unfallen rain. They made their way slowly across the garden, working and talking intently. Then the sky darkened, and the sun's light dimmed. Heinrich was glad when Brigita and the children returned, hands and pockets full of nuts they'd gathered for Keterlyn Diefenbach.

With a skyward glance, Marlein instructed, "Put them in the basket I left on the table inside, then come quickly. It will rain soon, and we must get these potatoes in first. It is getting too cold to get caught in a downpour."

Heinrich returned to his task of digging holes, no longer going at it slowly. Conversation could wait, but the potatoes couldn't, as the family's survival of the winter might very well depend upon them. He could always ask her for help with his sister later, but the way his heart welled at seeing some measure of peace in Marlein's was new and pleasant and allowed no room for trivial concerns.

# 10

The next day, Keterlyn Diefenbach made her way unsteadily from her room. Her limbs ached with inactivity, but she did not mind, for her heart no longer ached. It had descended into a blessed numbness.

Yesterday had begun so well. She even found some enjoyment working with her daughters in the garden. And that girl Brigita—she was good for Marlein: a friend and a helper. Because heaven knew Keterlyn was no help. Still, it would be nice today to work in the garden after a rain. Messy, but sometimes the squelch of the mud was enough to balance the dry expanse inside her. Almost.

Lethargy slowing her movements, she trudged into the kitchen. Her husband had left for the shop hours ago, and Marlein was working, always working, at the table. Her strong hands shaped brown barley dough into loaves, gentle yet firm. Leonetta and Aldessa were helping her, while the youngest three children sorted chunks of wood.

"Good morning, *Mutter*," Marlein greeted her as she used a shoulder to nudge a strand of hair away from her cheek. Keterlyn believed her daughter's smile to be genuine, but so much guilt hindered her own ability to push past the clinging sadness; her return smile was lacking.

"I thought I would work in the garden today," she offered timidly.

"Again? Are you certain that is a good—"

"Yes," she insisted. Worry pressed at the back of her mind. "What if yesterday's rain washed away the potatoes like it did the grains of barley three years ago?"

"Potatoes are quite a bit heavier than grain, *Mutter*," Marlein said, the placating tone of her voice clear, "and I think the rain was not so very hard."

For a heartbeat, Keterlyn considered relenting, but her heart tightened at the idea. "Even so, I wish to be certain."

The two women stood looking at each other. A mother who was less than a parent, and a daughter with much more to bear than she should have. Still, Marlein meekly stepped back to her place as daughter.

"Yes, *Mutter*."

Keterlyn reached for her shawl, hanging by the door. Wrapping it around her shoulders, she crossed it over her bodice and tucked the corners into her apron at her hips. It would not be in her way as she worked. She opened the door and stepped over the threshold.

"Good morning," greeted a masculine voice, coming from behind. Keterlyn glanced over her shoulder to see Heinrich emerging from his little room next to the side door. She closed the door all but a handbreadth and paused to watch them and listen to the conversation. "Marlein," the young man continued, "how are you this morning?"

"I am well, thank you. Yourself?"

"Oh, fair to middling." He grinned charmingly, and Keterlyn's heart sank at his next words. "There's something I was hoping you could help me with, though, Marlein. Do you think I could have a private word with you?"

A private word with her daughter could only mean a request for courtship, or a proposal if he'd already spoken to Marlein's father.

"Once Brigita wakes, I'd be happy to step outside with you, if that will do?"

"Actually, I'm fairly certain your father left a crate of the beeswax candles ordered by one of the burghers—I can't recall his name, though. Perhaps we could make the delivery together?"

Keterlyn wished she hadn't stayed to listen. She wasn't ready to lose a daughter to marriage. Stumbling into her garden, she saw the freshly planted soil, hiding its treasure. When she looked closely, she could see one or two tiny green shoots. Some of the potatoes must have started sprouting before they were planted. She should have been the one planting, but she'd been overwhelmed when Leonetta had cut her hand.

It could have been so much worse. The blood oozed and dripped and pooled when she dreamt of it last night. It soaked her young daughter's dress. It made puddles on the ground. But then she was in her bed, and believed herself to be awake, until she looked down and saw the blood on her own dress, soaking into the straw mattress and leaving puddles on the floor. Babies of different ages, at least five of them, lay about her on the bed, eyes closed and bodies lifeless. She sobbed silently, for the voice of her cries had withered away years ago, leaving only numb horror in its wake.

When she finally awoke in the misty morning light, her one comfort was in hearing Marlein's voice in the kitchen, drifting through the door. Her shift was drenched in sweat and her body trembled, but her daughter's voice soothed her mind. Marlein was making food for the day and seeing to the children. Her dear, sweet daughter was doing what she herself would never be able to do again. For Keterlyn had no illusions of being able to escape the gloom that had settled around her like a funeral pall. No, it was hers to live under for the rest of her days. Until it claimed her.

The side door of the house opened, and she was brought back to the garden, the pungent aroma of the soil further anchoring her in the present. A deep breath dispelled the last of the thoughts clinging like cobwebs to her mind. She glanced over her shoulder to see Marlein emerge from the house, a crate in her arms. Heinrich waved in Keterlyn's direction before placing his hand on Marlein's elbow and guiding her around the house, toward the city. She watched as he took the crate from Marlein's hands as they rounded the corner of the house, and then Keterlyn allowed herself to sink to the ground.

It felt so final.

Marlein would be leaving them. For what young woman, more than capable of keeping her own house, would spurn the offer of a fine young man about to be a lawyer in favor of keeping her mother's house? Her mother who could not keep her own.

She was broken. So very broken, though she did her best to hold it close and keep it hidden. She'd been beautiful once, and while age and sorrow had somewhat dampened her beauty, she knew she was still considered to be a handsome woman. She despised the contrast, the paradox of her life. Her hands itched to reach for her hair, for her face, to show physically what she felt on the inside. Torn. Ugly. Hands shaking, she reached up for her *Steuchlein* and pulled it off her head. But her arms were so terribly heavy, her movements unbearably labored. Lacking the strength to make her appearance match her feelings, she instead burrowed downward. The ground was soft, freshly tilled—it smelled alive, full of heady goodness, and she wanted to climb into it. But she couldn't, so she kept digging, potatoes being unearthed every time she plunged her hands into the cold, miry soil.

Yes, some of the potatoes certainly had sprouted, and she suddenly despised them for it. She herself was stagnant, good as dead, and here were tiny sprouts of life; the growth of the garden in the midst of an approaching winter hurt more than she could bear. Disgust with herself, the sorrow and sense of failure, welled up, threatening to choke her.

"I can't! I cannot do it," she sobbed over and over. Hands plunging into the garden beds, she clawed at every potato she could find.

Her life was designed for a purpose, but it didn't work as it should have. So many of her children had died. As many dead as were alive. And the pain ate at her, consuming her until there was nothing left. Nothing for her husband. Nothing for her children. Nothing at all.

# 11

The sun was well on its way across the sky, creating such brightness behind Heinrich's head as they walked that Marlein could scarcely look at him. It was certainly nothing to do with the unknown topic of the impending conversation; she knew that whatever he wanted to ask her was nothing to do with her, particularly. Still, she found it necessary to take a calming breath as he lifted the crate from her arms. Unsure what to do with her hands, with nothing to carry and nothing to occupy them, she clasped them together under her apron—a fresh one after yesterday's mess.

He began by saying, "You said yesterday that you've put up most of the harvest, yes?"

She nodded, surprised that he'd caught her passing comment last evening. The children had been tucked into bed, and the adults were sitting about the cheery fire, mending in her and Brigita's hands, candles to be shaped in the men's hands. "Though it's more of a cycle; there's always work to be done."

"Of course," he agreed, but made no attempt to say more or bring the conversation to its purpose.

After they'd taken several steps, she ventured, "How are your studies?"

"They are as one would expect—enthralling and exhausting simultaneously."

"Is that so?"

"Always." He sent a crooked grin her way, and her foolish heart flipped in her chest. Marlein looked away and silently scolded herself.

They were approaching a small copse of trees near the wall of the city. Heinrich gestured with a tilt of his head that she should precede him into the trees. She stepped carefully, following no real path, as the trees were not thick and most people stayed on the road and avoided the trees. The crate was burdensome, though, and so it seemed he felt a direct route was best. She wondered at his failure to consider the same for their conversation.

"The lectures are excellent, of course, and the work is certainly manageable," Heinrich explained. They emerged from the trees and began following the slight curve of the wall that would lead them to the city's eastern gate. "Sometimes, though, I wonder whether I'm merely chasing fancies."

"Surely the study and practice of law is a noble pursuit," she countered. Her heart ached at the thought that he might be questioning himself. His kindness to her family—helping with the candles when he really was under no obligation to do so—put her in mind of her father. Both men were so quick to help another whenever a need was discovered. It seemed to Marlein that such a quality would elevate a person's pursuits, whatever they may be.

"Oh yes, of course it is. Father Martin studied law before entering the Augustinian order." They were nearing *das Elstertor,* the gate for the road to Elster, a town to the southeast of Wittenberg. It sat on the Elbe River like their own Wittenberg. "Did you know that about him? He told us the story once, of how he was traveling back to school, nearly finished with his studies, and got caught in a storm. He prayed to St. Anne to save him and promised to enter a monastic order if he survived."

"I remember he once mentioned it during a homily."

"He has a fascinating mind. Intelligent and such a sharp wit, but never thinking highly of himself because of it." He stuck out an elbow for Marlein as they approached a large fallen tree near the wall. She gingerly placed her fingers in the crook of his elbow and stepped on and over it.

"He is a good priest. When *Mutter* lost the last one, he came to perform Last Rites for her." They were approaching the gate, and both greeted the guard. After they passed into the city, she said, "Are his lectures as engaging as his preaching?"

"Very much so; I enjoy the theology lectures perhaps more than those of my law professors. I had to receive permission to sit for some of his lectures because it is not my course of study."

"Are you thinking of changing?"

"No." He gave a small, self-deprecating laugh. "Not seriously. I am nearing the end of my studies, and Brigita needs me to provide for her."

"Ah yes." She knew well the complexities of desiring one thing while putting all of oneself into doing what was needed.

They were passing the university, and Marlein asked, "Do you have a lecture to attend today?"

"Yes, but not until later; I've plenty of time."

They continued up the *Kollegienstrasse*, passing the City Church and the *Marktplatz*. After turning down a side street, where the burgher lived, Marlein suddenly felt glad that Heinrich had accompanied her on this delivery. The street they turned down was narrow and dark, the sun being blocked by the two-story houses on either side.

"Marlein," Heinrich said as he stopped to place the crate on the ground, "are you well? That is, you seem sound of body, but I know that you are tired. Don't try to deny it—your eyes tell me the truth. With the days shortening, I know your mother's moods will be sinking, if they've not begun already."

She was taken aback by his direct question and the evidence to support his concerns. In the past, inquiries into each other's well-being had been superficial, despite the closeness of their association. With a concerted effort to sound calm and unaffected, she opened her mouth to refute him. As she spoke, though, Marlein heard her voice sharing what she'd had no intention of divulging.

"Mother had a spell yesterday." Once started, she was powerless to stop the torrent. "She was startled when Leonetta cut her hand, and I think with her efforts in the garden all morning, it was too much for her. That's why when you returned, no one else was in the garden. I'd sent Brigita to tend the children while I got Mother into bed. Once Leonetta was patched up, the children wanted to pick flowers for Mother, but they are just about gone. So they gathered nuts."

She finished rather abruptly, but could not think of anything else to say. Comments on her fear for her mother's mind seemed too much. A casual remark as to the recurring nature of such happenings seemed inadequate. She simply waited, fighting back tears.

"I suspected as much," he finally said, his voice low and perhaps a bit dark. "I do wish that I could take you away from—"

"Please, do not speak of such things."

"What do you—"

"You already do too much," she interrupted again, this time reaching out a hand to almost touch his shoulder. She stopped just short of the contact, but she observed a small shudder pass through his shoulders anyway. Marlein quickly hid her hands beneath her apron again. "Forgive me, but you're under no obligation to us. You know my father was reimbursed for any expense we've had in housing you, and you are here to study, not run errands and help a spinster."

"But that's not—"

"You are so kind. And your care for your sister so very admirable. Such inquiries after my welfare are . . . unnecessary." She looked down to find that she had twisted her apron around her hands. This was not going as she had expected. He had made no offer, no advance, and so she could not refuse anything. And yet, his kindness and care were nearly suffocating her. She hoped desperately that he understood her meaning. *Unwanted. Unbearable. Because it could never be.*

His eyes peered into her own for a brief time, and she wished she were shorter. Had it been her father, Matthäus, or even Sïfrit standing this close to her, she could simply lower her head to hide her face. And she desperately wanted to hide, for he would certainly suspect that her words did not match her feelings. How could they? He had lived with her family for several years now and never once had shown himself to be anything but a good and honorable man. Surely her fierce blush was giving her away?

She nearly wept with relief when he stepped back and bent to pick up the crate once more. They were about to start walking again when the door of the house to their left opened with a bang and out stumbled a woman. Her eyes were a luminescent hazel beneath her uncovered copper hair, her lips ruby red, and her dress made of a finer wool than even Heinrich's school clothing. Marlein recognized her as Arna Buhr, the daughter of a baker. The bread he offered was often moldering because he only roused himself to bake on occasion, otherwise spending his time in a tavern or passed out in his doorway, slumped against the doorframe. It was odd seeing Arna in such fine clothing. She glanced at the two of them before ducking her head and hurrying from the alleyway.

"That's strange," Heinrich commented before startling her by stating almost too matter-of-factly, "It is concerning my sister that I wished to speak with you."

With an effort, Marlein forced her thoughts to focus. "Yes?"

"I fear something is the matter. She seems downcast."

"I've not noticed anything out of the ordinary."

"That's just it. You didn't know her before." He shifted the crate to balance on one shoulder as they neared the door. "She was always a cheerful, outgoing girl. You have always reminded me of her. Of the girl that used to be."

They stepped up to the door Arna had left open. Heinrich closed it before banging his fist upon its solid wood to announce their presence. It was opened quickly, and Marlein's mind reeled while Heinrich exchanged the crate for several coins. What did he mean by this?

Walking through the city again, they were both quiet, thoughtful. Marlein did not know what to say. Heinrich was occupying her thoughts far too often, and she hoped that she would find a way to distance her thoughts from him. They continued in silence, but once they were outside the city wall, approaching the copse of trees, she risked a glance at him. He was worrying his lip between his teeth, but shot her a small grin when he slanted his head sideways and caught her eyes in his gaze.

As they reached the trees, he stopped so suddenly that she couldn't help but wonder if he'd planned to stop there all along. His warm hand carefully grasped her elbow as his eyes searched hers.

"Could you be persuaded to talk to my sister, to see if anything's the matter? She is so very changed from who she once was."

Marlein's face felt too warm, and she had a strong urge to pull herself from his gentle grip. But he was concerned. The worry etched lines into his face, and his eyes were clouded with uncertainty. She found herself thinking that she would do anything in her power to remove such an expression from his face.

"Of course, Heinrich. I'll speak to her."

His answering smile told her of his gratitude and of the great danger in which she found her heart.

\*\*\*

Heinrich was glad to hear her answer, though he never doubted that she would agree to help. Marlein was the sort of person who was driven by something larger than herself to do good. Her father was similar in that. Before hearing Father Martin's ideas of grace and his distaste for indulgences, he would have thought Marlein would surely have a surplus of merit like that of the saints. Now, he wasn't sure what exactly to think. About grace or Marlein.

They continued to walk, Heinrich offering his arm whenever there was a particularly tangled portion of brush or a fallen tree they needed to step over. He knew Marlein to be entirely capable, but found himself thinking that perhaps people were not made to be strong alone, but in community. At the least, that was what living at the Diefenbach home had taught him. They worked to support and encourage one another, and the whole seemed stronger for it. He liked the idea of helping the one who bore everyone else's burdens, even as he appreciated that she was willing to aid him with his own.

The pair emerged from the small wood, and he saw her family's house in the near distance. Her mother's figure was crouched near the garden, just visible beyond the house's corner. From this distance, they could not see what she was doing; he supposed it likely that she was searching for weeds. She tended to her garden fastidiously, almost obsessively.

"My father was much affected by my mother's death," he found himself saying. Marlein glanced questioningly at him, but said nothing. "He was always fairly quiet, but after she had died, when Brigita was just two years old, he never really recovered. I was ten years old and vividly remember the contrast. Our house changed from a place of light and laughter to a tomb of shadows and regret. He blamed himself, though the sickness could just as easily have taken him. We all were afflicted with it, but she was the only one who never recovered.

"After she died, he lit candles in church to pray for her soul. But if we needed light in the house, we were allowed a tallow taper—only one. The house was always dim and dismal, but Brigita was a bright spot for me. I did my best to care for her, but an elder brother is not a mother, nor even a father."

"She speaks very fondly of you," Marlein interjected.

Heinrich smiled appreciatively. "Thank you. It was never easy for either of us, but we treasured each other. She helped me trim my quills when I started Latin school and listened to me recite the letters and words I was learning. She took it very hard when I left for university, though she tried to hide it from me. I wrote to her often, though her reading skills are rudimentary at best. Simple words and short notes seemed to be all she could manage to read. I ought to have worked harder to help her learn, but my own studies occupied much of my time."

"You did the best that was in you, which is all any of us can do."

Heinrich hummed something like agreement, though her words struck a chord in him. Unfortunately, it was not a pleasant one. "Do you . . . do you think that it is ever enough, though?" he asked eventually.

"What do you mean?"

"Well, the church teaches that we do what is in us, and God will see to what we lack, through the merits of Christ and the saints, eventually cleansing us for heaven in purgatory." The words of Luther echoed in his head, disquieting the beliefs he'd held for so long. "Sometimes, though, I think that it is never enough."

"Surely you don't think that Christ's sacrifice and the merits of the saints are not enough." He could hear the alarm edging into her voice.

"Indeed not." They walked silently for a moment. "But for my part."

"I see." From the corner of his eye, he saw Marlein quickly look away from him, as though embarrassed. When she spoke, her words were halting. "I often feel similarly. I do all that is in my power to help my family, to support my father and to heal my mother, to care for my siblings. But my father is still tired every day when he returns from the shop. My siblings still cry for their mother. And my mother does not recover." She spoke the last sentence on a whisper, so quiet that he scarcely caught it.

"Father Martin says that Christ does all."

"But how can . . ." She trailed off, and he followed her arrested gaze, confused at how she'd been so distracted as to stop midthought.

They had reached the garden, and when he saw what had caught Marlein's attention, all thought of continuing their discussion flew away. Keterlyn Diefenbach lay beside the garden bed, her dress muddied and the ground upturned. Potato pieces were lying haphazardly all over the place, and the woman's silent sobs racked her body.

Marlein gasped. Her eyes were wide and watery, her hands fidgeting with her apron. "How can I help?" he asked quietly.

"Thank you, but . . . you can't. I . . . I think you'd best go. Perhaps see if Brigita and the children would want to go on a walk? I need to get her cleaned up and to her room."

He nodded, wishing he could offer . . . something. He wasn't sure what, but something more than the sympathetic glance and gentle squeeze of her elbow that he did give. He realized suddenly that he was annoyed with Keterlyn Diefenbach. She, whether she meant to or not, was adding to her daughter's burden and keeping her from a new, more pleasant way in life.

A way that would go alongside his own.

CHAPTER

# 12

Brigita was settling into her new life. She eagerly performed tasks with which she was familiar and watched carefully as Marlein demonstrated things she needed to learn. She often asked Brigita to help with things at the house or garden—but seeing to the children was her favorite task. She had no younger brother or sister, and after her father died, she lived with the Alscher family, whose sons were all grown. Her experience with children was limited up to this point. Therefore, getting to know the little ones at the Diefenbach house was certainly a happy aspect of her newfound living arrangements.

She knew that the Diefenbach household had its share of difficulty; seeing Marlein lead a silent, ashen-faced Keterlyn through the house and into her room had made that clear, if Brigita had doubted it before. But it was still much more pleasant a place to live than any place she had to this point. Marlein was kind, and sharing a room and chores with her was pleasant. But learning about the young people now in her life was fascinating. Seeing the world through their eyes almost rid her of the feeling that she had lost a part of herself along the way.

The morning after Keterlyn's episode, Brigita led the children out to look for wild carrots to pull up and bring back for winter food.

"Be careful, Aldessa!" scolded Leonetta when the girl was peering into a hole in the ground. "It could be an adder's den!"

"That's not likely," scoffed Aldessa, her blue eyes sparking. "See how big it is? More likely, a hare lives here. Maybe we could trap it for supper!"

"Come, children, remember what Marlein said we were to do?"

"Carrots!" cried Herlinde.

"That's right." Brigita dropped to her knees in the grass. "Now, who can tell me what we are to look for? I grew up in a city and haven't seen so many plants ever."

"Didn't you grow your food?"

"No, we traded candles that my *Vater* made for food in the *Markt*. I've never seen a carrot in the ground."

"Well," offered Leonetta, "the good part is underground, so you don't look for that. Look for the green part."

"The hairy leaves!" Aldessa cried, giggling.

"I was telling her," groused Leonetta.

"You can both tell me. I'll need all the help I can get!"

"Here's one," called Maria, several paces from the path they'd been following. She held aloft a plant with a fringe of green at the top that connected to a thin, pale orange root. "See?"

"Very good, Maria!" Brigita cheered. When she first met the serious little girl, she assumed she was one of the Diefenbach children. When Matthäus had come to collect Maria that evening, though, she could immediately see the resemblance. His hair was dark brown where his daughter's was a dark blonde, but they had the same soulful brown eyes. Like they'd both lived much longer than their years.

"Can we all find some? Marlein asked that we bring back as many as we can."

They all set to work, pulling carrots. Several times, Fridolin pulled up grass or some other plant instead of carrots, but Brigita smiled at him as she took it from his pudgy little hand. When he turned to look for another, she discreetly placed it beside the basket rather than in it.

\*\*\*

Matthäus banked the fire in Master Diefenbach's shop and hefted the two crates of candles. He was on his own, Sïfrit having gone to the tavern and Master Diefenbach to his house, but he didn't mourn the loss of company. Even Heinrich was absent, having told him that morning that he intended to return to the house as soon as his lecture was dismissed. Something about concern for Marlein after her mother's difficulty the previous day. He didn't offer much in the way of explanation, but Matthäus was all too aware of the struggles that the family endured.

Closing the door behind him, Matthäus bent to once again lift the two crates. It was not a difficult task, given his size. He headed east out of town, greeting several craftsmen closing their shops for the day. He planned to collect Maria from the house, help with the trimming of the candles, and return to his and Maria's room above the shop for the night. In it was the entirety of his earthly possessions, aside from his daughter. She was his most valuable: the only thing remaining from the life he had hoped to carve out with his late wife.

After he passed through *das Elstertor*, Matthäus stepped off the road to head northward and fought back a smile. Even now, nearing the end of his time with the master candlemaker, he could scarcely believe his good fortune in acquiring this apprenticeship. It was generally unheard of for a man his age to be taken on, let alone a widower with a daughter. But he needed a way to provide for Maria, so he had applied to Diefenbach's fatherly side. Now, several years later, he was nearly finished with his obligations to the man and could soon strike forth on his own.

In a corner of his room sat a frame he had made for dipping candles. Shaped with two cross pieces and pegs along the top to hold the wicks, it had taken him a good three weeks to make it just as he wanted. He planned to add a handle to the top later. Recently, in the evenings while Maria slept, he had been working on carving a set of molds for tallow candles. From a large block of hardwood, he painstakingly carved out the slender but deep hollows for the tallow to fill. Perhaps someday he would be able to devise a way to create a mold for beeswax candles; the softer makeup of the beeswax made it difficult to extract them from a mold. For now, though, tallow alone could be molded.

He had been saving for the vats and cauldrons needed for melting the tallow and beeswax . . . that was, if he ever was able to afford to work with beeswax. To start, though, he planned to travel from house to house with his small vat, melting down people's tallow and dipping their candles right there, until he could afford a shop of his own. Having a shop would make the care of his daughter much easier; having her in the shop with him rather than traveling about with him would certainly ease his mind.

Unless he took a wife.

It was not the first time the thought poked at him. It was the first time, though, that his thoughts did not go to Marlein.

He was nearing the Diefenbach house and saw Brigita walking with Maria, Aldessa, and Herlinde. The young woman smiled easily at the children, who were playing a game of chase. As he neared her, he was reminded just how much taller he was than the petite woman. He felt like a lumbering giant beside her, but that faded away as she caught his eye before looking back at the girls.

A smile broke across her face, quickly chasing away the sadness that clung to her. Matthäus felt as though he had been socked in the gut.

"They have been playing like this all afternoon," she confided. "I do not know where they get the strength!"

"Yes. When I tell Maria that it is time for sleep, she has wide eyes and starts chattering like a bird."

Brigita laughed and the sun broke through the clouds. "'Tis the same with these two."

Both grew quiet, watching the girls play. Matthäus subtly shifted the crates in his arms.

"Oh, I am sorry! You probably didn't mean to be caught up in talking with me. Go on to the house with those, and I'll bring the girls in shortly."

Matthäus wanted to protest, to say that he was more than capable of standing with the crates for a little while. But the sadness had once again clouded Brigita's face, and her sunny smile was hidden. Hoping to spare her feelings, he nodded and left.

The house was quiet in the absence of the three girls. From the side door, he could hear Marlein and Leonetta on the other side of the hearth, giggling as they prepared supper. Master Diefenbach sat near the fire with little Fridolin on his lap, making faces at the chubby, blond toddler. The elder man looked up as Matthäus carefully placed the crates in their usual spot in the room.

"You are home later than usual," Diefenbach said slowly.

Matthäus looked more closely at him, trying to decide whether the man was speaking in disapproval. "I wanted to be sure the shop was tidied before I left."

"Sïfrit could not help?"

Matthäus almost asked how he knew, but stopped himself. Instead, he offered, "He helped until his friend came to collect him."

"I see." Diefenbach settled the small boy against his chest, coaxing his head to rest upon his shoulder. Matthäus had done the same with Maria many times, until she grew nearly too long to fit beneath his chin. "There will come a time that you take on your own apprentice."

"Oh, I can't imagine—"

"I can, because you are a good worker, and careful with what you craft. You will be a master someday, sooner rather than later, and become a member of the guild wherever you settle." Rather than argue further, Matthäus simply waited to see what else the man would say. "You will need to learn mastery over the art of compelling others to do as you bid them."

"I should have forced Sïfrit to stay until all the work was finished."

"You are not the master yet. And perhaps the extra sweeping and scrubbing will serve to remind you to be more assertive next time."

Matthäus nodded, though he doubted it would help with Sïfrit.

Brigita returned with the children then, Heinrich following them in through the side door, and soon it was time to eat supper. The children shared bowls as they crowded around the table in the kitchen, and Marlein spooned out a hearty mutton stew before carrying a bowl through to her mother. Everyone in the house, and likely many in the town, knew of Keterlyn Diefenbach's difficulties, though probably not to their full extent.

Matthäus finished his bowl quickly, thinking how little meat he and his wife ate in the few months they had together before her death. Maria was just a tiny baby and did not remember her mother at all. He looked across the table at his daughter, who looked so like his Petrissa. Brigita was scraping the last of her own stew into the bowl Maria shared with Herlinde. He shot a questioning look Brigita's way.

She flushed a bit before saying, "My appetite has been off lately; I can't eat another bite."

Rather than answer, he offered a smile of thanks as he tore off a chunk of the bread on the table and used it to sop up the last of his meal.

Supper was finished, and Marlein, Brigita, and the girls began cleaning up. The men set to their own work nearer the fireplace. Matthäus began by cutting two candles apart from where they were joined by the same wick before moving on to shaping the base.

Slightly apart from the women and children, surrounded by the quiet, comfortable conversation of two men he respected and whose company he enjoyed, Matthäus easily settled into the evening routine. It was a place of peace amid his tumultuous thoughts.

Petrissa died just over four years ago, and pain still gripped him at the thought of her kind smile and her sweet voice that no longer echoed in his memory. His love for her had been as consuming as the fire that took her life, and he had never with any earnestness entertained the idea of marrying again. She had been light for him, and now his world was shrouded in darkness.

The candle in his hands was nearly finished. He wrapped his palm around the freshly cut base, allowing warmth to seep into the tallow. Once the candle felt more malleable in his hand, he used his fingers to smooth the rough edge from the cut. With a final inspection, he was satisfied with the candle and leaned toward the pile of finished candles the men were making. As he took another one, ready to be cut and smoothed, he allowed himself a moment to gaze into the fire, burning cheerily in the open hearth. Its brightness hurt his eyes as it shone in the dim room, and the pain seemed fitting to him.

# C H A P T E R

# 13

Willeic Gwerder had been away when the candles were delivered, exiting from the front door of his home, where the neighbors would be sure to see him. When he returned later, his manservant brought him to the table where he'd left the crate, and Willeic shouldered the servant out of the way and snatched up a candle. His dark eyes, matching his hair, perceived how even and smooth it was, the paleness of the beeswax charming him like the pale cheek of a woman not required to labor out of doors. Willeic begrudgingly acknowledged to himself that the coins paid were well worth the candles they'd purchased. Finally, he could rid his home of the stench of tallow candles and enjoy the sweet perfume emitted by the beeswax candles that would light the rooms.

His wife would be pleased. She'd done nothing but complain of the foul smell since their wedding. When she was pregnant with their son, she'd gagged and retched several times each day, blaming the tallow candles. But he couldn't afford the costlier beeswax when he had to keep his mistress happy along with supporting his wife.

Arna Buhr was a rare beauty with her flashing hazel eyes and hair the color of copper. He'd been taken with her a year after his wedding to Salmey, and decided that if priests could pay a penance to keep a mistress, so could he. His Baptism after his birth had cured his original sin, according to the priest presiding over the *Stadtkirche Marien* at the time, and if he paid enough coin and performed enough penance, he was certain he could balance the scale for an early release from purgatory, if he had to go at all.

Having these candles was a sure sign that he was balancing the scales. Such a luxury surely indicated his success in life—both in the realm of his trade in crafting leather items and in the realm of his eternity.

Willeic carried the taper over to the wall where a sconce held a tallow taper only half-burned. He held the new wick in the flame until it caught. When he held the candle aloft, the flame quickly settled onto the candle, bright and steady. He liked to think of it as representing his life. He was accumulating all he needed for pleasure and comfort in this life and ensuring he would be set in the next, as well.

"Take the tallow taper, Lukas; you can use it in your stall if you need light."

After the manservant took the tallow, with a disrespectful quirk of his brow and frown on his face, Willeic pushed the beeswax candle into the sconce and smiled. He had a thriving leatherworking craft, a son and heir, a marriage to the daughter of a wealthy man, and a mistress who kept him satisfied. Yes, his life was progressing very nicely indeed.

*** 

Marlein's eyes took in her family's small field. She told herself that she was merely looking to be sure it was ready to rest for the winter until planting time in the spring. But her eyes strayed to where Heinrich and the children were gathering wood on the edge of the stand of trees at the opposite side of the field, near her family's cottage where Emnelda, and her parents before her, lived. She saw him bend to speak in Aldessa's ear, and the girl jumped and ran to deposit her armload of wood on the woodpile nearby. Most of the wood they gathered, though, went into the cart Heinrich had taken to help them haul it home. Several moments later, he spoke to Maria, who carried her load of wood to the woodpile, as well.

Marlein shook herself and turned toward the small building and pen where they kept the pigs. The weather was still fine, for now, but she knew it was only a matter of time before it would be too bitterly cold to gather wood at any time but midday. In the meantime, there were three sows to prepare for market. Their small herd had done well this past year, and she and her father had agreed to give one to the monastery as part of their tithe and have the butcher prepare the other two for their own family's consumption.

"Steffan? Are you ready?"

The hired hand, nearly as old as her father, nodded. "Yes, Marlein. Here, open the gate for me, if you please? I'll need to get them out one by one. Think Heinrich is near finished with the cart? After I drain 'em, I'll need it to get 'em to the market."

Marlein nodded yes to both of the chatty man's questions and moved to the gate. After Steffan got the large sow out of the pen, grunting and likely swearing under his breath a bit when she knocked him into the post, Marlein latched the gate behind him. "I'll be in the hall, sorting reeds to dry, if you need anything," she said.

Steffan grunted an answer and herded the sow around the corner of the house, smacking the animal's side lightly with a long, narrow stick when it moved away from him.

"Yes, I'll be in here," Marlein said aloud after he had left. She was glad her father had hired the man to see to some of the chores. She knew how to slaughter a pig, but had no desire to do so if it wasn't necessary. Steffan would do very well on his own.

She shivered when she heard the sow squeal before all was silent.

Breathing deeply, Marlein moved to the pile of reeds she'd just collected. Spacing them out along the floors of the hall, she left narrow walkways in the living areas of the house and wider ones where animals would need to be moved about; it wouldn't do if they were to trample the reeds that would provide thatch for their roof.

Steffan stopped her twice to help with the other sows, but she had finished with the reeds just as Heinrich and the children tramped in through the door.

"Mind the reeds!" she called out, moving to the hearth. "You must all be hungry after such hard work. I'll have some food ready soon."

She unwrapped the bread she'd baked that morning using barley from the summer's harvest, and took some cheese and hard sausage from their respective places. After cutting it all and arranging it on a board, she invited the children to sit at the table.

"Heinrich, where's Brigita?" she asked when she noticed the young woman was missing.

"She decided to stay with Emnelda for a time," he answered as he joined them at the table, "to help her sort some of the herbs she'd gathered. She mentioned something about enjoying the time she spent in the infirmary with Sister Margreth."

"I see. Well, since my father isn't here, would you speak the blessing?"

Heinrich nodded and began to pray. "Lord God, our heavenly Father, we thank Thee for the food here provided for our nourishment, and for the hands which prepared it. Bless it to our bodies, and even as we gather together to be nourished, gather near to us and keep us in Thy care. In the precious name of Christ we pray. Amen."

"Why did you pray so funny, Heinrich?" asked Aldessa.

Mortification washed over Marlein, even though she had been wondering the same thing. But Heinrich merely laughed.

"I suppose it does seem funny, being as it wasn't what we typically say. Father Martin has been encouraging us to pray from our hearts, to pray about anything that troubles or upsets us, and to give thanks for the things we appreciate. He said that the apostles encouraged the early Christians to pray all the time, so I have taken his suggestion to heart."

He smiled at the children first, then leveled his gaze at Marlein. Her face warmed and she wanted to look away, but could not quite manage it.

"I've been especially thankful for the . . . friendships . . . I've found here in Wittenberg." His smile turned into something more playful as he added, "And so I've spent a great deal of time talking to God about those friends in prayer."

Marlein tore her gaze away and snatched up the board with food on it. "Cheese, Heinrich? Before the children gobble it all up?"

He chuckled as he took a piece, but she wasn't sure if it was in reaction to her half-hearted attempt at humor to diffuse the moment or to her discomfort at it.

"I want cheese, please!" cried Herlinde, and Marlein held out the board in the little girl's direction.

When everyone had been served, Marlein took some food for herself and sat back on the bench, trying to covertly watch Heinrich as she chewed. He had been around a lot lately. Not that his presence was rare in previous seasons, but neither had he made it a point to be available to help with chores or to occupy the children if she was working hard at finishing some task or another.

It could be that it was Brigita he was attempting to stay near; after all, he had expressed concern about her health. Marlein felt a stab of guilt at not having found the time to talk to her, but her days were so full lately that there was scarcely time to even say "Good morning" before they were hard at work. Threshing the rye Steffan harvested had started the busy season of preparing, but it certainly wasn't the end of it. There was so much to do, from pulling out winter clothes and figuring out what fit the growing children to hunting and drying and storing food to keep them through the winter. Her family was not as bad off as many in the countryside—Diefenbach owned his own land and could take wood from their trees whenever it was needed for their hearth, and any animals Steffan or her father hunted on the land could be consumed for food. But she also knew that some of their winter provisions would go to the hungry in the area, for they always did.

The thing that confused Marlein the most was Heinrich's time. He didn't have extra time on his hands, or she'd have thought he was merely hanging about because he needed activity to fill his days. But the other night, she arose just as the church bell tolled midnight in the distance because Herlinde was crying for her mother. As Marlein left her and Brigita's room in the dark, she saw light spilling from beneath Heinrich's door. If he was up late in order to complete his studies, why on earth would he be wasting his time helping around the house?

# 14

The floor was chilly beneath Johann Diefenbach's feet as he hurried to dress for the day. His wife was still abed, as she was most mornings when he rose, and tiny Fridolin snuggled into her bosom. He knew she found comfort in the tot—more than she found in him.

He heaved a sigh as he sat on the trunk to pull on his *Hosen*. This particular pair was the first of finer wool that he'd bought for himself; they were made of red and blue, each leg made from a piece of red and a piece of blue wool. With the recent increase in the success of his trade, he was finally able to provide for himself and his family some of the finer things, finer wool for their clothing being one of them. Still, he knew he would trade the best wool in a heartbeat if it would help his dear wife.

He couldn't blame Keterlyn, not really. She had been given a great deal of hardship in her life. Her suffering surely would shorten her time in purgatory, though. He wasn't sure what he thought of Father Martin's ideas of mercy and grace—what was the point of good works if not to work out one's salvation? Still, Diefenbach was not a learned man and figured he should leave the theological thought to those more qualified than himself.

He stood and pulled the long jerkin over his head, tied a belt around his waist, and bent to stuff his feet into his shoes. Many of the younger men seemed to favor the shorter doublets, displaying their legs with a newer style of dress. He preferred the older, skirted doublets and jerkins, though. His wide, floppy hat completed the outfit— for most days of working, he did not dress so carefully, but today was a meeting of the town council. Because he had not been selected to sit on it until very recently, he wanted to be sure he represented himself well. His dear Keterlyn's sufferings were no secret in town, but he knew that if he gave any hint of the extent of her despondency, they might reconsider his own fitness for such a position.

Diefenbach left the house, snagging a piece of bread he was pretty sure Marlein had left out for him the evening before. Walking to his shop was usually a good time to plan the activities of the day, but this morning his thoughts remained in the house, with his wife and family.

Over fifteen years had passed since he and his Keterlyn had lost their third-born at such a young age. Hers was not the last of the tiny graves dug for their family. Each loss remained fresh in his heart. He remembered thinking after this latest babe, though, that so many others suffered too. It did not lessen his pain, but neither was it amplified at the knowledge. It simply existed, awareness beside heartache. He found some solace in his work in the shop, but it was the times when he reached out to help alleviate the suffering of others that he found the ache in his chest subsided, just a little.

It was with great earnestness, therefore, that Diefenbach desired to contribute his voice to the plans for Wittenberg's future. The relationship between the poor and the emerging burgher class did not need to turn sour as it had been reported to in other towns—master guildsmen burning the livelihood of others who dared operate apart from their guild. Yes, quality must be ensured, but not at such a price and not as an excuse to disable a competitor. Surely there was a better way.

\*\*\*

The weather was changing; Heinrich could feel it in the air. It was sharp and cold in the mornings, warming minimally with the rising sun, and then cooling off again in the late afternoon. In very little time, the people of Wittenberg would be expecting the first snow.

Only a few days had passed since he and Marlein returned to her house to find her mother in the garden of uprooted potatoes. When he had seen Marlein that evening after returning from his lecture, her eyes had grown a bit hollow and her shoulders drooped more. Even so, the potatoes had been replanted the following day, but Keterlyn Diefenbach still had not emerged from her room.

And Heinrich's frustration with the woman continued to grow.

He could see the toll her melancholy was taking on Marlein. Her sunny smiles for him had grown rarer, and she seemed too weary most days to even meet his eyes. Their once-easy friendship now felt forced, and he sometimes wondered if it had become entirely one-sided. But surely, she was just tired.

Even so, he was gratified to help her as much as his studies allowed, while wondering even as he did why Keterlyn could not exert herself. After lectures, he hurried back to the house so he could offer to help carry things, to occupy the children so Brigita would be free to assist Marlein in the kitchen, or whatever was needed. His friends at the university had stopped asking him to come to the tavern for supper, instead bidding him goodbye with annoyingly knowing smiles as he fled the lecture hall.

The only one who seemed unconcerned with his behavior was Luther. He'd stopped Heinrich after class, asking if all was well. Heinrich had offered a brief explanation that his host family was working to prepare for winter, and he felt he should help. They helped so many in the community, and he hoped he might aid their efforts. Luther gazed at him for a moment or two, chuckled a bit, and grinned as he commended both Heinrich and the Diefenbach family for their kind consideration for their neighbors in need. Heinrich didn't give it much thought at the time, but as he left the lecture hall just now, Luther had called after him, "Give my regards to your Marlein Diefenbach."

Heinrich's face had warmed, but he merely waved, not knowing how to answer the man. Did he talk about her so much that even his theology professor knew more of his heart than he himself did?

When Heinrich reached the house that afternoon, he went through to the kitchen, stopping to greet Leonetta, who was sitting near the window and working hard to copy words onto what appeared to be a wide leaf. Marlein was at the near end of the table, busy with a large piece of fabric, several open crates scattered about the floor near her.

"What are you writing, Netta?" he asked as he stood beside where Marlein was bent over her needle and thread.

"My name," the girl replied, looking up from her work. "*Vater* says that the world is changing, and even though women can no longer be guildmembers, he thinks girls should at least be able to read and write."

"That is very true. Father Martin thinks that people should be able to read the Bible for themselves. Would you like for me to copy out a verse for you to practice writing?"

"I would!" she cried, eyes alight and a smile curving her lips.

Heinrich found her smile to be as contagious as her elder sister's, though for a different reason. "I shall go do that right now, then."

"Thank you!" She returned to her task before suddenly lifting her head again. "Oh! Do you think you could write the verse Father Martin spoke of during Mass last Sunday? About the sparrows and how God cares for them?"

Heinrich chuckled, knowing which passage she meant and how much she loved watching animals and learning about them. "Yes, but I'll need to ask Father Martin first to help me find it. I only have a book of the Psalms and then the Letter to the Galatians and the Letter to the Hebrews. But I know a psalm that speaks of thirsting for God in the same way that a deer thirsts for fresh water. Shall I copy that for you until I can ask about the other?"

"Yes, please!"

Heinrich was about to turn and go, but paused. He reached out, grasped Marlein's forearm briefly, and gave a gentle squeeze. She looked up, startled, and he grinned playfully at her. "Good afternoon to you too, Marlein. Didn't mean to ignore you."

She smiled back a bit, and while it was nowhere near as bright as he wished it would be, it was genuine. Heinrich rushed to his room to change into work clothes and write down the first verse of the forty-second psalm for Leonetta. He had to scratch out his writing several times due to mistakes; he purposely ignored the reason behind his hurried movements.

Back in the kitchen, Marlein had disappeared, and Leonetta was now working on the large piece of fabric in her seat near the window. Three crates full of food, packed and ready for winter, sat in a neat row on the table.

"Here is your verse," he said as he slid the slip of paper across the table toward Leonetta.

"Thank you!" She looked at the words and suddenly Heinrich's face warmed. He should have taken his time and written carefully, so that Leonetta could easily read the words she was only just learning. "'As the deer' . . . what is this?"

He looked where she was pointing, even though he knew the next word. Relieved that his writing wasn't too terribly illegible, he read aloud, "'Pants.' Thirsting for something."

"'As the deer pants for flowing . . .'"

As Leonetta continued to read, Heinrich turned to the crates arranged on the table. He tested the weight of the first, guessing it was full of sacks of grain.

"You read that very well," he commented after she finished. "Do you know what it means?"

Her face was screwed up in concentration as she answered. "That he wants the Lord as badly as a deer wants water?"

"And how badly does a deer need water?" Heinrich lifted the crate.

"Well, I suppose they need it to live, right?"

"And the psalmist here says that he needs the Lord in the same way. That apart from God, there is no life."

Leonetta grinned at him and he smiled back, glad he could make at least one of the Diefenbach girls smile so brightly.

"Well, I suppose your sister wants these put up, yes?"

Leonetta nodded, intent on her sewing again, so he carried the crates to the ladder. Soon he'd stored the other two as well, finding places for the crates in the increasingly cramped space above the rafters. As he came down the ladder the last time, ducking to avoid hitting his head on a beam, he saw Marlein setting out two bowls, presumably a reheated portion of what she'd prepared the previous night.

"Thank you for putting those up," she called as he walked down the hall toward the *Flett*. "I made a basket for the men at the shop and sent Brigita to take it to them while the little ones sleep," she explained when he approached the table. "They ate already."

"Is your mother feeling up to coming out to eat?" He forced his tone to remain even and not reveal any of the aggravation he was harboring.

"No." Her movements stopped, and she stared down at the piece of bread in her hand, which she had just unwrapped from a square of cloth. "I just checked on her; she's fast asleep with Fridolin."

"Ah." He wasn't sure how else to respond and was glad when Leonetta changed the subject.

She cheerfully announced, "I am hemming my new dress."

Marlein smiled indulgently at her sister, and Heinrich asked, "Are you now? What a lovely color."

"She has been a good help to me, especially lately, and I thought she deserved something nice." Marlein set out the bread. "She ate with the other girls. If you'd like, we can eat now."

The two young adults sat opposite each other at the table, and Leonetta leaned closer to the window, squinting at her stitches. Heinrich offered a prayer for the food before they began to eat.

"I suppose you sent Brigita to the shop so you would not have to interact with Sïfrit?" he said with a studiously conversational tone.

Marlein looked up with wide eyes, shooting a sideways glance at her sister, who was ignoring them. An amused grin then turned up the corners of Marlein's mouth as she said quietly, "Oh, not at all. I do so enjoy fighting off the attentions of a man so much younger than me, not nearly finished with his obligation to my father, and so full of himself that he cannot imagine why I would not be thrilled at the prospect of giving him my undivided attention when there is always something pressing to do in the house."

"Is that so?" He scooped another bite into his mouth, chewing and swallowing before he said, "In that case, perhaps I should learn more confidence and inflate my perception of my worth. And though my age cannot be helped, I do find myself obliged to your father for his generosity in hosting me."

"Oh no, I'm afraid you are much too kind and honorable to ever catch my attention. Nothing but pompous youths will do for me."

Her cheeks were rosy and her smile seemed privy to some secret, but he supposed it could be due to the warm room. Either way, the glow in her cheeks and the life in her eyes warmed his chest to almost uncomfortable proportions.

Deciding to tone down the playful banter before it grew beyond his control, Heinrich inquired, "Are you and Brigita getting along well?"

"Much better than I could have hoped," Marlein grinned. "We have much in common, not the least of which is our mutual affection for young Sïfrit."

"So, he's won my sister from me too?"

"I'm afraid so," she said, not quite succeeding at hiding the playful grin that stole across her face. "You'll be left all alone, with no wife and no sister, forced to teach the study of the law to unruly university students day after lonely, miserable day."

"No sister and no wife?" he couldn't help but tease. "I had not known that Sïfrit planned to make my sister his sister. As for a wife, I can only assume you mean yourself. Funny thing, though, I was not aware you were considering marrying me. In fact, had I known, I would have put more effort into our courtship."

He felt his chest swell as she was clearly bested in her own game, her face more flushed than could be attributed to the warm kitchen or to enjoyment of a verbal sparring match. She busied herself with pushing a piece of potato about her bowl, back and forth and around, before she ventured to raise her eyes to meet his. Once she did, he winked before saying jauntily, "Oh, but neither Sïfrit nor I ever stood a chance against your loyalty to your family."

She looked at him, her gaze open and vulnerable, her smile trembling minutely and falling before it faded away entirely. He almost apologized for the bumbled jest. But then her lips quirked into a small smile before she looked down at her bowl again. He'd forced himself to keep his expression neutral, but the truth was that the comment had slipped from his lips before he even had time to realize that it stemmed from a more frustrated place than he cared to admit.

Thinking that perhaps a subject change was in order, Heinrich asked, "Have you had a chance to speak with Brigita yet?"

Marlein looked up, regret washing over her face before she shook her head in the negative.

"I don't suppose you've had time recently," he allowed, "with all the things needing done before winter sets in."

"I have been rather distracted." Her tone was miserably apologetic and stirred his heart. "I am sorry, Heinrich."

He reached across the table to clasp her hand. "It's all right. Really, her color has improved, and she seems to be gaining weight. My worry was likely over nothing."

Marlein nodded a bit, but said, "Possibly, but I said I would speak with her, so I will be sure to do that soon. If for no other reason than to put our minds at ease."

Heinrich thanked her before focusing his attention on his food. Marlein was a young woman of great value, but she had made it clear to all who suggested it was time she marry: her time was her family's. Her heart was with them and could not be swayed. She had bound herself to their care, to her mother's care, and much as a part of him would love to attempt to win her, he knew she could never live with herself if she left them. And despite the personal aggravation it caused him, Heinrich could never live with himself if he was the cause of it.

***

Heinrich hadn't asked Marlein to be his wife. While she couldn't imagine whyever not—he constantly looked at her with silly moon eyes, so marked was his interest—Keterlyn was grateful he had decided to wait.

But it was only a matter of time.

She had tried, several times, to force herself out of bed after uprooting the potatoes. But she could not face her family. Had she really done that? She remembered wanting to see if there were any weeds to pull, wanting to lose herself in the easy rhythm of caring for her garden. The nurture of the plants seemed all she could manage anymore. Her sorrow was a mantle about her shoulders, heavy and unyielding. Even walking was a tiresome chore.

But now even her plants didn't want her. She'd snatched them from their safe, comfortable home. Just as some of her babies had left their safe, comfortable home long before they were ready to emerge, long before they had grown to the forms they were supposed to. She'd insisted on holding them, each of them. Emnelda, her face long and weary, had cleaned the tiny, lifeless bodies with infinite care year after year, wrapped and placed each one in her arms.

Though years separated them, each was etched on her heart and her memory. Sometimes she thought of them in rapid succession and relived the precious moments she had with them almost all at once. Other times, she thought first of her daughter Niesenn, who would have been eighteen had she lived longer than two years. Then was Friedank, her second son, born a year after they buried Niesenn and three months too early. Emrich followed not long after Friedank, and Albreda after him. The three girls survived, and little Fridolin. After him, she thought the babe she was carrying would survive, but when the time came to deliver, Kaetherlin's tiny body was still and lifeless. Keterlyn's heart broke, and she wished she was buried with her tiny babies.

Life pressed too hard, sorrow clouded too thick, and even the air she breathed was poison. Keterlyn was a woman broken.

# 15

Heinrich had assured Marlein that he didn't mind that she'd not had opportunity to speak with his sister, but her failure to do so still pricked at her conscience. She woke the next morning determined to speak to Brigita before the evening meal. The early morning would normally have afforded her the opportunity, but the younger woman slept soundly while Marlein readied for her day. She splashed water on her face before dressing in an old, threadbare gown. When Marlein pulled up the covers on their shared bed, Brigita rolled over and burrowed beneath them.

She had not been there for even two weeks, but had settled well into the Diefenbach household. Brigita carried more than her weight with the chores that she did, and her patience with the children was a great help. While there had not been opportunity for the private conversation that Heinrich had requested, Marlein felt a true bond with Brigita and had come to look on her as a sister. Having her there had raised Marlein's spirit to such a degree that she'd even found herself jesting with Heinrich yesterday.

Leaving their room, Marlein stepped to the door beside hers to peek in on her sisters. Since Leonetta's birth, she and Marlein had shared rooms; but when Brigita arrived, Leonetta began sleeping in the room with the youngest two girls. They all slept soundly that morning, and Marlein crept in to cover Herlinde, who had kicked the blanket away from her. After closing their door quietly, she went out to bring in firewood from the pile outside. Raising the grate, Marlein carefully placed some small pieces of wood near the brightest embers and waited for them to catch fire. Once they were blazing, she added larger chunks of wood a couple at a time until the fire was hot enough for cooking.

Next, she set up the pot hanging over the fire and made a simple gruel, keeping the noise down as much as she could. While her father was already gone and her mother and siblings could sleep through anything, Heinrich seemed to be a light sleeper. He had never complained about her waking him, but more than once she had dropped something with a loud bang, and he came out of his room soon after. This morning, though, she managed to start the gruel without any mishaps. While it was cooking and thickening, Marlein dashed down the row of stalls to be sure Steffan had fed their animals and see whether the chickens had laid any eggs.

"You rascals!" she cried when she found no eggs. "See if we don't have chicken pies for supper in a few days if you don't start laying soon. I know it's cooler than you'd like, but you can huddle together for warmth!"

Marlein hurried back to the kitchen, standing by the fire for a moment to warm her hands; she supposed she could not blame the chickens too much for not laying when that end of the house was so much colder than this end. The outside air was not as brisk as it had been the previous evening, and she guessed that once the sun rose, it would be one of the last warmer days. With the harvest stored safely, today she would finally get to the washing. Before long, the children woke, and shortly after that, everyone was up and preparing for the day.

After everyone broke their fast, Marlein and Brigita bundled up the washing into a small cauldron and a large basket. Their party of seven—the two young women and the five children—trekked to the deepest part of the stream running along the western edge of the woods behind their house. When they neared the bank, Marlein sent the five children into the surrounding area to gather sticks for the fire. As they went, she set down the small cauldron, heavy even though it held only a few bed linens in it, and uncovered the small ring of stones they had used to contain the fire the last time they brought out the washing, a few months ago. It had been much warmer then.

"Marlein! Marlein! Look at the big stick I found!" She looked up from her task to see Aldessa half dragging a branch larger around than her arm and twice as tall as she was.

"My, Aldessa! I'm shocked you can even carry that!"

"I'm a big girl!" she exclaimed, puffing out her chest. "Of course I can."

Marlein smiled at her sister. "Well, I'm afraid it is too big for our little fire, for I've nothing to chop it with and it is too big to break."

"Should I take it to the house?" She jumped and turned, the branch swinging widely and her pale hair catching the sunlight.

Marlein warmed at her sister's eagerness to help. "If you like. Just hurry back."

"Yes, Marlein."

"Oh, and Aldessa?" The five-year-old stopped in her tracks, swinging the branch again and making Marlein glad she'd already stepped a few paces away from her. "I seem to have forgotten to bring fire. Could you please take a taper from the box, light it from the embers in the hearth, and bring it in a lantern?"

Aldessa's eager nod was her answer, and she turned and started for the house.

"She is a good girl," murmured Brigita. "She reminds me . . ."

Marlein waited a moment, to see if she would finish her thought, but when Brigita started to busy herself with clearing brush from the fire ring, she gently probed, "What does she remind you of?"

Brigita peeked over her shoulder, meeting Marlein's eyes timidly before turning away and saying, "Myself. When I was younger. It isn't that I think she is like me now. I'd never think that."

"I do." Marlein scooted from her crouched position on the other side of the ring of stones until she was within arm's reach of Brigita. "I see a great deal of all my sisters in you. Kindness to all, enjoyment in helping, sweetness of spirit."

Brigita's shoulders were stiff, and she repeatedly shook her head almost as soon as Marlein had started speaking. "It's kind of you to say, but you really don't know me very well."

"I know what your brother has said of you. And I know what I've observed."

"But much can be hidden, even from those who know you well."

Confusion clouded Marlein's mind, but she couldn't ask what Brigita meant by her words because the children were returning, arms full of long, slender sticks and a few thicker ones.

"Is this enough?" asked Maria, dropping her pile where Marlein indicated, just a few steps away from the ring. The other children followed suit, even little Fridolin throwing down a handful of tiny twigs from his chubby hands.

"For now. Can you each take three sticks and break them into pieces about as long as your forearm? And Herlinde, your thicker pieces there will be good to make the fire burn hotter. Can you put them in our ring here?"

As the three-year-old did so, Marlein glanced over at Fridolin, who had a stick in his mouth, chewing slowly on the end. "Oh no, Frid! We mustn't chew them; they're for the fire."

She gently pried the stick from the boy's hand and led him to the ring. Arranging the sticks, she explained to the children that the small ones would catch more quickly, but also burn out faster. Once the larger branches caught fire, the smaller ones would be embers and ash.

"Now, we just wait for Aldessa." Marlein sat back on her haunches. "Why don't the rest of you children go and see if there are any fish in the stream. If there are, we will catch some and cook them here while we wait for the laundry to dry."

They scurried off, Leonetta holding firmly to Fridolin's hand.

Seeing an opportunity, Marlein drew up her courage. "Forgive my bluntness, Brigita, but it seems that if I dance around the issue, there will never be the chance to ask. Are you well? Your brother is concerned for you."

Brigita's face paled and her eyes widened, reminding Marlein of a cornered hare. "I . . . am not . . . certain that . . ."

"Here's the fire!" called Aldessa, startling both women from their uneasy pause.

"Thank you, dear. The other children are looking to see if there are any fish. Why don't you join them?"

Marlein busied herself with lighting the fire in the ring, then carefully stoking the flames and adding branches as the tiny twigs were burned up by the growing flames. She knew she had been blunt and abrupt with Brigita and wanted to give her a chance to collect herself.

"Heinrich is right," Brigita finally said. "Something happened. Something . . . something I'm not sure I can tell him. Though he'll know soon enough."

"Would you like to tell me?"

"There are fish!" shrieked Leonetta as the children came barreling toward them.

"Mind the fire!" called Marlein, her heart thundering as she thought of one of the children tumbling headlong into the fire. "Very good, then. We must first gather some water for the washing, then see if we can net some of the fish."

The children gave a cheer as Marlein stood and hefted the bucket to gather the water.

"Now, Leonetta, I would like for you to gather the water. You know to dip the bucket carefully, to get the cleanest water, yes?" The girl nodded and headed toward the water. When Brigita followed to help keep an eye, Marlein turned to the others. "The stream is cold and deep enough that the little ones won't be able to stand with their heads above water, so Aldessa, you need to keep them back while Leonetta gets the water."

The younger children moved to the field to the west, chasing one another and laughing, while Marlein situated the cauldron above the fire. Bucket by bucket, it was filled with water and started to steam. As Leonetta ran to the other children, Marlein used the laundry paddle to stir in lye soap and then grabbed one of her father's shirts from the top of the pile. Once it had been submerged in the hot water, Brigita dropped another shirt into the cauldron, and Marlein used the paddle to stir them around.

"You didn't see any stains?"

"No. I'll set any with stains aside, and go beat them on a rock in the river once I take some for rinsing."

Marlein nodded.

"So, Brigita," she said as she worked a third shirt into the water. "Will you tell me what is troubling you?"

Brigita had been picking up a shift of Marlein's but at the question, her hands fumbled and she dropped it, right beside the fire. "Oh no!" Brigita cried, bending to pick it up. "I'm so sorry!"

"Brigita!" Marlein set the paddle on the ground, taking the chemise from her. "Please don't give it another thought. Clearly, I upset you, or you'd never have reacted like that. Please, tell me. Maybe I can help."

Brigita hesitated a moment, wringing her hands. Finally, she drew an audible breath and said, "I doubt you can, but thank you for wanting to." She overturned the basket with her load of the washing, then held it out while Marlein lifted the dripping shirts from the cauldron.

"Just set it down," Marlein instructed. "We can carry it to the stream after we've washed a bit more."

Brigita nodded and snatched up a small chemise from the pile, placing it into the water for Marlein to soak and stir. "You are right that something is troubling me." She was quiet for a moment. "I am certain that nothing can be done, at least not that I would accept . . ."

Marlein purposely kept her voice quiet, as when she spoke with her mother during an especially bad spell. Gentle. Pouring as much care and love into her voice as she could. "Can you tell me?"

Marlein swirled the clothes in the water several times before Brigita answered.

"You will not see me the same." She twisted the shirt in her hands.

"And you cannot know that unless you tell me," Marlein countered, wiping away some sweat trickling down the side of her face. The air was cool, but the fire was hot.

"Perhaps. But Diefenbach or my brother will send me away."

Marlein lifted the clothes with the paddle, allowing them to fall back in before starting to stir in the other direction. "Is this a sin for which a confessor might be able to instruct you in penance?"

"I fear telling even a priest, for what will I do when he tells me I cannot be forgiven?"

"Surely your sin is not so great as that." Marlein remembered then something that Father Martin had said in the sermon a couple of weeks ago. "God's mercy reaches farther than we can stray."

"I . . . I cannot be sure of that."

"I promise you, Brigita, I will do all I can to help you."

"Please wait until you've heard before you promise something like that," she whispered. "Hope is too precious, and the loss of it too costly."

"Very well." Marlein gave one last vigorous stir to the clothes in the cauldron before lifting them once more with the paddle, pausing to allow most of the water to drip back into the cauldron, and finally shifted the dripping clothes into the basket. As Brigita placed more in the cauldron, Marlein located each of the children with her eyes, assuring herself that Leonetta was keeping charge of Fridolin.

Brigita seemed to have gathered her courage then, for she began speaking. Her voice wavered and her words started haltingly. "When our father died, Heinrich offered to leave school." Brigita paused while Marlein pushed the dry fabric into the water, bubbles of air escaping and bursting on the surface. "He said that he could return later, though I'm not sure I believed him. Our neighbors offered to let me stay with them, though, and it seemed a perfect arrangement. Alscher and his wife are good people, with three sons and no daughters. The thought was that I could help her with the house, and they would provide me with food and shelter. It worked well . . . for a time."

Marlein looked sharply at Brigita, alarm causing her heart to race. "They did not mistreat you?"

"Oh no! That is, not really." Brigita choked on the words. "I did not . . . I'm afraid that . . . I mistreated them."

Marlein's alarm did not abate, but she waited as patiently as she could, stirring the clothes in the cauldron, then lifting them to the basket. She willed her heart to calm, and sweat tickled her back as it dripped down her spine, under her chemise and bodice.

As Brigita held up a shirt of her brother's to search for any stains, she continued, "After a time, their middle son, Nikolaus, started to pay me special attention. It was nothing, really, but he would bring me a flower when he came back from delivering the metal items that his father made. Once he gave me a length of ribbon from a trip he made to Hamburg."

"That was kind of him," Marlein allowed cautiously. The words spoken seemed innocent enough, but Brigita's tone alluded to a different path the story would take.

"It seemed so," Brigita conceded, "but then he began to expect . . . repayment."

Marlein's stomach twisted uncomfortably.

"He'd ask to hold my hand when he carried something for me." Her voice had dropped to just above a whisper. "Or for a kiss when he gave me a flower."

"And when he gave you the ribbon?" The words were spoken before Marlein knew they were forming.

Brigita's face flushed and she twisted the linen in her hands. "He asked for something that left me with child."

# 16

Marlein could not force words through her lips. Her whole face felt numb, shock having spread from her mind through her body like a paralyzing venom. Brigita gazed anxiously back at her, her frail shoulders trembling and her eyes wide with fear. They slowly filled with tears, until it was too much for them to hold and the shiny drops spilled over onto her flushed cheeks. Marlein was shaken from her stupor and stepped forward to embrace Brigita, who was now sobbing. A glance over the girl's trembling shoulder revealed that the children were still a safe distance from the river.

Saying nothing, the women stood together, Marlein rubbing small, gentle circles on Brigita's back until her sobs subsided.

"How—" Brigita started to say until a hiccup interrupted her, "how can you bear to look at me, much less touch me? The church teaches that virginity is a virtue to be extolled, and I've thrown mine away."

Marlein forced away the cringe that wanted to creep onto her face at such blunt talk, instead offering a small smile. "First, you must tell your brother. He knows something is the matter, for he asked me to speak with you." Marlein drew a deep breath, turning to practical concerns, as they were easier to address than the confusing questions swirling in her mind. "Are you certain, then, that you are with child? Is it possible that something else is at work?"

Brigita shook her dark-blonde head. "My courses have been absent for some months now, and the last time was before . . . before it happened."

Marlein nodded, trying to remember what she'd learned from her mother. "Have you felt the quickening at all?"

Brigita shook her head and her face turned red as she countered, "But I've been sick for the same amount of time, and my bosom has grown and hurt terribly until recently."

Marlein took her time considering. The signs were consistent with what she knew of a pregnancy, but there was always the possibility that something else was at work. "Perhaps we should have Emnelda examine you? She was a trusted and respected midwife at one time."

Rather than agree or not, Brigita asked, "But no longer? What happened?"

"She grew old without marrying and bearing a daughter to aid her, and can no longer go to laboring women." Marlein supplied only the most basic information of what had happened before redirecting Brigita back to the topic at hand. "She will be able to help you determine."

"Perhaps I should." Misery then fell like a pall over the girl's face. "But I fear Heinrich hearing of it. I would not be able to bear it if he wanted nothing to do with me."

Marlein had a difficult time imagining Heinrich disowning his sister, knowing how kind he had always been with her family. "I haven't sent you away, and neither will your own brother."

Brigita seemed to consider her words before asking, "Will your father, though?"

"I cannot say for certain, but he is a kind and compassionate man, and I believe that even if he decides it would be best for you to leave our house, he will see to it that you are cared for. He will not cut you off from our family entirely."

"Even if this is true, I do not see how I can be forgiven. Virginity is allowed to be surrendered only inside the holy bounds of marriage, for those who cannot remain pure outside of marriage."

"Father Martin has said many times that the estate of marriage is a good and honorable one." Again, Marlein fought back the urge to squirm uncomfortably and answered the easiest of Brigita's protests, rather than the one at the heart of the matter. She knew those sorts of relations happened inside marriage and outside of it, but due to her own circumstances, had never given much thought to it one way or another. She was unprepared for a conversation such as this.

"But I am not married!" Brigita's cry was loud enough to draw the attention of the children. Marlein waved to them, smiling as widely as she could, and they returned to their game of chase.

When she turned back to Brigita, the girl seemed ready to break down sobbing, her lip trembling and tears flowing silently from her eyes down her smooth cheeks. Marlein hurried to say, "Regardless, the first thing that must be done is to tell your brother."

It was many moments before Brigita said quietly, "Perhaps you are right."

"I know that I am." Marlein returned to stirring the clothes in the cauldron before lifting them with the paddle. Again, she counted the children as the water drained from the clothes.

They carried the basket of washed clothes between them and started to rinse the pieces one at a time in the gently running stream. The cold water was refreshing after the heat of the fire, and they worked in silence for a time.

Marlein lifted the garment she'd rinsed and began to wring it out with her hands. Speaking aloud the thoughts she'd been pondering, she mused, "You clearly are not in love if you ran from him. Does he love you?"

"Love?" Brigita laughed then—a short, disbelieving sort of snort that startled Marlein. "Not at all. More like he was afraid I'd tell some-one what he did."

Marlein started to nod her head as she pulled another shirt from the basket. As Brigita's words sank in, though, she wondered at them. "You mean in sending you away rather than marrying you after con-ceiving a child?"

Brigita was silent long enough that Marlein looked over at her. Their eyes met; then Brigita spoke. "No. I was already set to leave for some time. We . . . it happened shortly before I left, so he likely doesn't even know."

Swishing a shirt in the water as if she could wash away unpleasant memories, Brigita continued her tale. "After I left the Alscher fami-ly, I went to a convent outside Schönebeck. Once I was there, I had no thought of him coming after me; why would he? Sister Margreth helped me write to him, explaining that I . . . that I couldn't remain with their family after . . . More than two months passed with no word from him. Then he arrived late in the evening, and I had to flee through a door on the other side of the convent."

"You fled from him? Did you think he would cause you harm?" Marlein's heart clenched as she watched the girl's face twist with worry. "Do you have reason to believe he would follow you?"

"He is searching for me. During my journey here, while I was hid-ing, he came very near. Near enough for me to hear him, and he talked of returning to Magdeburg to begin a more careful search."

Marlein nodded but had difficulty connecting her thoughts enough to form a question. The entire situation seemed off, and while she hoped that Brigita was not keeping anything from her, it seemed almost certain that something else was at work.

"I went to the convent well before they expected me. I begged to be allowed to stay, and they assigned me to work with Sister Margreth in the infirmary after I took my initial vows. I missed my courses a couple of weeks after that. After the second time, I spoke with Sister Margreth, confessed to her what I did and what I suspected. She offered me a potion that might end the pregnancy, or the chance to leave. Because I had not begun my novitiate period yet, she pointed out that it would be easier for me to leave right away than after I took my final vows."

"Did you consider . . ?" Marlein trailed off uncomfortably.

"I'm not sure. Possibly?" Brigita gave an uncomfortable chuckle that fell flat. "I think I was mostly shocked at her offer. I'd heard rumors of what sometimes happens in some convents, between a nun and the priest. But to have it confirmed . . ."

"It is rather startling," Marlein offered.

Brigita smiled sadly. "It is. But not all convents are like that, and not everyone in them. It is exceptionally difficult for some, I suppose. I had not even committed to that life or entered the convent before I fell, so I cannot think ill of them."

Marlein's heart ached at the sorrow filling Brigita's eyes with tears, so she gently called her back to the present. "And you chose to run?"

"I did." Brigita expelled a breath heavily and pulled the garment she was rinsing from the stream's water and began squeezing out the water. "Sister Margreth found the dress I came in and an old cloak, as it was summer when I arrived. She also packed some food for me."

"I am glad God sent someone to aid you at that time."

Brigita stood and shook the shirt out with a loud snapping sound. "I doubt it was God. I've sinned, terribly. I can't imagine that He'd have helped me escape."

Something in Brigita's words lodged in Marlein's mind, like a pebble in her shoe, but she could not decide what she didn't like about it. She kept silent as Brigita called for Aldessa, who was playing with the other children some twenty paces away.

"Can you manage to lay this out over the bushes there?"

"Yes, Brigita." Aldessa smiled adoringly at the older girl and took the shirt.

Brigita took another garment from the basket and started the rinsing process again.

"This will be faster when the children are older," Marlein commented. "Though I am thankful for your help, with more than just the laundry."

Brigita looked up from the water and smiled. "If you want to go wash, I don't mind staying here to rinse."

Marlein wondered whether Brigita simply did not want to be interrogated further about her circumstances, but aloud she said only, "That is a good idea. Thank you." She stood, but before turning to go to the fire, she added, "I am glad you told me, Brigita, and please do tell your brother soon; delaying will only give us less time to find a solution."

Laying a hand of comfort, of solidarity upon Brigita's shoulder, Marlein waited for a response, but the other girl merely nodded, keeping her head bowed to her work.

# 17

Discomfort squirmed in Brigita's stomach, and for the first time in several months, it wasn't nausea. As she knelt by the stream, rinsing each piece of laundry, she could not account for Marlein's kindness to her. They had continued working together after her confession, and once everything had been washed, Brigita finished rinsing while Marlein caught and cooked some fish, joking that the men were on their own for a meal today. After, Marlein took the rinsed clothes and spread them out on various thickets and bushes to dry. Throughout the time, Brigita watched fearfully for the change in behavior she was sure would come. How could Marlein not treat her differently, now that she knew? Brigita was a fallen woman, left with the direst of consequences for her wantonness, and yet Marlein had offered comfort. Help, even. She did not know what to make of it.

Her uncertainty was banished and her confused thoughts scattered, though, by a loud shriek.

"Marlein! Marlein!" sobbed Leonetta from nearby.

"What is it, Netta?" Brigita asked, being nearer to the girl.

"Dessa's been bitten!"

"Where is she?" Brigita asked, rising to her feet and catching the seven-year-old by the shoulders as she stumbled to a halt.

"By that tree! I told her it was an adder's nest!" Leonetta's face was flushed and her eyes glassy with tears.

"It will do no good to be angry now, dear," Brigita mildly reprimanded. "She'll know now, but the best thing you can do is run and fetch your sister. I think she took some of the rinsed clothes to lay out on the thicket."

Both looked downstream and saw Marlein, shaking out a dress and carefully arranging it on the tangle of barren branches edging the field.

While Leonetta sprinted toward her elder sister, Brigita turned and ran to where the other children were gathered around Aldessa's quivering form.

"You've been trying to make friends with an adder, I hear?" Brigita crouched down beside the girl as she spoke. The five-year-old's hair was mussed, and sweat was beginning to gather in tiny droplets along her hairline.

"N-no, I-I th-thought it was a ha-hare's hole . . ."

Aldessa trailed off into a wail, but Brigita kept her voice calm and low as she worked at removing Aldessa's shoe. "I see. Did you know that before I came here, I helped Sister Margreth in the infirmary? While we were there, one of the novitiates was brought in after she was bitten by an adder."

The little girl finally quieted, then hiccuped and swiped her sleeve across her nose. "No, I didn't know that."

Brigita nodded and peeled off the stocking. "Well, then you'll never guess what Sister Margreth did to help."

"Did she suck out the poison?" asked Aldessa.

"How did you know that?" exclaimed Brigita, smoothing the girl's pale hair as she did so.

Aldessa giggled a little and hiccuped again. "Because I do. What's wrong with my ankle? Why does it burn so much?"

Brigita looked down at the wound and was glad to see that while the skin around it was red and swollen, it had not spread very far yet. "The poison the adder put in your ankle is what's making it burn. Lie back, and lift your leg. Yes, that's it." She supported it at Aldessa's knee and foot, careful to avoid the inflamed area. "Now, let me see if I can do it as Sister Margreth did."

Brigita lowered her head and sealed her lips around the wound. She breathed out harshly through her nose, then began pulling blood—and hopefully the venom—from the wound into her mouth. Suddenly, she was afraid she might retch and stopped to spit several times into the grass beside them.

"Is it yucky?" asked Maria, wide-eyed.

Brigita shuddered and managed to say, "Very. Tastes like metal," before steeling herself to begin again. She remembered Sister Margreth pulling three mouthfuls from the novitiate, so it was her aim to do the same for Aldessa.

Just as she spat the third mouthful away, Marlein came barreling into the area. "Oh, Aldessa! I'm so sorry!"

"Brigita is helping me," said Aldessa, and Brigita turned just in time to see the relief flood Marlein's face.

"Should we get her to Emnelda's?" Brigita asked.

"Yes. Yes, of course. Thank you, Brigita, for thinking so quickly. Here, I'll carry her; can you follow with the children?"

"Of course, but may I wash out my mouth first?"

"Oh yes! Certainly. Come along then, children." She was already some ten paces away. "We'll see you there, Brigita!"

Brigita hurried to the stream, stopping behind a bush to retch onto the ground. It seemed her time of sickness was not quite over after all. When her stomach settled again, she knelt once more by the water, cupping her hands and bringing some of the clear liquid to her mouth.

She sucked in the water, swished it around, and spat onto the ground. The water ran pink and nearly turned her stomach again. She breathed through her nose until she felt settled, grateful that her mouth was clean again.

She stood. Three shirts remained in the basket, so she shook them out and set them out to dry. When there was nothing else to be done there, Brigita started toward Emnelda's tiny cottage.

***

Emnelda was carefully wrapping string around the stems of some branches of sage. The plants' growth had slowed considerably as the weather cooled, but so long as it produced new leaves, she would harvest it. With winter coming, plenty of people would need its curative power as coughs and tender throats became more common.

Her fingers ached as she fumbled the knot on the last bunch of it and tossed it into the basket beside her stool.

"I'll sit a spell," she said to no one in particular, though her orange-striped cat meowed at her. "Yes, I'm not as young as I once was."

She carefully rubbed her knobby fingers, thinking as she did that she ought to put some salve on them to help with the pain.

A loud knocking startled her into rising quickly from her stool. Once upon a time, she would have sprung up, but as it was, she stood and hobbled over to answer the summons.

"Oh, thank heavens, Emnelda!" Marlein cried, carrying one of her sisters.

"Whatever is the matter, Aldessa? Not making your sister carry you for no reason, are you?"

"No. A snake bit me!"

"Heavens! And Leonetta was just here the other day with the cut on her hand." She cleared the table off as she spoke and motioned Marlein to set the girl on it. Meeting Marlein's eyes with the question of how serious it was, she said aloud, "How is your sister's hand healing, then?"

"Very well, I think," Aldessa answered.

"Yes," spoke up Leonetta from the doorway. "I helped carry sticks for our laundry fire. And dip water from the stream for the washing."

"I carried a very big branch," piped up Aldessa. "It was taller than me!"

As Aldessa spoke, Marlein nodded over the girl's head to communicate to Emnelda that her wound had not yet progressed to a dangerous point, though of course it could worsen if left untreated.

"Isn't that something?" Emnelda clucked as she began to examine the wound. The two puncture marks from the adder's fangs were not too close, indicating an older snake who'd already settled in for the winter, and though they looked painful, they were not as deep as others she'd seen. Thankfully, it was not a younger snake; those often were more frightened, and any self-respecting midwife knew that the fear made their venom deadlier. Even so, the redness and swelling should have been worse than it was. "Why is there not more swelling around the wound?"

"Oh, Brigita sucked out the venom!" spoke up Leonetta. "She said it tasted icky, but she wanted to help. I told Aldessa that it was an adder's den, but she wouldn't—"

"That's enough, Leonetta," warned Marlein.

Emnelda chuckled and patted Leonetta's head. The girl was growing like a weed, already up to her shoulders. "I'm sure she's learned her lesson, Netta. Now let's see about treating the wound."

She hobbled over to a shelf, made by her father for her mother when she was a midwife for the women of Wittenberg. It was built with a boxlike shape, and an added piece of wood across the front ensured the small bottles and small casks it held were less likely to be knocked from their place.

"Now where is the St. John's Wort?" she asked herself. She'd harvested it wild last June and boiled it down to make a decoction. "There you are!" She snatched the gray stone cask from its place and pried off the lid. "We will make a poultice for the wound, and I'll also mix some theriac for her to drink."

Just then, the door opened and Brigita entered the cottage. "I'm sorry I took so long; I set out the other shirts to dry before I came."

"Thank you," murmured Marlein, holding tightly to Aldessa's hand.

Emnelda's interest peaked and she asked, "So, you are the one with the fortitude to suck out the venom."

The young woman froze, arm outstretched, as she reached for Aldessa's other hand. "Well . . . I . . . just did what was needed."

There was an air about the girl that Emnelda noticed immediately. Under the concern on the girl's face was a misery. Perhaps it was worry about Aldessa's life, Emnelda considered, but there was a weariness that spoke of weeks or even months of misery. As Emnelda hurried to gather the other ingredients, she recalled something she'd heard just the previous week. "When Father Martin comes to visit me, he's taken to teaching me more about the ways that God helps us. In Christ, of course, but also working through people to help us." She paused, waiting until Brigita's eyes lifted to meet her gaze. "What just happened was God helping that child by using you. Don't dismiss what He calls good."

Brigita's expression was skeptical. Rather than comment on it, though, she indicated the cask in Emnelda's hand. "St. John's Wort?"

Emnelda blinked and continued with what she was doing. "Yes. For a poultice."

"Would you also give her theriac?" Brigita's voice was detached and matter-of-fact, almost desperately so.

"I just told the others we should." Emnelda almost laughed. "Have you worked under a midwife before?"

Brigita had spotted a relatively clean piece of linen hanging to dry by the fire and shook it out as she answered. "I assisted in the infirmary of a convent for a short time. Would this work for the poultice?"

"Yes." Emnelda accepted it from her proffered hand. "I keep dried items in the box by the fireplace. Would you go find balsam seed and anise? I have gentian and rue out already."

Brigita nodded and hurried to the fireplace, where she crouched and began searching for the items among the herbs and other botanicals in the box. Emnelda began mixing the poultice and moved to secure it around Aldessa's ankle. Marlein bounced Fridolin on her hip as she shuffled Maria and Herlinde out of the way to allow Emnelda access to the wound.

"It's getting rather crowded in here," Marlein managed as Fridolin began to fuss in her arms. "Aldessa, would you mind if Brigita and Emnelda stay with you while I take the other children home? I'll come back as soon as I can."

Emnelda watched as Aldessa looked first at her, then at Brigita. She smiled and answered, "Yes. And I'm sorry, Netta, for not listening to you."

Leonetta's eyes grew glossy and she bit her lips before she answered. "I'm sorry for being bossy. I love you, Dessa."

The girls smiled at each other, and Emnelda wondered, not for the first time, what it would have been like to have a sister, or even a daughter. Would they have been close like the Diefenbach girls?

"Here you are, Fraulein Steuben," Brigita said, bringing Emnelda from her thoughts.

"Thank you. And *Emnelda* will do just fine. No one else calls me anything but my given name." She took the items and began measuring portions into the small pot she hung over the fire. "Please fetch the wine, then stay beside Dessa. Let me know of any strange behavior," she requested while pointing a gnarled finger to the wine's location. Taking it from Brigita, she poured a small amount into the pot, just enough that it would hold the dried ingredients she continued to add. Gentian and anise were the last to go in, then she waited for the mix to boil a few minutes, then poured it into an empty cask.

"She seems to be doing just fine," Brigita commented after she'd settled by the girl.

"You did well, removing the venom so quickly." Emnelda placed the cask in Brigita's hand. "Give her some now, and again every few hours until it is gone. It should help rid her body of the rest of the poison."

Brigita nodded. "Thank you. This could have been much worse."

Emnelda waved away her thanks. "God grants healing according to His will. We are just the tools of that." She took the cask back and held it out to Aldessa's lips, while Brigita raised up the girl's shoulders so she could drink. "I noticed when you brought Netta here with her cut hand that you seem quite knowledgeable about healing. How long did you work with the Sister?"

"Only a couple of months," Brigita whispered as she lowered the girl's shoulders.

Emnelda kept her voice well within the scope of casual observation, hoping to hide her keen interest in Brigita's story as she commented, "You seem to have picked up quite a bit."

"Some. I did enjoy my time with her." She kept her hands busy and eyes distracted as she fussed with smoothing Aldessa's hair and straightening her skirt.

Emnelda nodded. "You did very well today."

Again, Brigita embodied discomfort. She shrugged her narrow

shoulders, then buried her hands in the folds of her skirt. "I should probably get her along home. Should I report back tomorrow with her progress? I'll come immediately if fever sets in."

Emnelda nodded, unconcerned with Aldessa's health; the girl was lucid, and the swelling was minimal and not worsening. Rather, she wondered about Brigita and why she could not acknowledge a compliment or raise eyes to her own.

C H A P T E R

# 18

When Heinrich heard that Aldessa had been bitten by a snake, his first thought was for the child's welfare, and immediately following that, he wondered if it would send Keterlyn into another fit of deeper melancholy than she had heretofore displayed. But then Marlein hushed his questions as to Aldessa's welfare, whispering her intent to keep the incident from her mother; she reasoned that the poor woman needn't be bothered with it.

*Poor, indeed.*

But Heinrich hid any inclination to scowl and heard Marlein's whispered report on what had happened, leaning in closer than usual to hear her low voice.

In very few days, it seemed that aside from a bandage making her stocking bulge a bit at her ankle, Aldessa was just fine. Her limp was gone, and in just a couple more days, the bandage had been removed as well, Keterlyn none the wiser. Heinrich supposed it was easier to keep things from the woman when she so seldom emerged from her room.

On Aldessa's first day without the bandage, Johann took her and the other children to the shop; he said that he needed help sorting the latest batch of candles by size.

"You know as well as I do," intoned Marlein drily as she pulled a canister the size of her palm from the shelf on the wall, "that he had those candles sorted as they were made."

Heinrich chuckled, happy to have some time with Marlein and his sister. "He just wanted to give you some time; you've been working so hard."

Marlein started to protest, but Brigita spoke up as she entered the room, tying an apron about her waist. "She has, but we won't be lazing about today." Under the apron, she wore an old but warm dress of Marlein's that had been taken up to accommodate her shorter stature.

Marlein smiled at Brigita before bending to retrieve the lone cask of flour.

"All right, I have nearly everything for supper. I hope the hens have some eggs for us, or I may have to go begging, if any of the neighbors have a surplus."

Heinrich reached for her wrist, gently squeezing before he even knew what he was doing. Marlein's questioning eyes met his. Swallowing his chagrin at acting without thinking, Heinrich pulled up one corner of his mouth in what he hoped was a convincing grin. "I'll get the eggs."

Marlein didn't speak right away, but bemusement overtook her features. "Do you know how?"

"Yes. Don't you remember teaching me last year?"

"Hm." Marlein withdrew her hand and pretended that the lid on the cask of flour needed adjusting. "I suppose I did. Thank you, then, Heinrich."

He nodded, plucked a basket from where it hung on the wall near Steffan's stall, and moved toward the last stall on the left. The chickens were often given free rein in the yard during the warmer months and only came in to their roosts when night fell. But now that the temperatures were dropping, they had taken up permanent residence in the stall, huddling close to keep warm. Theirs was the farthest stall from the house because it smelled worse than everything except the pigs, whose stall was beside theirs.

Heinrich unlatched the half door and hurried in, pulling it shut behind him before any of the hens escaped. "Good morning, birds," he said softly. He remembered Marlein telling him to speak quietly and to pitch his voice higher to mimic hers, or the hens would likely be uneasy with him.

Glad Steffan had already cleaned the small space filled with the cackling, squat birds, he stepped slowly over to the roosting boxes that had been built years ago. Two birds had left an egg each in their nests, so he started by carefully taking those.

"Now for the trickier part," he murmured.

He clucked his tongue quietly at a hen in the nest beside the one where the egg had been left. When she didn't squawk at him, he reached carefully under her, patting around for any eggs. Her soft feathers tickled the hairs on the back of his hand; he felt her squirm and removed his hand.

"Just hold on," he tried to soothe her while reaching out his hand once again. "Marlein needs more eggs—ow!"

The hen had pecked his hand. He jerked back, empty-handed, and examined the bright-red blood oozing from the wound.

"And this is how I am rewarded for my troubles?" he groused.

With a frustrated grunt, he thrust his hand under the hen below the one with the now-ruffled feathers. When she pecked his forearm, he gritted his teeth against the pain and continued searching with his hand. Triumphantly, he withdrew two eggs from that nest before moving on to the next.

When he brought the basket back to the *Flett* for Marlein, he had a full dozen eggs and as many peck marks. Thankfully, he'd become quicker as he went and not all his wounds were as deep as the first.

As he approached, the two women were chatting on the other side of the hearth.

"I'm so glad you don't appear to have suffered any ill effect from pulling the venom from Aldessa's wound," Marlein was saying. Heinrich had heard of his sister's heroics and smiled. He started toward them as Marlein continued, "If you'd become ill, who knows what evil might have touched your . . ."

Brigita met his eyes over Marlein's shoulder, and as Marlein turned around to face him she trailed off, her face slowly flushing a dusty pink. They stood so close he could see the blonde tips of her eyelashes.

"What might have happened?" Heinrich asked, curious about the vein of concern running through Marlein's words and the deep flush rising on his sister's face. Their odd behavior indicated something more serious than a momentary illness. "Evil might have touched her what?"

"Oh . . . nothing in particular." Marlein stepped away from him, and Brigita turned to peer at the fire. She cleared her throat before continuing. "Her . . . life?"

"I fail to see what you mean. Her life was in danger?"

"She's been feeling unwell until recently," Marlein elaborated. Her answer seemed a bit too rehearsed, though, and she wouldn't meet his eyes as she spoke. "It would be a shame for her to grow ill from the venom after so recently recovering her health."

Heinrich looked from one woman to the other. "What is going on?" he asked directly, even as he wondered if this was somehow related to his request that Marlein talk to Brigita.

"Oh, you know how women can be about the health of those dwelling in their households."

Before he spoke them, he knew his words were unkind, but Marlein was keeping something from him and he couldn't check his tongue. "This is your mother's household."

Marlein's face grew pinched at that, but she merely shrugged in a show of nonchalance. Stepping back into the corner made by the bench and the wall, she turned to finger the tapestry hanging on the wall and countered with, "You understand what I mean, Heinrich. She has just regained a healthy glow and is no longer so frail-looking. Besides, she must keep her strength up for when her time comes . . ." Her startled eyes stared back at him and told Heinrich that she'd said more than she'd intended.

"Her time?" He stepped closer to where Marlein had retreated, effectively trapping her. She would have to either stay put or step very close to him to move away. He doubted that she would step away. "What are you two hiding from me?"

Brigita had followed behind him. While he hadn't turned to look at her, he felt her petite presence behind him. Marlein stared over his shoulder, presumably at Brigita, some silent exchange passing between them. Finally, Marlein nodded and said, "Why don't we go to the garden? I need more wood for the hearth, and it would be good to check the potatoes. I doubt the ground has frozen completely yet, but it would be good . . . to check . . . on them." She flushed again, which Heinrich didn't understand but made him all the more suspicious. In the years he had lived with the Diefenbach family, Marlein had blushed only a handful of times. Something was really upsetting her for her to flush so.

Rather than argue with the change in venue, Heinrich sighed as he stepped away from Marlein and to the pegs near the side door, retrieving the women's cloaks and handing them off before stepping into his room to retrieve his own.

Outside, the air was crisp and chilled, but not biting. The sun shone pale in the almost white sky. Marlein immediately crouched down to dig her fingers into the ground, pulling up a rather small potato.

"Another week and I suppose we'll have to bring them in. I wish the cold had held off for a bit longer."

Heinrich simply watched the women. Marlein straightened, wiping her fingers on her apron while Brigita stepped toward the woodshed adjacent to the garden. When his sister had disappeared around the other side of the structure, he turned to Marlein.

"What is this about?"

"It isn't my story to share."

He wanted to be angry—really, what right had Marlein to keep from him something so clearly concerning his sister—but could only admire her loyalty and integrity.

Brigita emerged from the shed then, a bundle of wood in her arm, and said without preamble, "I am with child."

Heinrich was stunned. "What? How can this be? You came to us from a convent!" He heard his voice rising with every word, but was powerless in the face of the building indignation inside him.

"I-it was before the convent." Her voice was barely a whisper, and through the haze of his rage, he almost missed how pale she had grown. "When I was with the . . . the Alscher family."

"You welcomed the attentions of that—"

"I . . ." She shuddered out a breath. "I am sorry, Heinrich."

"I am so deeply ashamed, Brigita. It is, perhaps, a good thing our poor father is dead for the shame you have brought on us." His words flew like arrows from the bow of his contempt. But spitting the poison from his mouth did nothing to improve the situation. Heinrich's heart felt heavy, so very heavy, as he attempted to look at his sister, but failed. "I feel as though I don't even know you."

"Heinrich!" Marlein nearly shouted his name, and he was brought up short. He'd nearly forgotten she was there.

Heinrich rounded on her. "And you, Marlein! I'd have expected better of you. To keep this from me, to deliberately—"

"As I said, it wasn't my story to tell." Marlein's voice was at its usual volume again, but there was a sharp authority to it that was foreign to his ears. "You might do well to observe your poor sister."

He finally forced his eyes to the young woman he'd thought he knew. Brigita's eyes were downcast, her head bowed, and her slight shoulders trembling.

Marlein plunged onward. "That is not the posture of a wanton woman, but a broken one. She understands her sin; she is repentant. How can you berate her so?"

Something shifted painfully inside of him, and he looked over at Marlein. Good, kind Marlein, eyes shining with unshed tears and face so earnest and open. Her gaze held nothing but disappointment for him, though.

Heinrich wished desperately that things could be different. He wished that Keterlyn could handle herself, that Marlein wasn't tied to her home, and that Brigita hadn't just thrown another wet log into the fire of his life. Soon, it would be popping and smoking, obscuring his plans and what he'd perceived to be his purpose. For what could life hold for her now but to secretly deliver the child and then hope that a convent would take her in?

"Listen to her." Marlein's words were whispered gently, kindly. She stepped close, placing her hand gently on his arm. "Give her a chance to explain. Sometimes, things are not what they seem."

Feeling simultaneously hot and cold, Heinrich nodded, reached up to squeeze her hand, and watched Marlein carefully transfer the bundle of wood from Brigita's arms to her own before retreating into the house. Turning to Brigita, finally ready to listen, Heinrich heard her speak of her sorrow, her shame. His heart melted in the face of her tears. And suddenly, he didn't mind a popping, smoking log, because it was his sister.

# 19

Brigita's relief was a thing alive. The weight, once removed, was so great that she did not know how she had carried it until this point. Her brother's disappointment was a terrible thing to endure, but still less than her own. And he was not casting her off. In fact, at this very moment, he was embracing her. She breathed in deeply of him, so comforting: the sweet smell of beeswax, the slightly noxious odor of the tallow, and a musky tang that mixed with the wool and wood smoke that clung to his cloak. She never wanted to leave his embrace. For the first time in months, she felt entirely safe and protected. And honest.

At length, though, she forced herself to step back. While she was overjoyed that her brother was not about to disown her, there were still things to consider, to decide.

She broached the subject by mentioning, "Marlein suggested that perhaps Emnelda Steuben would have an idea of where I could go."

"Yes, that was wise of her to consider that." Heinrich's face was still flushed. "Do you . . . do you wish to keep the child, or leave it with a convent or monastery?"

"I do not know." Brigita looked down, feeling the full weight of her shame. "When he . . . when it happened, he said that he loved me. That it was good to do, because we loved each other, that he wanted to marry me."

Relief washed over her when Heinrich said nothing and, in contrast to a few moments before, waited patiently for her to continue.

"Afterward," she continued, "I left for the convent. When I arrived, I asked Sister Margreth to help me write to him."

"Did he reply?"

She shook her head. "Not in so many words." Feeling the fear and anxiety of that night crowding in, she wrapped her arms around her scarcely expanded midsection to hold her elbows and said, "It was late one evening, at least two months I'm sure, since I arrived at the convent. I'd come to feel safe and secure, despite the fear that I might be . . . with child." She whispered the last words. "I was in the infirmary helping Sister Margreth. There was a commotion in the front, and we heard the prioress speaking with some men. I recognized Nikolaus's voice, and it didn't sound like he was there to marry me; he said that he needed to confront me about false allegations he believed I was about to make against him. I was so frightened, Heinrich!"

He reached to pat her arm, and she longed for him to hold her again that she might recapture the safety and warmth of those moments. Knowing how infrequently displays of affection overtook her brother, though, she did not expect it and forged onward. "Sister Margreth agreed with me when I told her I was afraid to let him know I was there. We heard the priest coming, and before I knew it, she threw a dress at me and told me to change quickly, while she packed a bag of food and some coins. As I pulled on my old boots, she sketched out a little map to help me know where to go."

"And you got away before they found you." His brows were furrowed, and his tone implied that he'd spoken more to let her catch her breath than to confirm his thoughts.

"Yes. It was quite late, and my dress and cloak were dark; the hood hid my face. I stayed in some trees nearby until I saw them leaving the convent, then took off in the opposite direction—away from Wittenberg and north, past Magdeburg. I hoped Nikolaus would be staying the night in Magdeburg and tried to move ahead of him, walking all night until I came to a little village in the morning. I'd wanted to make him think I was going home, rather than here. I knew he would overtake me if he knew where I was actually going." She shivered lightly.

"Shall we walk around a bit?" Heinrich asked. "Might help stave off the cold."

Brigita nodded, happily taking her brother's arm when he offered it to her. They began to walk around the small field. "I made sure to speak to a few people, merchants who would be out when he eventually passed through. I told the baker I was traveling from the convent to Braunschweig and asked if he could spare a small piece of bread for me. After that, I started on the road toward the west again, sure that some of those I'd spoken to were watching me go and would be suspicious of a woman traveling alone and on foot. After the road bent around a small wood, I hid again and waited for Nikolaus to pass. When he did, riding a horse fast and hard, I started east again, went around the village, and kept to the outskirts of the other villages I came to. It took me several days, trying to stay off the roads and not be seen. I even was lost once."

Heinrich mused, "I wonder that he didn't come here first."

"He didn't want to alert you if not necessary." At her brother's questioning glance at her, Brigita explained. "I heard him speaking with his brother when I was in Coswig. I hid in a shed with a goat, and they were right outside. I'd used up my food and was sure they'd hear my stomach growling! But he decided to turn back to see if they'd missed me."

"I see," Heinrich murmured. "Do you think he will come here eventually?"

Brigita had been avoiding thinking about that possibility, and Heinrich mentioning it brought the aversion she had to seeing Nikolaus again crashing down on her like a wave of icy winter water. "I do not know," she managed. "I hope not, but I fear he will."

"Then you must not be out by yourself any longer," Heinrich stated while patting her hand where it rested on his forearm. "Either I or one of the other men will accompany you with the children on outings." She opened her mouth to protest the bother of that arrangement, but he insisted, "Marlein will agree. Did you tell her about the men following you?"

"No, I did not wish to alarm her."

"We must tell her and see what is to be done." He paused a moment, then added, "We must tell Diefenbach as well."

Brigita felt dread settle in her stomach, churning and mixing with the aversion, fear, and disgust already residing there. She knew she would have to tell people eventually, but did not look forward to seeing their care for her turn to disdain. "Can we wait until after Christmastide?"

"Will you be able to hide your condition that long?"

"I think so. I've only just started getting larger through my middle, and Marlein has altered this dress and the other she gave me to hide it well. If worse comes to worst, I will keep my cloak on and say I am chilly."

Heinrich considered her a moment. "Very well. We will wait. But we must tell them after Christmastide. Soon after."

# 20

Advent would be upon him in just over a week, and Luther sat—as he had many times already—to explore the texts in Scripture concerning the promised Messiah. There were so many to choose from. The first time he was given the opportunity to read Holy Scriptures for himself, he felt as though he was trespassing on holy ground. He was a sinner, such a sinner who often found that he despised a God who would condemn poor sinners to hell while simultaneously threatening them with the righteous judgment of Christ. But after he read, and read, and read some more of the Word, his eyes and heart were opened to a truth he desperately needed to know: that God was a God primarily of love, not of wrath. That Christ came to bear the sins of the world, not to exact punishment for them. That salvation had been accomplished—fully— for the whole world, and when a person's heart was softened by the Holy Ghost and faith given, that person could believe. Which was the only requirement for salvation. God gave that which He demanded because of His great love. He knew that people were unable to meet the requirements for righteousness . . .

A late-migrating bird perched on the window near him and cawed, bringing Luther from his thoughts and recalling him to the task at hand. He pulled his Vulgate, the Latin translation of Scripture, closer and began searching for the words of the prophets that pointed to the Savior.

"There are so many," he murmured to himself, "that I cannot possibly use them all in the few weeks of Advent before Christmastide. Why do we not celebrate Advent for more weeks?"

"Father Martin?" asked a voice at the door of the room where he was working in the university's building.

Luther turned to see Heinrich Ritter standing in the door, clutching his soft, circular hat in his hand, nearly crushing the single feather that had been sewn into the band.

"What can I do for you?" he asked, setting aside the pen he had been using to make notes.

"I, uh . . . I've just come from lecture with my law professor."

"Ah. Does he still sniff every four sentences?"

The earnest student stifled laughter and replied, "I ought not to say."

Luther nodded, gesturing for Heinrich to be seated. The poor young man's face was so solemn, he'd hoped to interject some humor and could not keep it entirely at bay as he said, "Of course. Silly of me to have asked."

The young man smiled briefly in reply as he perched on the edge of the nearby bench.

"What is troubling you, Heinrich?" Luther asked.

"There is . . . a situation . . . that has developed."

It was unlike the student to stumble over his words so much. When he didn't continue, Luther prompted him, "And that is?"

Ritter drew a deep breath as if steeling himself to utter the words before exhaling as he stated, "She is pregnant."

"Marlein?"

Heinrich's head jerked up, his eyes confused. "What? No."

Luther said nothing, wondering who the young man could mean, if a woman being pregnant affected him enough to cause such duress and difficulty in expression.

Heinrich laid his hat across his lap and grasped his knees. "My sister, Brigita. She just told me yesterday, and while I know what she has done is a sin, I can't help but wonder whether there is more to her story than she told me. Perhaps more than she even realizes."

Luther considered for a moment. "Do you believe her to be unrepentant?"

"Hm? Oh no, it's easy to see that she is, as Marlein pointed out to me none too gently."

Amusement forced a chuckle through Luther's lips. "Forgive me, young Ritter, but I can imagine that scene. Marlein forcing you to see reason where your own sister is concerned."

Heinrich's smile was rueful. "Yes, I behaved badly when Brigita first told me."

"Her willingness to divulge the information would indicate a positive point, I should imagine."

"True. I could not see it at first, but Marlein was quick to open my eyes."

Luther burrowed his hands into the folds of his robe, as he was accustomed to doing. "Do you seek counsel from me?"

"Yes?" Heinrich looked down as he moved his hat from his lap to hang it on one of his knees before leaning his forearms on his legs and clasping his hands. "Maybe. . . . I'm not sure. I think I just wanted the opinion of someone older and wiser."

"I'm not ten years older than you and not likely much wiser," Luther returned on another chuckle. "Though perhaps my education and office give some added insight." He waited a moment to see whether Heinrich would speak first and possibly elaborate on what was at the heart of his dilemma.

"How can I ensure," blurted Heinrich just as Luther was about to speak, "that this does not create difficulty for her, or for me? I've worked all my life to care for her, and now this. I cannot think what will become of her once knowledge of this becomes public. The shame of it may very well spread in such a way that life could be very difficult."

Taken aback, Luther asked, "Make life difficult?"

"For her, obviously, but I will not be unaffected," Heinrich explained. "Even Marlein—I mean, the Diefenbach family, could suffer repercussions from this."

Luther noticed that it was the third time Ritter had referred to Diefenbach's eldest girl, and by her given name no less. But he decided against mentioning it to him; the young man had weighty enough thoughts. Instead, Luther continued, "And what does Diefenbach have to say about all this?"

"We've agreed to wait until after the season of Christmas has passed."

"We?"

"Brigita, Marlein, and I." Heinrich tilted his chin up to stare at the ceiling and sighed deeply. "It seems such a heavy weight."

"And you do not bear the brunt of it."

Ritter looked at him again. "What can you mean by that?"

"Your sister is the one most affected, the one carrying the burden, literally as well as figuratively."

After a moment of silence, Heinrich nodded, but said, "Perhaps, but it still does not help with the question of how to handle it all, how to mitigate the difficulty."

"Sometimes," Luther said slowly, knowing his words would be difficult ones for him to hear, "we cannot mitigate difficulty in life." Heinrich stared at him, saying nothing. "Sometimes, we must simply plunge with both feet into the difficulty, knowing that our Lord goes with us."

Confusion coloring his face, Heinrich hesitated slightly as he said, "Into it?"

"Perhaps, at this point," Luther said as gently as he could, "it would be best to ensure your sister receives plenty of good food and is as comfortable as possible until such a time as you are able to speak with the Diefenbach family about it, as she is under their protection for the time being. Don't borrow tomorrow's trouble for today, young Ritter."

\*\*\*

Willeic mounted his horse, a smug smile curving his full lips and distorting his other features to something sinister. He had certainly found a treasure today, and not just at the run-down little tavern at the edge of Jüterbog. She had been a welcome distraction and a fun change of pace from his consistently pleasant mistress and his dull but ever-available wife. No, the treasure making him smile had cost him less than that, and it earned him complete freedom from any consequence.

Johann Tetzel had told him so.

He had been preparing to leave for Wittenberg and passed through the town's square, where the Dominican friar was preaching. The theatrics were impressive, his company wailing loudly and his banners depicting the wretched state of those souls consigned to purgatory. For a moment, Willeic had felt a tinge of panic at the thought of how many sins he had on his soul.

But no, he had been paying his penance, and now he wouldn't even need that. His salvation was secure because he had done his part, balancing the scales, with this one indulgence from the Pope himself, Christ's vicar on earth.

"What a fortunate man I am," he said to his horse as he patted the satchel strapped to the saddle, where his indulgence had been carefully stored. He spurred his horse homeward, eager to enjoy the new freedom this document would grant him.

# 21

Several days passed without Brigita's condition being exposed, and Heinrich began to think that perhaps Father Martin's suggestion to wait before deciding on any course of action was wise. He still worked to help ease the burdens borne by both Marlein and Brigita, spending nearly all his spare time at the house rather than with his fellow students, taking supper exclusively at the house and spending only as much time at the university as was required by his lectures and studies.

Despite Heinrich's reluctance to meet his friends for supper at the tavern, one cold day between lectures, he ran into Romauld in the *Marktplatz*. Heinrich had planned to spend his spare hour at Diefenbach's shop, but paused upon hearing his friend's voice.

"Heinrich! What a happy coincidence! I am about to meet Karl for a meal before our lecture. You must come with us."

Heinrich considered his options. Often, Marlein brought bread to her father's shop for the men now, and he enjoyed meeting her there. However, she had been quite steady in maintaining their friendship as it was. Namely, a *friend*ship. Perhaps it would be best if he didn't bother trying to steal a few minutes with her.

"Very well," he said.

"Excellent!" Romauld's grin was wide, and Heinrich couldn't help grinning in return. "Let's go, then."

The two strolled toward the tavern, discussing what Luther had said during the previous lecture about the Letter to the Hebrews. Then Romauld abruptly changed the subject. "Do you think he will call for a split with the papacy?"

Heinrich was brought up short. "Why do you say so?"

"Well, it seems unlikely that Rome will give serious consideration to his concerns. I've heard Tetzel has been complaining about him, and he's one of the Pope's favorites, what with how much revenue he brings in for St. Peter's."

They arrived at the tavern, and Heinrich followed Romauld into the dimly lit interior. A single wood door sat in the center of sturdy stone walls. Inside, dark timbers framed the interior walls and contrasted against the pale, off-white of wattle and daub. Karl was already seated and was struggling to hold places for them at the crowded table. The tavern's single table was long and stretched the entire length of the room. Benches on either side were nearly filled with noisy patrons. Several circular iron chandeliers rimmed with tallow candles hung above the table, giving off light and odor. Heinrich sank onto the bench, once so familiar, but now uncomfortable and strange. He handed a coin to the serving girl, who brought a bowl of stew and a hunk of bread that looked to be a day old. He missed Marlein's bread.

"So, Heinrich," Karl said once they each had food and a tankard of ale, "finally able to pull yourself away from your lovely *Mädchen*?"

Heinrich scoffed as he pushed some of the stale bread into his mouth. After chewing and swallowing, he corrected his friend. "She isn't *mine*. She belongs entirely to her family."

His two friends laughed and he wasn't sure why. Rather than try to figure it out, he washed down the dry bread that tried to stick in his throat with a healthy gulp of watery ale.

"Is it true Father Martin's been invited to dispute at Heidelberg in the spring?" Heinrich asked to change the focus of his friends' interest.

"Indeed," Karl said around a mouthful of mutton. "We are hoping he will decide to defend his Theses."

"Do you think that likely, since they call several significant practices of the church into question?"

"It may be more likely that he presents something less . . . incendiary," Karl answered.

"Will they give him a chance to defend them, though?" Heinrich asked. "At some point?"

"I cannot say."

Just then, the sound of wood smacking against stone alerted all to the door's forceful opening, and Sïfrit strode into the tavern. Heinrich observed as he swaggered over to where his friends sat at the end of the long table and ordered a serving girl to bring him two ales. The first, he downed quickly before starting on his second. Heinrich was able, for the most part, to listen to his friends' conversation until Sïfrit and his loud friends suddenly began to speak about women. They shared one conquest or another before one turned to ask Sïfrit how he was faring with Marlein Diefenbach.

"She allowed me to walk her to the gate today," he boasted. "She is a cold woman, but I'll warm her eventually."

Heinrich's reaction was immediate. He was up and out of his place on the bench within the space of two heartbeats and towering over Sïfrit in another. "What did you say?" he snarled.

"Heinrich?" the younger man asked. "I haven't seen you in here in a while—"

Heinrich grasped the collar of Sïfrit's doublet, yanking harshly upward so that he was forced to stand. Though Sïfrit had a few inches on him, Heinrich had breadth and fury on his side. "You've decided you can say such things about a good, honorable woman?"

"N-no, I just—"

He yanked on Sïfrit's doublet and snarled, "Just *what*?"

"I was just joking with my friends."

"Were you now?" He glared at the other men, still holding on to Sïfrit's doublet. "Didn't sound like a joke to me."

"Heinrich," said someone from behind him. "Come on, we'd best head to the university."

He turned to see Romauld and Karl behind him, Romauld having spoken and grasped his arm. He hadn't even felt the touch. Swallowing thickly, Heinrich released Sïfrit and took a step toward the door.

"*Ja*," one of Sïfrit's friends baited them, "scurry on back to your university, and leave the real work to the real men."

"My *Vater* was a candlemaker," Heinrich said. "I work alongside Diefenbach as much as I can between studying and lectures."

"You work alongside his daughter, you mean," taunted Sïfrit.

Heinrich and Romauld exchanged a glance, and Heinrich nearly reached for Sïfrit again. Romauld coughed, and Karl reached a staying hand to rest on Heinrich's shoulder. With a heavy sigh, Heinrich took a step backward. They gathered their hats and left.

"Hot-headed, boastful, obnoxious little—"

"It's probably best to let it go," murmured Romauld.

Heinrich forced himself to keep quiet for a moment, then expelled his breath in a hissed sigh. "Probably."

The admission did nothing to ease his annoyance, though, nor slow his racing heart. Either way, he would be sure to keep a closer eye on the little knave.

They arrived at the university in very little time, and the three students filed into their places. Soon, Heinrich was engrossed in Luther's lecture.

They were continuing their study of the Book of Hebrews, and today the good doctor directed his students to the tenth chapter.

"'And let us consider how to stir up one another to love and good works, not neglecting to meet together, as is the habit of some, but encouraging one another, and all the more as you see the Day drawing near.' Now, you all are aware of my commentary on 'good works,' so I shall not harp on it at this point." There was a collective chuckle around the room. "Let us instead, as the author of this letter instructs, consider what it means to stir up one another to love and to encourage one another as Christians. How do we do this?" Luther asked as he shifted upon the stool. "One way to do this, as Paul suggests in Galatians, is to bear with one another's burdens. How many of you have ever struggled to carry something?" He waited, staring students in the face, and raised his own hand. "I have." At length, a few reluctant hands went up into the air, followed by more and more until the entire room was full of men acknowledging weakness. "When someone comes to share that burden, to take half of the weight onto himself, how much encouragement did you receive? Our sinful inclination is to want others to bear with *our* burdens, to make allowances for *us*, to allow us leeway and grace, while we hold them to impossible standards."

Luther stood, gaining momentum in his speech. As he continued to speak, he paced across the front of the lecture hall.

"This is what those who preach indulgences do. They hold people to unattainable standards and threaten the terrors of purgatory. But we cannot expect true piety from them; charity, righteousness, chastity, love—they are not required to keep such standards of living, but are given lesser sentences than other men. But this is not what the Holy Scripture teaches.

"I know you have only this Letter to the Hebrews before you today, but how strongly I desire for you to have the entire Scripture! Perhaps someday, but for now, listen to these passages." He moved back to the podium. "From the fifteenth chapter of Romans: 'We who are strong have an obligation to bear with the failings of the weak, and not to please ourselves.' It would seem to me that Rome would rather it say, 'We who are strong have an obligation *from* the weak, that they bear with us to please us.'"

Several of the students chuckled, but Heinrich felt unease growing in his gut. Not because he believed Luther to be wrong, but rather because he was right.

"Yet that is not what Scripture teaches. We must look to God's Word, His own testament, for our only source of what is right and true.

"Let us look now to the First Letter to the Church in Thessalonica, the fifth and last chapter, where we read, 'And we urge you, brothers, admonish the idle, encourage the fainthearted, help the weak, be patient with them all.'"

As the professor spoke, darts of discomfort found their mark in Heinrich's heart. Admonishing, encouraging, helping, patient . . . was he truly any of these? Admonishing Sïfrit, rather than just being annoyed with him. Encouraging Keterlyn, rather than resenting her. Helping Brigita, rather than simply shielding her.

"What encouragement is there in this false piety of Rome? I would not speak so plainly of the Holy Father himself, but the more of Scripture that I read, the more I am convinced. We must return to God's Word for the source of all that we do in ministering to God's people. Which brings us to the First Letter of St. John, the fourth chapter: 'And this commandment we have from Him: whoever loves God must also love his brother.'

"This is where we see, without exception, the heart of the Christian faith: love. God's love for His people, and His people's love for one another, and for the world. We are to bear one another's burdens, to stir one another up to love and good works. That is to say, we are to admonish, encourage, help, and be patient, *in love.* Because He has loved us with so great a love, poured His mercy and grace on us in the life, works, suffering, death, and resurrection of His Son, the Christ, we are to love one another. We are to carry His love to the world. The broken world, the world lost in its own pleasure, its own slothfulness, its own weakness and despair. Because He loved us with an everlasting love."

Luther continued, and Heinrich managed to write most of what he said. But his mind was reeling.

Did he love? Did he bear with the burdens of others?

What of Keterlyn's burdens? Sïfrit's? even Marlein's?

Conviction was painful, to be sure. Unpleasant at best. Heart-breaking at its worst.

And yet, Heinrich could not begrudge its dawning.

After the lecture ended, he took his time packing his supplies, waving off the teasing of his friends. When the room had nearly cleared, with jittery hands and his heart in his throat, Heinrich approached Luther.

"Father Martin?"

"We are making a habit of meeting, are we not?" Luther chuckled as he finished collecting his books. "What is troubling you, young Ritter?"

"I . . ." Heinrich nearly lost his nerve, but then grasped to the hope he had that reminded him of Christ's love. The love that Luther read of in the Book of John. "I want to ask about your lecture."

He tried, he truly did, to catch one of the swirling questions in his mind, but they all escaped him.

"Ask away," teased Luther after several moments of silence had passed.

"Easier said than done, Father Martin."

"Hm. Well, shall we retire to the garden, then? Perhaps the fresh air would help to clear your mind?"

Heinrich nodded, murmuring as he preceded the man from the

room, "He is as kind as he is knowledgeable."

"Oh, I am rarely as kind as I should be, and so much knowledge yet to gain. But I am glad to share what I know and point you to Scripture for the rest."

Heinrich felt his face heat. "I hadn't thought you could hear me."

They were silent as they strolled to the monastery's garden. They passed a friar who was scrubbing the floor at one point, and later another laden with linens to be washed. The corridors were dark, calm, and peaceful. Heinrich felt the tension ease in first his neck, then his head, as they walked along.

"Allow me to carry my books to my cell, and I shall return in a moment, young Ritter." Luther held open the heavy door leading to the monastery's garden as he spoke, and Heinrich nodded in answer.

Outside, the cold washed over him and blew away the cobwebs of his mind. Suddenly, he knew just what he wanted to say to Luther. As he waited, he walked about the paths of the garden, letting his eyes roam the stone wall, partially covered by creeping vines. His fingers trailed the near-dead stalks in the back corner plot. The chill in the air sharpened the earthy perfume of freshly turned soil mixed with kitchen waste. It was the aroma of decay turning into something to support life. Heinrich hadn't learned to appreciate that until several months after coming to Wittenberg; previously, he was only used to the odors of the city: waste, musk, and filth.

"Young Ritter." The words, though spoken softly, startled Heinrich as though they'd been shouted. Luther laughed. "I suppose you were very deep in your thoughts indeed, if you did not hear me approach. I've a clumsy, heavy footfall."

"I know what to say now."

Luther nodded, the hood of his habit wobbling a bit from where it hung on his head. His dark eyes reflected the afternoon daylight as he looked intently at his student.

"I am beginning to believe," Heinrich began, "that everything I've been working toward is false."

"What do you mean?"

"Well, what you said today about bearing one another's burdens." Heinrich began pacing the corner of the garden. "I have long wanted to bear my own and my sister's, but no one else's. And even when my sister's burden was not the sort I wanted to deal with, I was of a mind to send her away, at least until Marlein talked sense into my dense head. And even Marlein! I resent Keterlyn for her suffering, and Marlein, to an extent, for not being free to walk away from it. And Sïfrit, Diefenbach's apprentice . . . I can't abide his presence."

Luther did not speak right away, but stood calmly watching him fidget, and Heinrich suddenly felt foolish for baring his faults so quickly and so fully.

"So, Heinrich, you've found that you aren't perfect."

He wasn't sure what Luther meant, but remained quiet, hoping his next words would explain.

"You are an excellent student, and from all I can see, a devoted brother. However, you are not perfect, no matter how you seek to surround yourself with perfection."

"I wouldn't say—"

"Of course, you wouldn't," Luther stopped him. He withdrew his hands from the folds of his robes and studied his fingernails, scraping some dirt from under them before continuing. "But tell me. When you learned that your sister was missing, what upset you the most? The agony of her spirit or the public effect of it?"

Heinrich knew the answer and remained silent because of it.

"And when you realized your feelings for Marlein, were you concerned for the effect of her mother's sufferings on her or for the hindrance it was to obtaining what you wanted?"

Heinrich nodded. "I see what you mean."

"And Sïfrit?"

Heinrich began to wonder if Luther meant to drag each of his confessed faults to the fore for discussion and dissection. "Do you see him as a brother in need of patient guiding or as a competitor for the hand of Marlein Diefenbach?"

"Yes, Father Martin. I see your point." Heinrich heaved a long breath and turned to run his hand over the ivy growing on the wall. "I am learning that I have a great deal to learn, still."

"Oh, do not be so hard on yourself, young Ritter. For we are all continuing to learn. We are as little children in God's eyes, so how would we ever know all there is to know?" Luther chuckled and slapped Heinrich on the shoulder with a friendly hand. "This is simply the Law doing its work on you, telling you that you are a sinner."

Heinrich nearly grunted, but stopped himself in time; he did not want to add disrespectful noises toward a man dedicated to the service of God to the list of sins he had committed. Instead, he hummed and hoped it sounded like thoughtfulness was behind it, rather than frustration.

"But do not fear, for God's Word does not leave us here." Luther reached and pulled a leafy branch from the ivy. "Remember the second half of the passage? By bearing burdens, we fulfill the law of Christ. That law isn't like the Law that condemns, but is that which binds us to Him, the only place salvation can be found."

"It's a law that tells us to love?"

"Yes." Luther pointed the leafy branch he held at Heinrich. "The night when Jesus was betrayed, He instituted Holy Communion, but He also instructed His disciples to love one another. He set an example by washing their feet, the task of the lowest servant in the household. He, our Lord and Master, did the task of the lowest, so how much more should we do that which is distasteful and burdensome to us?"

Heinrich understood what Luther was saying, but still felt the weight on his heart, telling him that what he'd thought would suit him and, he'd supposed, please God was wrong.

"What am I to do then? I have confessed sins before, but never have they bothered me to such a degree."

"That," Luther announced as he handed the ivy branch to Heinrich, "is your conscience responding to the prodding of the Holy Spirit."

"I thought the Spirit gave gifts?"

"Yes. Is not recognition of sin a gift?"

He hadn't considered it as such before, but supposed it could be. "If it leads to repentance?"

Luther nodded. "Repentance itself is a gift. And the forgiveness that then comes with Confession?"

Heinrich shrugged.

"And here is the heart of the Christian faith." Luther began strolling about the garden, and Heinrich hurried to catch up and keep pace with him. "We are sinners, unable to do a thing to help ourselves. That is the truth of it: as dead as these stalks that will next week be taken out and burned. Even good works and penance are helpful only after the Holy Spirit has worked repentance in our hearts. Left to our own devices, we would continue, assured of our own goodness and ignorant of the great disparity between what we think is good and what God calls good."

"And none of us is good."

"That is correct. But He doesn't leave us there, in the despair of our realization. That's when the sweet balm of the Gospel comes to restore us."

"How?"

"In the Word of God, read or spoken. It is Christ's work. Scripture says that He is the vine and we are the branches connected to

Him. That branch," Luther indicated with a nod at the one in Heinrich's hands, "will begin to wilt and fade soon. When we are disconnected from the Word of God, from Christ, the same happens to us. Do you know, the more I read of the Holy Scripture, the more I see that Christ is at the heart of it all. More than the saints. More than even God's wrath. So often when a judgment is pronounced on the children of Israel, there are also promises of a Savior to come. Everything God does in the midst of the Israelites is either preparing for or pointing to the coming of the Son of God."

"But for this feeling I have, what can I do?"

"You've already confessed. Are you ready to receive absolution?"

Heinrich nodded.

"In the stead, and by the command of Christ, Heinrich, I forgive you your sins. Strive to bear the burdens of those God has placed in your life, relying on Christ and the blessings of His Spirit to enable you to do this good work."

"Because it is the command of Christ?"

"Yes. And because it is good for your neighbor. We are made to live in community together, to encourage and sharpen, to bear one another's burdens."

"How do I bear another's burden? Aside from not being annoyed by it?"

"Ah. You think it will be that easy to change your feelings in that regard?"

"Well, no."

"How might you bear Keterlyn Diefenbach's burden?"

Heinrich racked his brain for an idea. "Pray that God would lift it?"

"It is always good to pray for those in need," Luther nodded as he folded his hands in the wide sleeves of his robe. "But God would also have us give to those in need, comfort those who mourn while reminding them of the hope that is in Christ, and build up one another in our speech."

"Perhaps trying to talk to her? Help her to know she is not alone in her grief."

"That is an excellent place to start. One who is suffering from melancholy should not be left alone too long or the devil may find a foothold."

"And perhaps I ought to spend some time with Sïfrit besides when we have no choice but to be together. Exemplifying a better way may show it to him?"

"Excellent," he nodded. "We all have burdens. For some, it is ignorance. For others, grief."

"And still others, regret or loss or despair."

"Or even something as basic as aging."

"Like Emnelda Steuben."

"Yes. She has borne what she can of others' burdens for a long time, but now that her own burdens grow heavier, few are there to aid her."

Heinrich nodded, his head filling with ideas faster than he thought he could likely implement them.

"Well, young Ritter, I am afraid I shall be late to evening prayers if I do not hurry, but do come to me again if you need further aid."

"I will, Father Martin. Thank you."

Luther shook his head. "Do not thank me, bumbling fool that I can be. Instead, thank the good Lord that He saw fit to use my mouth to speak His Words of forgiveness and encouragement."

Supper was just being cleaned up, and Brigita had been doing her utmost not to worry for Heinrich. But if Nikolaus Alscher had caught up with him, or if he met with trouble walking from the city to the house . . . She really should have told her brother everything.

"He most likely met some friends for supper at the tavern," Marlein soothed her as she glanced toward the side door for the twelfth time since supper began. "Heinrich did that quite often when he first came to us."

"But he hasn't now that I'm here?" Brigita despised the possibility that she had so disrupted her brother's life.

"No." Marlein paused while wiping down the table. "That's odd. I hadn't thought of it much, but it's been several months at least. . . . He usually eats at the house now."

Brigita didn't comment, but from the far-off look in Marlein's eyes, she imagined that she might be puzzling out the exact time and reason for Heinrich's sticking more closely to the house than he did initially. Brigita herself, though, could guess the reason. Hiding a small grin despite her concern for her brother, she returned to her task of dumping the last of the roasted pork into the pot near the fireplace. It would simmer over the coals all night; in the morning, Marlein would add some beer and possibly an apple and some potatoes, and it would be ready for another meal tomorrow evening.

Heinrich arrived home just as the sun was beginning its descent in the sky. Its rays pierced the dim interior of the house when he opened the door, alerting everyone to his presence.

"Sorry I'm late," he said as he removed his cloak. "I stayed after lecture to discuss . . . Father Martin's lecture."

Brigita offered a smile, but remained silent, cutting a sideways glance at Marlein. She was, after all, the woman of the house, and it would be more appropriate for her to offer Heinrich a meal. Never mind that Brigita's heart danced with joy whenever she saw the sweet, shy interactions between her brother and her dear friend.

"Um, there's some bread. . . . I think Brigita just put the last of the roast into the pot for tomorrow. Maybe you'd like some cheese, too?"

Heinrich nodded before making an excuse of changing his clothes and disappearing for a time.

"Well," Marlein said, suddenly more flustered than Brigita had ever seen her. "I think I'll retire now. The last few days are catching up with me. Please be sure to scatter the coals and lower the grate over the fire before you retire."

She had shut herself in their room before Brigita could even think of how to keep her there.

"Where's Marlein?" Heinrich had returned from his room, wearing the jerkin that Brigita told him last week she thought Marlein favored.

"She said she is tired," Brigita said, deciding not to elaborate on her suspicion as to the real reason behind Marlein's sudden disappearance. "So the lecture was engaging?"

He smiled at her, took some bread and cheese, and poured himself a half stein of beer before sitting at the table. "As always. If it was as lucrative a profession, I think I should have studied theology, rather than law."

"Can you not still?"

He shook his head. "Not if I wish to provide for you. I do not wish to inconvenience the Diefenbach family more than we have already."

"But Marlein says she enjoys my company and appreciates my help. Would it not inconvenience her further for us to leave?"

Heinrich chewed his bite of bread, considering her thoughtfully. "You are quite determined, though about what I cannot decipher."

Brigita shrugged, a grin spreading widely across her face. "Tell me, Heinrich, about your discussion with Father Martin."

She watched as he took another large bite, chewing slowly while she waited. Eventually, he swallowed, drank several gulps of beer, and let out a small belch. Brigita quirked her brow at him, chuckling when he rolled his eyes at her.

"So?" she gently prodded.

"Well, he spoke today of Christians encouraging one another, of bearing one another's burdens, as there are verses in Scripture that address just that."

"And?"

Heinrich sighed. "You must understand that I am still determining what this all means in my life. . . . But I've reached the conclusion that I have not been bearing the burdens of others."

Brigita was confused. "But you have been working for years to provide for me."

"Yes, while being entirely unaware of the burdens of others."

"What do you mean?"

"Well, as your brother, your provision and security are my highest priority." Heinrich took a bite of cheese before continuing. "But as a community of Christians, we are to bear one another's burdens, and not only those that suit us. I would gladly bear, say, Marlein's burdens."

"Because you care deeply for her," Brigita interjected.

He leveled a reproving stare at her, but did not refute her statement. "But Sïfrit, for example . . . I find that he annoys me more than inspires me to any sort of help or sympathy."

"But he is obnoxious."

"And ignorant," Heinrich agreed over the rim of his stein before he took a drink. "That is his burden."

"How are you expected to bear the burden of another's ignorance?" Brigita knew she was not as learned as her brother, but the very idea seemed ridiculous.

"I suppose by helping him to learn," Heinrich replied. "As I said, I am still working to understand what this means, but I am certain this is something that God's Spirit is urging me to wrestle with."

Brigita nodded, taking her brother at his word, even if she did not entirely understand what he meant. He'd finished his bread and cheese and tipped back the stein to drain the last of the beer. She swept the crumbs he'd dropped on the table into her hand and tossed them into the fire. It would not do to leave them to attract mice.

"Gita, I'm afraid I've also been remiss where you are concerned."

She froze, wondering if he'd somehow found out what she'd been keeping from him. "How is that possible?"

"Well, I've been more concerned with the impact this will have on your reputation and mine, and even that of the Diefenbach family. What I should have been concerned with is your heart. I cannot even begin to imagine the pain . . ."

As he spoke, Brigita felt her shame rise, warring with an equally strong sense of the loss she'd suffered. Her chance at making a good marriage, her sense of safety and security, and most of all, the days when she believed the best of the world. All were broken, if not shattered entirely. Hearing her dear brother acknowledge her loss, though, rather than refer to it all as a problem to be solved, felt like a warm blanket on a cold day, and she smiled through the tears she hadn't realized were falling.

"Heine . . ." She didn't know how to explain the rush of feeling, so she simply threw herself into her brother's arms, sobbing on his shoulder, and finally mourning that which she had lost.

# 23

Winter had come. While the snow had yet to make an appearance, the cold was setting in so ferociously with the sinking sun that it took Matthäus's breath away. More layers, made of heavier wool than his summer jerkin, helped some. His boots almost slipped on the frosty ground as his long strides carried him quickly from the Diefenbach house. He had just kissed his sweet Maria good night and would not see her for a couple of days. Diefenbach had helped arrange for some candle molds that Matthäus had made to be sold to a chandler in Jüterbog, and he was sending him to conduct the transaction. As he walked, his feet felt heavy despite their speed. His legs began to ache. Matthäus did not like leaving his daughter, but it was Brigita who filled his thoughts.

Last night, he had dreamt of her. Brigita's smiling face danced before his eyes, laughing and joyful, all traces of sadness gone. Then a storm came, darkening all and obscuring her face. He awoke as lightning struck, sending fire to the earth and setting the area ablaze. He lost sight of Brigita even as the smoke cleared to reveal a too-familiar old cottage. It was burning.

What had he been thinking, allowing himself to feel tenderly for her, even as the death of his wife clung to him? The guilt would follow him through his life and even past death, into purgatory. That is, if he was given the chance to be cleansed from it at all. But such morose thoughts did nothing to help him on his way. Besides, in purgatory, at least he would be with his wife.

Another thought came to mind, one that had been lodged in his brain all day. Yesterday, he had been speaking with the carpenter in the shop beside Diefenbach's, Metfried Lyngstrom. The man knew of Matthäus's hobby of carving, and they often discussed the benefits of various kinds of wood in carving and building. The carpenter showed him some very fine oak, which he had obtained in Jüterbog just the day before. While he was there, he heard Brother Johann Tetzel speak and purchased a plenary indulgence from him.

"What is the difference that you would purchase one so far from home?" Matthäus had asked.

"This Tetzel said this indulgence will clear away all sins committed, even for someone already dead. I did it for my mother, that she may be freed from purgatory's fires."

"Is that so?"

"Yes. He said he will be there for a couple days yet. I heard of him when the leatherworker Gwerder mentioned it at the tavern recently."

It was then that the idea had begun to form in Matthäus's mind. As he had worked through the day, the idea became more and more defined, until by this evening, it was a plan. He had only one more thing to do before following through on it.

He wished to speak with Father Luther first.

Heinrich had great respect for the man, and Matthäus had great respect for Heinrich. As he approached the City Church, imposing with its twin, rectangular towers and massive stone face, his heart thrummed from anxiety. He did not fear the place, exactly. No, he attended Mass faithfully and did his best to listen carefully to Father Martin's preaching. But the guilt that tailed him intensified whenever he approached the building. His steps slowed, and several people moved past him in the growing gloom of evening.

Matthäus was just about to turn back, standing as he was before the large front doors, when they opened, and a figure in the brown Augustinian habit emerged and closed the door behind himself. Luther was looking down at some papers in his hand, brow furrowed, and just before he ran into a dumbfounded Matthäus, he looked up. His soft, kind eyes met Matthäus's dull brown ones, and the immediate compassion on his face bolstered the young man's courage.

"Good evening, Father Martin."

"Matthäus Falk." There was good humor in his voice.

"Forgive me, I, uh, I must ask you something."

"Nothing to forgive in asking," Luther said, stepping forward and motioning toward the street that led to the university. "If you don't mind walking with me, I fear I am running late for evening prayers. I was preparing my sermon for Sunday, and I find sometimes that the church is quieter than the university."

Matthäus nodded and fell in step with the friar, but words escaped him.

"What is it you wanted to ask me?" Luther prompted after a moment of silence.

He almost made an excuse to leave. But the idea of being free of his guilt was too appealing—for surely if his dear Petrissa were no longer suffering in purgatory, perhaps the guilt would leave him. He forced the words, "I was told the Pope is offering an indulgence that will free anyone's dead relative from purgat—"

But Luther interrupted him as the compassion on his face transformed to anger.

"What lying dog told you that?" he nearly snarled.

"I-I was speaking yesterday to the carpenter, Herr Lyngstrom. He told me he purchased one for his mother."

"I'll need to talk to him."

"Please don't be angry with him!" Matthäus felt awful for anyone having to face the man's wrath. Luther's reddened face was distorted with something akin to rage, and he nearly thundered his words.

"But I've been preaching grace through faith! Has he not listened?" Luther then turned to peer into Matthäus's face. "And what of you? Have you been listening to my sermons? Perhaps I need to be more emphatic if it seems my entire flock does not take my words—God's words!—to heart."

Shame sat like a heavy rock in Matthäus's belly. "Forgive me, Father Martin. I did not intend to offend you, nor to sin."

With that, the compassion had returned to Luther's face. "No, forgive my outburst. The Lord has determined to teach me patience in the most effective method, it would seem. Tell me, why do you feel the need for such an indulgence?"

Matthäus shook his head, unsure if he could voice his hurt aloud. "It . . . it would be for my wife. She died some four years ago, when I could not pull her from a fire."

Speaking the words brought it all back in a rush. The heat, the fallen beam trapping him at the periphery of the blaze, her cries until smoke silenced them. Then someone else's hands reaching for him, pulling him from beneath the beam, back to where Petrissa's brother held baby Maria out of harm's way. By the time he could draw a full breath, his wife was long since gone.

Luther stopped walking and turned to face Matthäus. "And you think that freeing her from purgatory would purge your own guilt at not being able to save her?"

Matthäus had no words; he merely nodded.

"It is Christ alone that saves, Matthäus," Luther said, earnestly placing a hand upon his arm. "You cannot save your wife any more than you can save yourself from your guilt, real or assumed. Trust in His mercy, gentle husband, not the paper of a man. Trust in God's grace."

"Are indulgences bad, then?"

Luther turned and began walking again, and Matthäus forced his heavy feet to follow suit. "That is something I am still working out in my own mind. If one purchases an indulgence as an act of devotion, he does a good thing. But for salvation? It is Christ alone that saves."

"How can you speak so surely? Lyngstrom said that Tetzel is sure he can save souls with the indulgences."

"Look in God's Word," Luther advised. "You are a compatriot of Heinrich Ritter, are you not? He has his Letter to the Galatians from last year. And the Letter to the Hebrews that we are nearly finished with. Can you believe Advent is nearly upon us already? Ask to borrow one from him. He is a good fellow, eager now to share the loads others bear; I'm sure he will oblige you."

Matthäus did not have the heart to tell Luther that he did not know how to read German, let alone Latin. He supposed so great a man had much more on his mind than the literacy of a grown man. He simply nodded. "Thank you, Father Martin, for your time."

"If I have pointed one person to my Lord," grinned Luther, "it is time well spent."

The two shook hands, and Matthäus turned around to head back to his room above the shop. He feared he would not sleep very much that night.

Heinrich felt as though he could breathe again. From the earlier uncertainty as to his sister's whereabouts through worry over her health, he was finally seeing her face begin to fill out and she smiled more than she had since her arrival. The knowledge of her impending difficulty did not rattle him as it did upon the initial discovery. Even the shy smiles and lingering eyes between his sister and Matthäus did not perturb him. It seemed that life in the Diefenbach home was good for her, and he was content.

The weather was fine but cold as he stepped from the weaver's shop with a parcel of cloth tucked under his arm. Glancing down the street, he saw Matthäus striding toward him from the direction of the *Marktplatz*. He remembered that the man had been seeing to some business of Diefenbach's in Jüterbog, and likely had just returned.

"Good evening, Heinrich," Matthäus called to him.

"Good evening." Heinrich waited for him to catch up before offering his hand to shake. "How was Jüterbog?"

The other man's face fell as he opened his mouth. "Business went as expected."

"Why do you seem downcast, then?"

When he took a moment to reply, Heinrich looked up and saw that Matthäus was surprised. At length, though, his deep voice began haltingly. "The carpenter whose shop is beside Diefenbach's told me several days ago that he purchased an indulgence in Jüterbog for his deceased mother."

"Is that so?"

"Tell me, Heinrich." Matthäus's unease expressed itself in his crossed arms, furrowed brow, and pinched mouth. "Has Father Martin spoken in lecture about indulgences?"

Heinrich was unclear where this question came from, but he answered honestly. "He has spoken some of the danger of Tetzel's indulgences."

"But they are not Tetzel's—the Holy Father himself issued them!" The emotion behind Matthäus's response revealed a deeper investment in the discussion than mere curiosity would demand.

"Yes," Heinrich began carefully, not wanting to add to his friend's anguish. He had only just begun to see for himself the disparity between the teachings of Scripture and some of the practices of the church. Even so, as he wrestled with the ideas himself, he felt compelled by a force beyond himself—perhaps a Force beyond himself—to attempt to explain the problematic nature of the practice. "Father Martin is concerned that this particular indulgence could exclude true repentance. Potentially."

"Potentially . . ." Uncertainty again colored Matthäus's voice. "But not certainly? I don't see how something that the Holy Father has given to us could be anything but good."

"Consider this. If I bought one for myself, might it be for the sake of saving myself," Heinrich explained carefully, "rather than for the building of St. Peter's or for an act of devotion to our Lord?"

"I suppose," Matthäus allowed.

"And if one does this from selfishness, rather than repentance and devotion," Heinrich pressed, albeit gently, "would it not then be sin, rather than an act pleasing to God?"

Matthäus said nothing, but the discomfort on his face was plainly visible. Heinrich had never seen such tension in his friend, nor such deep furrows in his brow and frown lines around his mouth. They were passing the university, and Heinrich greeted several of his fellow students who were milling about, discussing some idea or another.

"Did you purchase an indulgence?" Heinrich finally asked as the pair passed through *das Elstertor*.

Matthäus shook his head and heaved a great sigh. "No, but I would have, had I not spoken with Father Martin before I left for Jüterbog. He urged me to trust in Christ's mercy rather than a man's paper."

"And so you should." Heinrich reached a hand to Matthäus's shoulder to communicate his sincerity.

"But will that deliver my Petrissa's soul from purgatory?"

Heinrich was unsure how to answer. Luther had not addressed the issues of purgatory or indulgences much in his later lectures; he spoke zealously of the Scripture passages they studied and the grace and mercy of God that they extolled. But indulgences, which had featured prominently in his Theses, seemed to fade in the brilliant light of the Word of God. At least for Luther. For his friend Matthäus, indulgences seemed to be at the heart of a crisis for him.

"I do not have answers for you, Matthäus. But I will pray that understanding be given you. Perhaps some study of Scripture would aid you; that is what Father Martin puts forward as the balm to his own sufferings."

Matthäus hesitated a bit before saying rather reluctantly, "He suggested that I ask to borrow your copy of Galatians."

"Did he? I suppose that would fit with who he is." Heinrich chuckled a little. "You are welcome to it. I feel rather guilty for not opening the volume since last year. Unfortunately, it and my notes are all in Latin, not German. But perhaps I could translate some for you in my spare time. The lectures will be in recess over the Christmastide."

Matthäus's distress seemed never to leave him, as his furrowed brows and frown returned. For a time, he remained stoically, if worriedly, facing forward as they walked through the cold countryside. Finally, though, he seemed to sag, the tension leaving his face and his body. "It would do no good," he admitted defeatedly. "I cannot read."

"But you conduct business for Diefenbach. I've seen you update his ledger."

"I recognize some words," he allowed, "and I can write and figure numbers."

"I see." Heinrich saw that admitting his perceived deficiency had cost the man no small amount of embarrassment. "Matthäus, it is nothing to give you shame. Only recently are merchants and craftsmen able to afford school, so it would stand to reason that not many can read."

"And I was not even of a merchant class," Matthäus remarked. "My mother and father were vassals on the holdings of the man whose land abutted Petrissa's family's land."

The two men were approaching the Diefenbach house and saw the children scattered around Marlein and Brigita in the trees along the edge of the field. Heinrich and Matthäus went into the house by the front gate. Heinrich greeted Jäger as they passed his stall and Steffan where he was sitting and carving what appeared to be a peg, perhaps to repair something in the house.

Heinrich left the package of fabric on the table before going to change into his simple jerkin. When he emerged, Matthäus was standing and staring into the embers of the fire, a thoughtful look upon his face. When he noticed Heinrich, he looked up. By unspoken consent, they headed back out through the side door to where Marlein and Brigita directed the children in gathering wood for the woodshed. Heinrich found his eyes following Marlein without even realizing it, until Matthäus spoke and he came to himself.

"Heinrich, may I ask you something?"

He glanced sideways at the other man, seeing his gaze riveted on Brigita, and was suddenly wary. Was he looking at her for the same reason Heinrich was looking at Marlein? Was Matthäus about to indicate interest in his sister? The man was a giant beside his tiny sister, but gentle and kind. Heinrich supposed that if she loved Matthäus, he would give his blessing.

"Would you teach me to read?"

"I must first speak with—what?" Heinrich thought that perhaps he did not hear the other man correctly.

"I asked," Matthäus repeated uncertainly, "if you'd teach me to read."

"Oh. I was thinking . . ." Heinrich trailed off, confused by his thoughts. He realized he'd been warming to the idea of Matthäus as a brother-in-law.

"I-I'm sorry," Matthäus looked distinctly uncomfortable, but Heinrich was slow in catching up. He'd not denied his friend's request.

"Why are you sorry?" he finally asked, deciding to address the most recent words first.

"You are already busy with lectures and—"

"As I said, we will soon be recessed for a few weeks. I am happy to help you." He reached out to shake his friend's hand while clasping his arm with his free hand. "Besides, if I have time to help Diefenbach with trimming the candles, surely I can make time for such a noble pursuit."

Matthäus didn't say anything for a moment, then a large smile broke across his face. When he did speak, emotion made his voice a little unsteady. "Thank you, Heinrich. Very much."

"Will you tell me, though," Heinrich asked, as they began walking through the garden toward the field, "why now? What is prompting this?"

Matthäus hung his head and studied his calloused hands. "I have lived for years with the guilt of my wife's death. I want to be free."

"Why are you guilty?" Heinrich and Matthäus had reached the far end of the garden and stopped at the small gate that separated it from the field beyond. "Have you gone to confess it?"

"'Tis too complicated a sin for confession. And likely too great for what I could atone."

Heinrich wanted to press him, but forced himself to wait patiently. Adopting a casual posture, he propped a foot on a large rock beside the gate and rested a hand on a picket of the fence. Finally, Matthäus continued speaking.

"We oughtn't have married. We loved one another, but Petrissa was of a wealthy merchant family. My father was a peasant. But we fell in love before we knew that. We met in the forest one day; I was gathering sticks for my family's fireplace, and she was gathering nuts. We talked as we completed our tasks. The next week, we met twice. She hunted for berries while I gathered larger pieces of wood for a building project I'd been hired to do. But we talked and laughed, and agreed to meet the next week. Before either of us knew what had happened, months passed and we loved each other."

Heinrich was surprised. Matthäus always struck him as a steady sort of fellow, not ruled by emotion or carried along by flights of fancy. "All this, without knowing who the other was, who the families were?"

"We knew each other, our temperaments and hopes." Matthäus's tone was tense and defensive. "Perhaps I ought to have asked her father's permission to court her after a week or two, but you know me; can you imagine me asking to speak to her father?"

Heinrich grasped Matthäus's arm and pulled him a few paces away from the field, in case any of the children had wandered close. A quick glance around told him that wasn't the case, but he still questioned their good judgment at conducting such a conversation in the open. "So you seduced her in secret?" he hissed.

"No! Her honor was intact on our wedding night. We'd kissed before, just a little after we decided to wed, but nothing more." He shook his head and followed Heinrich toward the front of the house where they would be afforded more privacy. "We married in secret and lived separately until we could show that the marriage had been consummated and her family could not force an annulment. Six months after we married, she was growing great with child. We went to her father and allowed him to read the marriage certificate. He had no choice but to acknowledge it. He refused to bless the marriage, but did give us a small cottage on his property where we could live. I started an apprenticeship with a nearby carpenter and woodcarver, but just a few months after Maria was born, our cottage caught fire."

He trailed off, and Heinrich almost asked what happened next, when it dawned on him: Matthäus's heavy breathing, glassy eyes, and red nose and ears.

"I woke first and shook Petrissa awake. She woke up and started for the door. I went to get the baby and ran from the cottage. I didn't realize that Petrissa had turned back."

He was quiet for a time, thinking of what Heinrich could only guess. The men's breaths created puffs of steam in the cold air, and the silence was magnified by the tension and the cold.

"I broke free of the cottage. Maria was crying, which told me she could still breathe. Some of Petrissa's brothers had already seen the fire and had come running from her family's house. I thought they'd taken her. We all shouted back and forth a bit, but finally I understood that they hadn't and Petrissa was still in the house. I dumped little Maria into the arms of the nearest brother and ran back into the house. I yelled for her, and finally heard a faint cry from the bedchamber. She was caught under a portion of the ceiling that had fallen. I tried to get to her; I did! But the main beam of the roof fell then, knocking me down and trapping my leg. I couldn't get to her, and I couldn't get out.

"I don't remember much after that. I remember her cries, then her screams. I remember tears on my face, and wondering how I could make tears when my mouth was so dry and painful. Then she stopped screaming, and someone was pulling me out.

"Her brothers were furious. Even after I recovered enough to talk, they wouldn't listen, that I had thought she had run out ahead of me. They blamed me for her death—but no more than I blamed myself. When we went back to clear the ashes and see if anything could be salvaged, we found her remains. She was holding this in her hand."

He pulled out from beneath his jerkin a small, wooden cross attached to a thin strip of leather. The cross was carved of one piece of wood, with excellent proportions and sanded or worn smooth, though its ends were marred with black in a few spots.

"I'd made it for her just a few weeks after we met. She wore it all the time, even when she slept. I'm not sure why she'd taken it off that night."

Heinrich did not know what to say. He'd had no notion of the pain his friend carried. But he did know what Luther would say. He would point the broken young man to the Christ, to His Word in the Holy Scriptures.

"Let's start tomorrow morning."

Matthäus glanced up at him for the first time in a long time. "What?"

"Tomorrow morning, we will start reading the Holy Scriptures together; you will learn to read as we progress."

\*\*\*

Nikolaus had been living in Wittenberg for two weeks now. He hadn't yet spoken to Brigita—he knew if he went to her when she was with anyone else, she wouldn't submit to him. That family protecting her stuck to her like a bunch of hungry dogs to a person who tossed them scraps. Or perhaps it was the other way around: Brigita was the hungry dog, sniffing around the wealthy family.

Either way, he hadn't been able to get her alone. Though once, he nearly had. She was walking back to the house she was staying in from the cottage at the edge of their property—he'd learned all about the Diefenbachs from the smithy he'd been staying with: the upstanding burgher Johann, the melancholy wife, the passel of children, and their apprentice Matthäus and his daughter. He was sure there was another apprentice, but he'd not learned who he was yet. Asking too many questions about one particular family would cause suspicion. It was likely the other apprentice lived a similarly holy life as the rest of them.

The day after Nikolaus arrived in Wittenberg, he'd sought out the lesser-frequented of the three smithies hawking their wares in the *Marktplatz*. This one wanted someone to do his work while he sold in the market. Because Nikolaus knew the trade but would never have his own shop—unless he was able to secure Ritter's place—he was glad about the arrangement. Besides, this way, he could easily stay hidden from Brigita.

The last time he saw her, he'd not wanted any sort of lasting attachment. Now, though, he hoped to devise a plan to force a marriage. Working for another man wasn't ideal, but if it allowed him time to observe and learn her habits and patterns of travel while remaining out of sight, he would suffer it cheerfully. Besides, winter had arrived with a flurry of snow, promising to very soon make travel difficult, if not impossible. Having a warm place to stay and income, meager though it was, allowed some measure of comfort. And remaining hidden in the out-of-the-way smithy was in his best interest, at least for the time being. He thought he'd soon venture to the tavern, as neither Heinrich nor that giant Matthäus seemed to frequent it in the evenings.

It wouldn't do for Brigita to see him before he could devise a way to meet with her that gave him the advantage he wanted. Then they'd have no choice but to marry. He'd already destroyed any chance of her believing he loved her. If, however, he could guilt her into wedding him, it would work just as well. Perhaps better because he would have no need to pretend affection at any time.

# 25

In the days following his enlightening but difficult conversation with Matthäus—Heinrich would never have imagined the quiet, steady man held such depth of pain!—he was swept along with the tide of coming examinations. He did keep his word to Matthäus, though. In the evenings, while Maria listened to stories told by Diefenbach with the other children and Marlein and Brigita tidied the kitchen and prepared for the following day, Heinrich and Matthäus sat at the table and studied. Heinrich took a few moments each afternoon to copy letters and words onto paper for Matthäus to practice reading and writing, and Matthäus excelled at his tasks. Soon, his aptitude for learning prompted Heinrich to include Latin in the letters and words he was writing on the paper. Even with a second language added, Matthäus kept up. Heinrich believed that the other man may very well have been more intelligent than himself, but had never been given the opportunity to expand his learning. Helping his friend brought satisfaction and fulfillment like no other task.

Heinrich and Brigita had not spoken further concerning her condition, but as her face continued to grow rounder and her dresses grew snug around the middle, he no longer worried over her health, at least; he'd worry about the threat childbirth might be to her health when the time came. For the time being, though, her quick smile and growing closeness with Marlein assured him that her heart was well too.

The two women often shared understanding glances and warm smiles; whenever he witnessed such an exchange, it warmed his soul like a warm blanket on a cold day. His sister finally seemed to have a true friend, who for all appearances cared for her as much as he did.

When exams had been written and the university was in recess until after the Holy Days of Christmas and Epiphany, many of the students returned to their homes. Heinrich, though, had not traveled since his father's death. Instead, he made himself useful to Diefenbach and earned a small wage. He spent only a few hours each day at the candle shop, but he enjoyed his time with the other men, working together with their hands to make something useful. He even used the opportunity to subtly continue his lessons with Matthäus. He would use the tip of his knife to etch into the wax words that Matthäus struggled to learn, before dropping them into the pot for remelting. Or he would help as Matthäus wrote the accounts, finally recognizing the letters of the words he'd memorized.

In the afternoons, though, Heinrich was free to do as he pleased. One such afternoon, bright and chilly, the eldest two Diefenbach children accompanied their father on an errand to town while the youngest three played quietly near the side door. Keterlyn Diefenbach was resting quietly in her room, and Marlein decided to take the opportunity to prepare *Springerle* for the Christmas celebrations. As the special biscuit called for a finer flour than the hearty barley or oat types Marlein usually used for bread, she asked Heinrich to climb up to the storage loft to see whether there was any of the wheat flour left from the small bag they had purchased several months ago.

"No," he called down from the top of the ladder, "I don't see any."

"Are you certain?" she asked, stepping onto the lowest rung. "I was fairly sure I remembered only using about half of it when I made *Springerle* for the Messner girl's wedding."

"Well, you're free to come up and look," Heinrich joked. Giving a cursory glance about the cramped space, he turned to descend the ladder, intending to offer to ride into the city for some flour. Poor Jäger had been confined to his stall far too much lately. "Good heavens!"

When he'd turned, rather than the open space of the ladder as he'd expected, Marlein stood on the second-highest rung, her skirts gathered and tied in her apron strings.

"I-I suppose that makes for easier climbing," he choked out, unused to seeing quite so much calf on any girl older than Leonetta.

"Hm?" Marlein stopped her search for the flour and looked at him. When he snapped his eyes from her pink stockings to her face, she looked down. "Oh"—her voice was soft—"yes. I apologize; you fit so well into our household I sometimes forget that you aren't really family."

She quickly loosened her skirts from the apron strings holding them up and they fell with a *whoosh* that sounded much like the sigh Heinrich released at the same time.

"Here it is!" Marlein cried triumphantly, straightening from where she'd been crouched behind a couple of crates, rummaging through some old burlap sacks in the corner. In her hands was a small, half-filled sack of what Heinrich supposed was flour. "Let's just hope it is enough!" she chuckled.

Heinrich nodded, still feeling discomposed. Clearing his throat, he forced a smile to his lips and said, "If it isn't, I'll be happy to ride to the *Marktplatz* for more flour."

"Thank you." She smiled back. "Now, would you like to climb down first, or shall I?"

"I think you'd better," Heinrich said, barely containing the self-deprecating laugh that wanted to escape. He found it more and more difficult to be patient with his growing feelings for Marlein. And he wasn't sure any more why he had to be.

"Very well," Marlein answered, and Heinrich had a terrible time remembering they were speaking of climbing down the ladder and not commencing a courtship. "Do you mind carrying the flour as I'll be managing these unruly skirts?"

"Of course."

Once they both were on the ground floor, he handed her the flour.

"Thank you."

"I didn't do anything. You had to go find it," he reminded her.

"Still, it is more pleasant to climb with a friend than alone." She looked upward for a moment and shuddered. "I've never enjoyed having to climb up there. I fear falling, and the spiders and rats like it. That's why I keep so little flour; so easy for pests to get into it."

He nodded, smiling faintly at the smudge of dust on her cheek and the wisp of spiderweb in her hair. "Hold still," he cautioned, reaching for the spot just above her left ear. "There's a bit of . . ."

Rather than finish, he swept the spiderweb onto his fingers and showed her. If he wasn't mistaken, she had stopped breathing.

"Spiderweb," he whispered.

Marlein let out a ragged breath before whispering back, "Thank you."

She had been holding her breath.

"You're welcome."

"Why are we whispering?"

Heinrich shrugged and shuffled a little closer to her. Staring at her sweet face, the smattering of freckles across her nose and the curly wisps around her forehead, he shrugged again and began to reach for the side of her face.

"Another spiderweb?" she choked out, her voice strained.

He shook his head and reached farther.

"Oh!" Marlein's eyes had flown wide open, and she stepped back, leaving his hand just inches from its intended destination. She stepped back again, putting an arm's length between them. "I-I should get started. You . . . you'd mentioned riding for more flour. Do you think you could do that now? I should like to make a second batch tomorrow to have for the Epiphany, and there certainly is not enough flour for that."

She turned and hurried from him, went into her room to retrieve a coin, and awkwardly held it out to drop into his palm after she'd returned. Heinrich was disappointed, but reminded himself that he wanted to help her, to ease her burden. So he smiled, went to saddle his horse, and rode away from the woman who drew him like no other.

C H A P T E R

# 26

Marlein stirred the stiff dough in the bowl, thankful again that the spoon she used was carved of a sturdy wood. Her arms were beginning to ache, but she still worked to ensure all the ingredients were well-incorporated before she stopped and prepared the table to roll out the dough. The strenuous stirring helped her to find an outlet for the strange nerves that had arisen after her interaction with Heinrich that morning.

The side door opened, a cold blast of air washing over her. Marlein looked up from her work to see Brigita enter the kitchen, followed by her brother. Both had broad smiles for her.

"I had just arrived back with the flour and found Brigita in the garden, pulling up some potatoes." Heinrich set the small bag of flour on the bench at the table where Marlein worked while Brigita dumped her apron full of potatoes onto the floor near the side door.

"They're still rather dirty," Brigita murmured apologetically.

"That is just fine," Marlein said with a smile.

"Well, ladies," Heinrich announced, "I should go get Jäger; I tied him to the garden fence when I came upon Brigita. He won't like being left in the cold."

Marlein snatched a dried apple from the bowl she'd filled earlier to put with the pork for their supper, offering it to him. "Why don't you give this to Jäger, then."

After he left, Brigita came to peer into the bowl Marlein was stirring. "What are these?"

"*Springerle*. It's a stiff dough, but they hold the pattern of the mold well. They'll be rolled, stamped, cut, dried, and then baked tomorrow."

"They sound complicated." The doubt in Brigita's voice was clear.

Marlein laughed. "A little. But that's why we only ever make them for special occasions. Have you never had one?"

"Never," Brigita returned. "I've heard of them, but had no idea how to make them. My father was never one for frivolities."

Marlein wasn't sure how to answer, but was saved by Heinrich's return. Rather than address Brigita, she said to Heinrich, "Surely you aren't leaving him in the stall without a rubdown?"

Heinrich glanced over his shoulder toward the stalls before answering. "Steffan offered to get him settled for me. He said that his work is sparser in the winter months and would enjoy seeing to him." He stepped closer to Marlein and nudged her shoulder with his own as he peered into the bowl she held. "Jäger was most appreciative for the ride. I would pass on to you the thanks he gave me, but doubt you would want the slobber or head butt I received."

Marlein chuckled and lightly nudged him back. "You'd be right about that."

"What can I help with?" Brigita asked.

"Actually, there's not much that needs doing just now. I've been thinking: you two haven't had much time to talk lately. Why don't you go and take a walk around the countryside? Supper won't be for a couple more hours, so take your time. Brigita, is that cloak warm enough for you?"

"Yes." Brigita then surprised her by stepping close and wrapping her arms around Marlein's shoulders. "Thank you so much. I think I would have been completely lost without your kindness."

Marlein returned the embrace, glancing over Brigita's shoulder to see Heinrich watching them, a warm smile on his face. The women separated, and Marlein smiled fondly at Brigita. "You are most welcome. I do so enjoy having you here. You know, had my sister Niesenn lived, she would be near your age. Perhaps that has something to do with this bond I feel with you."

"We will be back in time to help with supper," Brigita said through her wide smile.

"Well, don't speak for me. You know I can't help, or Sïfrit would harp on me for days," Heinrich joked.

Marlein felt her face warm up, remembering the many times Heinrich had warded off Sïfrit's advances for her.

"I think she'd prefer your bumbling help around here over having to face him alone," Brigita countered, an impish grin on her face.

"Brigita!" Marlein couldn't believe the girl had been that direct and stared at her incredulously. "What a thing to say."

Heinrich laughed softly before saying, "Come, Gita. Let's leave Marlein in her misery and hope we return before Sïfrit arrives from the shop."

The two moved down the hall, presumably to look in on Jäger on their way out. Then the door opened and closed, and she knew they'd gone. Marlein turned back to her task with a sigh, feeling both relieved and sad that they would be absent for a time.

Marlein had just started to roll out the stiff dough when her mother appeared in her doorway.

"*Mutter!*" Marlein started to clean off her hands. "Can I get you something? Warm beer? Wine?"

"*Nein*, child," she answered, reaching toward Marlein a little before turning to a small stool situated near the fireplace. "But thank you. I'll just sit by the fire a spell."

"Are you feeling well?" Marlein carefully kept her tone neutral as she resumed the slow process of rolling out the dough. It would be about as thick as her pinky when she finished.

"Well enough."

The silence settled over them. It was not comfortable, but neither did it make Marlein uneasy. Every time she snuck a glance in her mother's direction, the older woman was watching her. Just as Marlein finished rolling the dough and reached for the *Springerle* mold she'd already dusted with flour, her mother spoke.

"You are a good girl, Marlein." The words were spoken in her usual direct tone, yet there was a layer of melancholy beneath the surface.

Marlein ached to speak freely with her mother, to ask how she could help her—for nothing she did seemed to be of any good. With the fragility of the pleasant moment, though, she feared it would shatter if she spoke the wrong words. "Thank you" was all she allowed herself to say.

"Someday, my girl, you will make a very good wife."

Marlein pressed the mold into the dough and searched her mind for where this might be coming from. Her mother seldom spoke of the future, and less so of a possible future where Marlein was no longer in their house. Had she overheard her conversation with Heinrich and Brigita? Or was something else spurring her to speak?

"You know my place is here," Marlein said carefully, lifting the mold, only to have the dough follow it for a bit, stretching and distorting the stamped image. "With you."

Her mother rose from the stool and came to stand at her shoulder. "See how the dough can't keep its integrity when the mold presses it down? Put it out to chill in the winter air for a little while. Don't let it freeze, though. Just firm up a bit."

Marlein looked sideways at her mother, her heart glowing warmly. How she wished every moment of every day could be like this. She nodded with a smile, scraped together the dough, and placed it back in the bowl. Once she'd set it on the stone stoop outside the side door, she closed the door and returned to her mother, who was still standing near the table.

"Are you hungry?"

When she nodded, Marlein hurried over to the hearth and took a bowl from the nearby shelf. In a pot hanging over the fire was a rich stew that had been simmering since after breakfast. Most of them had already eaten of it, but there was plenty left. She spooned out a healthy serving and handed it to her mother.

"Would you like bread too? I have some—"

"No, this is fine."

Marlein handed her a wooden spoon and watched Keterlyn dip it into the bowl, then raise it to her lips.

"This is good. You cook well, Marlein."

"*Danke, Mutter.*" When her mother sat at the larger table for eating, Marlein moved back to the table to clean up the mess. She smiled and hummed a little to herself, thinking that just maybe, her family was growing firm enough to keep its integrity despite the various things that pressed down on it.

\*\*\*

Willeic's fists banged on the flimsy door. It was barely enough to keep the biting mid-December wind out, so why could he not push it down? He pounded upon it again, the rough wood biting into the soft edge of his palm, though he couldn't bring himself to care. Arna would soothe it. But his wife was already suspicious. If Emnelda wouldn't help him, his wife's suspicions would be confirmed by the sight of Arna's small but swollen belly. He had no desire to share his wealth with some sniveling little illegitimate.

The door finally creaked open, interrupting his thoughts just as he raised his fist to hit it again. He stopped himself from hitting the woman's sallow face, but only just. Her surprisingly thick brows were raised and her pale blue eyes—so pale they were nearly white in the light of the moon reflected on the snow—assessed him.

"Yes?" Her voice rasped with disuse. He supposed that old Emnelda no longer had many visitors. Just the few who still sought her out for simple tinctures and salves. And the occasional patron such as himself. It was said that in her youth, she was a beauty and quick to rush to any expectant mother's birthing bed when the time came. But as he pushed past her, and she teetered precariously on her wobbly feet before catching her balance on a nearby chair, he saw that she was merely a shriveled shell. The warnings of some of his neighbors seemed foolish superstition when he stood before her feeble frame. A witch indeed!

"Now, old woman, I need a potion to make a little problem I have go away."

"You can't mean . . ." Her horror-filled eyes betrayed her understanding of the situation.

"I certainly can."

She said nothing for a few heartbeats—his thunderous and angry in his chest. Finally, her voice grated itself into his ears. "How far along is she?"

"I haven't a clue!"

She hummed and said, "Then are you certain?"

He scowled, remembering when he'd felt forced to feign happiness when Arna grasped his wrist and placed his hand on her barely swollen belly, smiling broadly at him. He pretended, swallowing his annoyance that she had allowed this to happen.

"No!" If that *thing* were allowed to reach birth, he would be responsible. "I ask you again: will you help me?"

When she didn't answer right away, he jumped at her pause and thrust his hand into the pocket tied beneath his cloak, reaching for a pouch of coin. Surely her reliance on the kindness of others for daily sustenance would sway her for him.

"Will this help persuade you?"

Her withered lips pressed together before she opened them in a snarl, revealing yellowed teeth. "No."

Rage swept over him in a burgundy haze, tinging his cheeks and the whites of his eyes. It pounded in his ears and turned his hands numb. He uttered threats, then pleas, before finally storming away.

"I will find someone else who wants my coin more than she does."

***

Emnelda trembled as she placed the bar back across her door, her hands scarcely able to grip the heavy wood. Once it was secure in its braces, she weakly lowered her frame onto the small, crooked stool near her hearth. She rubbed her hands over her upper arms, trying to catch some of the warmth of the low-burning fire. Fear blinded her already dim eyes to all in the room but the blaze.

The man's eyes, which she could barely see for the dimness of the cottage, had told her more than his silence. She'd asked how far along the babe was, and they had grown distant. He might not want it, but he could not deny its existence.

She knew of the herbs to make a tonic that would cause the mother to bleed until the baby died. But she could not find it in her to mix them. She had seen the aftermath of loss and could not aid with such a thing. Not only would it give people the satisfaction of evidence, for she knew what they whispered about her, but she couldn't end life. It was not her purpose. She ached to help life, to champion it, as much as she was able. She had no choice but to refuse him, and she did.

She could flee, because she knew that the man might very well retaliate for her refusal. But she had no choice. She would not leave her people, even if she wasn't theirs. The Diefenbachs had been good to her, though she could not offer anything in return. In fact, she feared she was the cause of much of their suffering. So many of Keterlyn Diefenbach's children had perished under her care, and she could not help the feeling of responsibility. However, despite her guilt, she was bound to them. Or perhaps because of it.

She would stay. And a good thing, too, as her bees would need her come spring.

# 27

Heinrich could not recall a more joyous Christmas in his adult life. The day had begun with the Christmas Mass and hearing Luther preach of the great mercy God showed in sending His Son. Not sent in judgment, but out of love. Not in wrath, but to bring mercy. Not in anger, but to create peace. As he watched the evergreen tree, decorated with dried flowers, being processed through the street, he could not help staring in wonder at what it represented: God present with His people, God bringing a new thing, new life, into the dead of winter, into the dead of a world perishing in its sin. God in flesh to bear the burden of man's sin.

After the procession of the tree, the families of Wittenberg dispersed and returned to their homes. Marlein and even Keterlyn had been working hard to prepare food for this most holy and joyous of days. As the Diefenbach family exited through the city gate to head homeward, Heinrich found himself walking beside Keterlyn.

"The weather is good today," he ventured, unsure whether she would answer. Conversation with Keterlyn was rare.

"It is," she surprised him by saying. "I remember one year when I was a girl, it snowed so terribly much, and we could not leave our house for fear of getting lost. Living with our own land for growing food is a blessing, but it doesn't come without its share of trials."

Heinrich nodded his agreement, while trying to think of how he might connect with the woman. They had so little in common, aside from Marlein.

"I know you and Marlein have been working hard to prepare for today," he offered.

"She's done much more than I," Keterlyn admitted with no small amount of chagrin in her voice. "But I did try to rouse myself."

"I am glad," Heinrich offered. "I know she . . . misses you."

"Thank you," Keterlyn murmured. She swallowed. "Life . . . has not been what I'd expected. I think . . . I know . . . that there are many blessings. I have security, no fear of hunger, which is more than so many others. But . . . I've still suffered."

Heinrich's heart was thumping wildly in his chest, more so than any proximity to Marlein had caused, though that had been considerable. No, his anxiousness had more to do with finding the right words. For so long, he'd seen Keterlyn's paralysis in her grief as something to push away or that he hoped would disappear. His heart thundered now, though, because he was beginning to understand that here was something he could instead take upon himself too. It wouldn't be easy, as their relationship had always been polite but distant. But if he took seriously Luther's and St. Paul's admonition to bear with one another, he knew that he needed to at least try.

"I know that I can't really understand what it is like for you," he began quietly, "but I've recently come to realize that God is love, and He desires for people to love one another as He loves us."

She nodded, though the doubt on her face belied her agreement with him.

"I've not done well," Heinrich continued, "but I want to do better." He reached sideways to touch her elbow with a couple of his fingers. "You are not alone, Keterlyn."

Keterlyn turned watery eyes toward Heinrich. She said nothing for a time, her eyes blinking rapidly several times, and her lips pressed tightly together. At length, she whispered, "Thank you, Heinrich."

They arrived at the house then and entered to enjoy a lovely feast. The *Springerle* were passed about, the sharp anise flavor bursting from the plain white biscuits. Roast goose, meat pies, potatoes and carrots, fine wheat bread, and other things that had been prepared were passed around the table in new bowls that Matthäus had carved, sanded, and waxed for the family. Everyone had their own bowl. Merriment filled the room, eliciting smiles from Keterlyn and even pleasantness from Sïfrit.

Before the evening of more feasting and singing hymns of Christmas, Marlein packed a basket to take to Emnelda. She had declined an invitation to be carried in a cart to celebrate with the family, but Marlein wanted to take some of the goodies to her. Dusk was settling, bathing the cold world in pale pink light. Marlein carried the basket, and Heinrich brought a lantern, in case the sun set before they were ready to return to the Diefenbach house.

"I think, Marlein," Heinrich said as they crossed the barren field, "that better food has never been made than what you prepared for us this Christmas."

He glanced sideways at her, seeing her cheeks already rosy from the cold and her nose bright pink.

"You know that the mulled wine makes anything taste better," she said, a smile fighting for prominence on her face. "Though I believe it might have been the fact that we each had our own bowl."

"It was kind and observant of Matthäus to carve bowls for your family." After a short pause, he added, "Well, whoever you eventually marry, he will be a happy man."

That was too much to say, he was sure. Her face grew rosier as her eyes widened; when she turned her head away, he opened his mouth to apologize, but they had already arrived at the cottage. Marlein knocked on the door, and they waited until the scraping sound of a bar on the inside being removed alerted them that she was home. One pale eye peeked through the tiny opening between the door and the post.

"Oh, 'tis you." The door swung wide, and he saw that Emnelda held a hot fire poker with a sturdy cloth wrapped around the end.

"Whatever is that for?" he asked as he followed Marlein into the tiny cottage. "Do you think a robber would come on this day of our Lord's birth?"

Marlein placed the basket on the table before crossing to the hearth. "Heavens, Emnelda! You cannot keep warm with so low a fire!" She took a log from the small stack near the edge of the hearth and placed it on the fire. "There, we shall have a cheery fire blazing soon!"

Heinrich watched, confused, as Emnelda started to protest, even going so far as to reach her arms out as though to grasp the log as the flames climbed up its sides, before she gave up and clasped her hands before her. "I do not have many logs, so I was trying to make them last."

"I can easily bring more for you," he offered. "In fact, I can use the handcart to bring some tomorrow and again on Sunday. With the cart here, it will be easy to use it to help you come to Mass."

"That is kind," Emnelda allowed, "but my back has been bothering me lately and all that jostling is more than I think I could take."

Heinrich exchanged a concerned look with Marlein; Emnelda had never refused an offer to help her to Mass. He knew that she delighted in hearing the words of Luther expounding on what the Scriptures taught about God.

"Very well, then," he said. "But I'll be by with the wood early tomorrow. You'll tell me if you change your mind?"

"I will."

Before they left, they brought in the rest of the wood from her small woodpile outside. Walking back to the house, Marlein asked, "She was acting oddly, yes?"

"Very." The blue of the sky seemed to deepen with every step they took, and Heinrich was glad he'd lit the lantern from Emnelda's fire.

"I can't think of what might be the cause." They walked in silence, feet crunching on the frozen snow. "Perhaps if Brigita were to stay with her, she would do better. She can help Emnelda until her time comes, then Emnelda can help Brigita when it does. Do you think that either woman would mind such an arrangement?"

Heinrich was impressed with her idea. When he looked over at her, her eyes reflected the lantern light, gleaming softly in the night. He couldn't help the fondness that softened his voice as he said, "It seems to me that Brigita will agree to whatever you suggest; you've quite won her with your kindness."

"Oh, I've done nothing." She looked away, hiding her eyes.

Rather than attempt to argue with her, Heinrich continued, "And it seems that if Emnelda is nervous about something, she would appreciate having another person about the place."

"It was very strange that she opened the door with the fire poker in her hand. And the door was barred! It is dark out, but she knew to expect us before supper; I told her as much when she declined our invitation."

He nodded but had no answer, so they continued in silence for a time. The evening was quiet, the calm of winter settling into his soul. Grateful for the time of refreshing, he knew that a season of difficulty for Brigita and therefore for him was on the horizon.

"Brigita is increasing," he commented, echoing his thoughts.

"Yes," Marlein agreed. "The dress she wears was only taken up because she is shorter than I am. But she fills out the rest of it. I would not be surprised if she can no longer lace it after just a few more days."

***

They arrived back at the house, slipping into the gathered group of people. The warmth of the room filled Heinrich's heart even as he munched on cakes and biscuits to fill his belly.

"I am glad to see you filling out so well, Brigita," Diefenbach said as he reached for another small cake. "You were such a waiflike creature when you came to us."

Brigita's eyes went wide and her face flushed. Heinrich looked at Marlein, whose face was alarmed. He quickly spoke up to distract from Brigita's flustered appearance.

"I am glad she is so well cared for here," Heinrich said, "and I know that she enjoys her days spent with Marlein."

Everyone nodded their agreement, but Heinrich did see more than one pair of eyes assessing Brigita speculatively.

Yes, they would need to speak to the family soon.

***

Keterlyn was glad when the festival of the Epiphany arrived, marking the end of the twelve days. She struggled every year at the celebration of Christ's birth. Guilt assailed her for the struggle, but she was unable to find joy. Making *Springerle* with Marlein had been a good moment in the preparations, reminding her of the time before she was so broken. It was good to feel useful. But Marlein was very capable, so Keterlyn's moments of usefulness were growing fewer and farther between.

Heinrich's kind words to her on the walk from Christmas Mass to the house had been a small comfort, but really, how could he help her? Still, it was nice that he sought out conversation with her every time she emerged from her room. There were days she didn't, but when she did, she could count on his company, even if her husband and children tended to avoid her.

It seemed her family had little need of a mother who most days could scarcely rouse herself from bed. She knew she was being unfair to them with those thoughts, but the knowledge did little to dispel them.

Without the garden to distract her, and the shortened days and cold weather keeping everyone indoors for much of the day, Keterlyn felt trapped. Especially when she heard Heinrich and Matthäus speaking together of God's Word and His love. It ate at her heart most uncomfortably, especially as she had nowhere to escape.

More than the house, though, her own thoughts snared her. Whispers of her failure to carry her babies, memories of pain and heartache, moments of isolation when the silence was louder than the screams she held inside . . . all conspired to pull her downward to a place she'd hoped never to return, until she feared ever rising from it again.

# 28

Christmastide's twelve days culminated in the holy day of Epiphany. During those twelve days, as no work was to be done, there had been ample time for leisure. Or in the case of Matthäus and Heinrich, study. He and Heinrich worked through the books of Scripture that Heinrich had in his possession, and it was as if his eyes were slowly being opened. The fear in his heart for his dear Petrissa was steadily being driven out by love. God's love for His creation was such that He did not keep back even His own Son, but sent Him as a sacrifice for all sin, for all time, for all of creation. Heinrich explained to Matthäus as Luther had once explained it to the students during a lecture. The word *repent* was being discussed, and the intention of the admonition of Christ to "Repent!" was not a thing to be done for individual sins as atonement. No, atonement had already been made in Christ's death on the cross and resurrection from the tomb. Repentance was something lived out in daily life, in which the old, sinful person was daily drowned in remembrance of his Baptism and the new person emerged to live a life that would glorify God and help his neighbor.

On the Epiphany, the entire Diefenbach household attended Mass. In light of his recent revelation, Matthäus enjoyed it for perhaps the first time since his Petrissa had died, and when the family returned to the house afterward for food and celebration, he made a point to walk with Brigita when Maria skipped ahead with Aldessa and Herlinde.

The sky had been gray and stormy the previous evening, as snow clouds rolled in to cover the earth with a fresh blanket of pristine, glistening white. A new day, everything clean and fresh and new . . . Matthäus could not help but believe that it reflected his life at this point. Fresh, wiped clear, the sins of his past covered.

"Careful of the ice there," he cautioned, offering his arm as Brigita neared a shiny patch on the snow.

"Thank you," she murmured as she tentatively took his arm.

"I . . ." Matthäus stopped and cleared the nerves from his throat before continuing. "I've noticed that you enjoy watching birds."

She seemed mildly startled, but not alarmed, as she replied, "I do. They always seem so carefree, so quick and beautiful."

He reached into a pocket hidden in his doublet and grasped the hard object he'd stowed there. "I hope it isn't too forward of me, but I carved this for you."

She let go of his arm to take the small object into her hands. Raising it to her face for closer inspection, her brows raised and a small smile ghosted across her lips, causing his shoulders to relax and the tension to ease just a bit. It faded entirely when she glanced up to meet his eyes—a rare occurrence.

"It is lovely." Her fingers traced the bird's delicate, outstretched wings—they'd been some of the trickiest things he'd ever carved; he'd even spent some of his carefully saved money to order a new knife from one of the finer blacksmiths in the city—and his heart swelled at the wonder in her eyes when she saw the detail he'd carefully etched into the hard walnut wood. "Did it take you long?"

"No, not really." He reached over to lightly touch the bird's head. "Lyngstrom had a small chunk of walnut leftover from a chest that someone had ordered. I traded him beeswax for it."

"Where do you get beeswax?" she asked with a chuckle.

"Emnelda gave it to me last autumn when I stocked her woodpile for her."

She smiled once again, but it faded as she asked, "Do . . . do you require anything in thanks for this gift?" There was a tremor to her voice that turned Matthäus's stomach for some reason that he could not identify.

"Of course not. If I did, it would be a transaction, not a gift."

Her forehead smoothed at that, and she looked up at him again, eyes crinkling at the edges with the fullness of her smile. "Then let me give you this: thank you, Matthäus, for the lovely bird."

"You are most welcome."

His heart swelled when, several minutes later, she tentatively reached to hold his arm again as they crossed another icy patch on their way to the Diefenbach house.

\*\*\*

After the recess, Heinrich once again began attending lectures and absorbing the wonderful knowledge offered by his professors, particularly Doctor Luther. His descriptions of what the Letter to the Hebrews taught left Heinrich hungry for more of the Word of God.

The time he spent studying with Matthäus was enjoyable as well. As he reviewed what he had learned and written about the Letter to the Galatians, he found that reading it the second time was just as fascinating as the first time. He still gave Matthäus words and sentences to read, and the man increased his reading speed and understanding. After he had finished what work he had for his own learning, and Matthäus had meticulously copied what Heinrich prepared for him, the two men would begin reading the Letter.

Sometimes Heinrich pointed to a phrase that Matthäus had learned and asked him to read it; sometimes he simply translated into German as he read aloud. They pored over the words, discussed and questioned and sought answers. On occasion, Diefenbach joined them, and every now and then, Marlein asked a question as she listened quietly while working in the kitchen.

One particularly frigid day, the two men sat close to the fire while Marlein and Brigita were preparing supper. The two men had just finished their work and were preparing to read the Letter to the Galatians again from the beginning. Heinrich paused to ask, "Would you prefer that we move to other things that would apply more to your craft? Do you know how to write *wax* and *candle*?"

"Oh no," Matthäus answered quickly. "Father Martin said that I should seek comfort in the Scriptures, that his comfort and confidence comes from there. I have, and I think it is working. The fear and guilt have faded already."

"Well, I suppose I can't argue with that!" Heinrich gladly turned to the beginning of the book and offered it to Matthäus, to see how much he could read. While Matthäus silently worked through a troublesome word, Heinrich's thoughts strayed to how much he enjoyed this. He almost wanted to abandon his study of law and turn instead to theology. The Scriptures, especially. But he could not, for his sister needed someone to provide for her, now more than ever. The niggling thought pressed, though: if he was unable to acquire clients because of her shame, how would he provide for her anyway? She desired to keep the child, which seemed an impossibility. Still, he would do what he was able to help her, to bear her burden.

Just as Matthäus managed to stumble through the first few sentences, Sïfrit wandered in through the side door. Heinrich noticed him pause when he saw them before ambling over to see what they were doing.

"Trying to teach this simpleton to read? Useless."

Heinrich watched Matthäus's face freeze, two bright red spots showing high on his cheeks. "I wouldn't say that, Sïfrit," he said when

Matthäus remained silent. "In fact, he has shown remarkable aptitude for learning. He is even reading some Latin."

Sïfrit said nothing else, but huffed a bit and strode past them to the table. He greeted the women, who were working on supper. Heinrich felt an unholy glee when both the young women answered with short, clipped words. He met Matthäus's eyes, and they both huffed out annoyed breaths before standing. With a tiny grin and a brief roll of his eyes heavenward, Heinrich looked over at the kitchen.

Brigita sat at the table near the window, wearing the thin cloak she had when she arrived. Marlein was chopping vegetables at the other end of the table, Sïfrit standing close behind her and peering over her shoulder. Heinrich read her annoyance in her clenched jaw and the jerky movements of her hands as she worked.

"Sïfrit, why do you not leave the ladies be?"

"Why do you insist on sticking your nose into my business?" Sïfrit glared at him before raising his hand to boldly rest it on Marlein's upper back, just below her neck. Her movements stilled, and Heinrich saw her eyes widen as Sïfrit leaned closer, until his shoulder pressed lightly against her back.

"When you keep sniffing around them like a dog, I make it my business."

This stopped the younger man, who finally stepped back from Marlein, though his hand remained.

"Heinrich, you may have a right," Sïfrit slurred slightly, "to warn me off your sister; I'll give you that."

"How gracious of you," Heinrich sneered, recognizing that Sïfrit had once again stopped at the tavern on his way to the house.

"But there's no reason for you to take offense at my talking to Marlein." His grin for Heinrich was provoking as he slid his arm around Marlein's shoulders. "Unless you have a claim on her?"

Fire burst forth in Heinrich's belly and raged through his body. With it rushing in his ears, his mind spun as he grasped at words, but nothing came.

"I am under my father's protection," Marlein spat out. "Sïfrit, you will remove your hand from me, and the two of you will in the future leave your fighting outside of my kitchen. I have plans for neither romance nor marriage and do not appreciate such a discussion of me when I am right here in front of you!"

The fire in Heinrich cooled instantly in the face of her ire directed at him too. Sïfrit backed away from her, hands and eyebrows raised, before finally turning and leaving through the side door, muttering something about returning to the tavern for supper. Heinrich watched, helplessly, as Marlein scooped up the vegetables she had been chopping and turned to drop them into the pot that was simmering over the fire. She gave it a quick stir and went back to clean her knife with a rag before replacing it on the shelf where the children could not reach it. He didn't know if it was merely his imagination, but her hands seemed to tremble as she performed the tasks. As she approached the fire once more, Heinrich saw that her eyes were unmistakably glassy and her face was flushed. Without a word, she stepped past him and strode to the side door, nearly running as she passed through it.

Heinrich felt heat once again, but this was of a different nature. Shame and regret coursed through his body, weighing down his limbs and numbing his mind. The anger from before tried to assert itself— really, how could Sïfrit be so forward, even in his cups?—but the newer feelings easily overpowered it.

One question remained, weighing on his mind: How could he lower himself to such a petty reaction?

"I . . . I think I'm not very hungry," he mumbled to Matthäus. "Tell Diefenbach I'll return later; I'm going for a ride."

# 29

Matthäus blinked several times, staring down the hall toward the front entrance that Heinrich had just led his horse through.

"Do . . . do you think they will be all right?" asked Brigita quietly.

He turned and looked at her. She still sat at the table, scooping meat into pastries and pinching the dough around it to make pies. She kept her eyes on her work, glancing up at him on occasion.

"I suppose so. They both are worked up. They'll calm." He turned to retrieve the book and then joined Brigita at the table. "Do you know where Diefenbach and the children are?"

She finished another pie and carefully set it on the wide wooden paddle waiting on the table. "They went for a walk, but should return soon; the sun will be down in little time and it will be too cold to be out."

"Do you mind if I practice reading?" Matthäus couldn't explain why he felt bashful asking the question.

"Not at all." She offered a small smile. "I wanted to tell you, I think what Sïfrit said was terrible. You are learning, and I admire that."

"It is your brother's doing," he admitted.

"But you don't have to put in the work if you don't desire to. I know making candles takes a great deal of time; I watched my father do it for years." Her face flushed, but she held his gaze as she spoke, and for several moments after Matthäus felt warm and a little uncomfortable with the praise, but mostly warm. He returned her smile, then cleared his throat and began to read, translating aloud to German as he went. Brigita made pies and listened to St. Paul's words first greeting the Christians in Galatia, and then chastising them for straying to another teaching. He stumbled over a few words, but when he looked up at Brigita, she simply smiled encouragingly. He had never seen her so unguarded and wished he could sit and read to her every day.

Feeling his face flush at the thought, Matthäus returned to reading St. Paul's description of his calling and subsequent preaching. Once he had finished the chapter, he looked up to find Brigita staring ahead of her, seemingly lost in thought.

"I would suppose," she said, looking down again to return to her work, "that St. Paul knew that after his work to destroy the Church, he must work all the harder."

"What do you mean?"

"Well, he had sinned greatly." She finished the last pie, wiped her hands on her apron, and sat facing him. "And after he was saved, he was so zealous. He had much to atone for."

Something in her face made him sad. "You know, I said something similar to Heinrich the first time we read this. He showed me another passage . . ."

It took him some time to find it, slow as he still was to recognize the words that the symbols made. But he was beginning to memorize some of them and eventually found what he was looking for, in the fourth chapter.

"He's writing to the people of Galatia because some are wanting to enforce the old law that all men are circumcised, but St. Paul says that God has shown him that it doesn't matter because for those that He called, all are the same: circumcised or uncircumcised, slave or free,

Jew or Greek." Matthäus felt that he was stumbling over his words and wished that Heinrich were there to explain it better. Still, Brigita's face was once again open, her interest evident. He forged onward. "He goes on, then, to say that people's slavery to sin, I mean, when they were lost in their sin . . . it makes them slaves to it, to the devil. But here, see what St. Paul writes? Oh, it's Latin. Um, he says that when the fullness of time came, God sent His Son to redeem those under the law . . . that's us—well, all people. And the redemption is complete. There's nothing we do in it."

"But we have to do what is in us to—"

"No. Heinrich told me that Father Martin explained it like this: God knew that we can't keep the Law, but Christ came to keep it and to take our sin. Like the sacrifices the Jews did for years in the temple, Christ is the sacrifice that redeems us. And we can't, so He did. And while Christians should do good works, they aren't what save us."

"But when sin is so great that it can't . . ." She trailed off, frustration wrinkling her brow. "Well, I don't mean to say that Christ's sacrifice isn't enough, but—"

"But that's where it leads, doesn't it?" he interrupted. "When Christ died, He died for all sin. Even what we think is too great. You see, I—"

He was about to say that he felt trapped, enslaved, for years by the death of his wife. If he had gotten to her, if he had been more careful when banking the fire, if he had not married her against her family's wishes . . . yet even that, he knew now, Christ had redeemed.

But he wasn't sure he could share such personal things with Brigita just yet. He liked her immensely, but didn't know if he was ready to share something so deeply personal.

"I have struggled with . . . something," he finally began to explain. "But when Heinrich said all this to me, it was as though a great weight was removed from my shoulders, a terrible stain from my heart. It still is working in me, changing my thinking, but I no longer feel trapped and weighed down by it."

As he spoke, Brigita's eyes had welled up, and by the time he stopped, her lower lip was trembling. "That is such a . . ." she began, but trailed off breathlessly. "I would enjoy learning more."

Matthäus dared to reach across the table and lightly squeeze her hands, where they were clasped before her. "I find that the more I read or hear from Scripture, the more the truth sinks into my heart. I would very much enjoy reading with you in the future."

Brigita smiled, tentatively, tremulously, before she nodded. "Let's plan on that, then. For now, though, I must get these into the oven."

She stood, climbing from the bench, and her cape fell behind her shoulder on one side as she maneuvered. Matthäus tried not to stare, but the way the bodice of her dress strained against the bump protruding from her midsection, it was difficult not to. Brigita moved to the oven and raked the embers out of the way, unaware of his stare, before returning to the table. It was then that she met his eyes.

He saw the moment she realized. His eyes had been flicking back and forth between her face and her stomach, and when they returned to her face the last time, hers were looking back at him. She'd seen him staring, and now he wanted to kick himself. But why? He hadn't done anything wrong. But she didn't seem the sort of girl to . . .

His head was spinning.

She quickly turned away, rounding her shoulders as she drew the thin material of the old cloak about her again. Her movements were jerky and clumsy as she carried the paddle to the oven and carefully placed the pies on its hot base.

"Um, I have to . . . Please take the pies out when they turn gold. I need to . . ." And she stumbled through the door of the room she shared with Marlein, closing it softly behind her.

Matthäus sat quietly for a moment, debating what to do. He figured he'd watched someone take things from the oven enough times that he would be able to do it. But he wondered if he should first talk to Brigita. Going to her in her room, though, certainly wasn't appropriate.

The side door opened, and he looked up hopefully. Marlein would be able to help. But it wasn't Marlein. Diefenbach bundled the children through the door. Maria saw him and squealed happily, running to him.

"*Vati!*" She hugged him tightly before pulling back. "We went to the candle shop today! Diefenbach took us, and I helped dip a candle!"

He looked over her shoulder to the older man, who was grinning as he helped the youngest girl, Herlinde, out of her winter wrap. "I gave them each a wick and let them dip it in the tallow."

"It was stinky! I dipped mine ten times. I counted. One, two, three . . ."

As she chattered on, Matthäus listened to her, but glanced over at Diefenbach several times. After he did so a third time, the older man raised his thick brows and grinned.

"Excellent, Maria," Matthäus finally managed to interject. "Why don't you and the other girls go and visit the horses? I think they are lonely."

"Where is everyone?" Diefenbach asked as he strode over to Matthäus. "I thought Sïfrit would be here for supper too, but I find that not only is he gone, but so are Marlein, Brigita, and Heinrich!"

"There was . . . an uncomfortable situation," Matthäus began. "Sïfrit was pestering the girls, and Heinrich stepped in. He and Sïfrit got into it a bit, verbally, and Marlein told them both to stop, that she didn't like them fighting like that, and she wouldn't be entertaining either one of them as suitors."

Diefenbach hummed. "And they all left?"

"Yes." Matthäus shrugged helplessly. "Sïfrit first, then Marlein went, I think toward Emnelda's house. Heinrich went for a ride."

"I see." The older man stroked his bearded chin thoughtfully.

"Do you think we should go search for them?"

Johann shook his head. "Marlein will be fine. If she isn't back by complete nightfall, I'll go with a torch to look. But I imagine she will be, for she isn't one to flee her responsibilities long. For now, let's go be sure the children aren't upsetting the horses."

Matthäus decided he wouldn't say anything about Brigita unless Diefenbach asked. In his mind, though, he could still see her rounded belly, so like his wife in the months before Maria was born. There was no question in his mind: Brigita was carrying someone's child.

CHAPTER

# 30

Heinrich hadn't exercised Jäger like he should lately; he'd been busy with his education . . . and with Marlein. He could see now how much his life had begun to center around the young woman. He rarely went to the tavern with his fellow scholars anymore. He hurried through his studies so that he might help carry things or round up the children for an outing, so that she had a few moments of quiet. Yes, he had long known her implied intention to remain in her father's house, to care for the family. She had said as much several times in the years of their acquaintance. To hear her say it directly to him, though, brought on other feelings entirely.

His animal raced across the frozen ground. He'd thought of going after Marlein, but what would it accomplish? They were headed in different directions, figuratively and now literally. Once he received his doctor of law degree, he planned to return to Braunschweig and would likely not see her again. The knowledge sat like a heavy stone in his stomach. Not even the exhilaration of riding, which usually cheered him, broke through the pall of melancholy.

The animal's black coat gleamed in the setting sun as he galloped down the path toward Wittenberg. He leaned back and gently pulled up on the reins as the packed snow gave way to poorly cleared gravel. Heinrich wasn't sure where to go; it was too late in the day to go for a ride in the countryside. He had no desire to eat or be around people, so the tavern was not an option. He allowed the horse to wander along Wittenberg's streets, even as his mind wandered.

"Why this pull to her, Jäger? Yes, she's everything I'd have wanted in a wife, but the one exception is too great to overcome. She won't— can't—leave her family. And I love her more for her dedication to them!"

The horse snorted and stomped his hoof when Heinrich pulled him up to allow a woman carrying a large basket, with two small children clinging to her skirts, to pass before him. Once they were out of earshot, he continued the one-sided conversation with his horse.

"I cannot remain here. My sister's shame will be revealed in very few weeks." He guided Jäger to the left. "Already she is showing too much for anyone to miss it if she isn't wearing her cloak. Her stain is mine, and I can't make it Marlein's as well."

Jäger continued following Heinrich's directions with the reins and pressure from his legs.

"She just said that she will not marry, that the very idea is repugnant." He knew his words exaggerated what she'd said, but his heart smarted after the exchange. He had been content for the time being to remain her friend, but somewhere, in the back of his mind, he'd always thought that someday . . .

Someday he would be able to hold her. To breathe in the scent of her. To touch his lips to hers. He stopped his thoughts abruptly, and shame burned him. He had never allowed his thoughts to wander so far, but they seemed to have a will of their own. Was this how Brigita's fall began?

Ruthlessly forcing his mind to his surroundings and away from their previous place, he realized he had arrived at the university. He wondered briefly whether Luther was there, perhaps studying in his cell or reciting prayers with his brother friars. With heavy movements, Heinrich dismounted from his horse, looped the reins around a post nearby, and pulled on the bell's cord.

The friar that answered his summons was a young fellow, his tonsure fresh and new and his face in need of a shave.

"Would it be possible to speak with Father Martin?"

He nodded, gestured for him to wait, and turned, his brown Augustinian habit billowing slightly as he walked away. Soon, Luther emerged from the door, his own habit older and more worn than the younger friar's, with ink stains around the fraying cuffs of his sleeves.

With a gesture for quiet, Luther passed through the door of the monastery and led the way to the university's courtyard. No breeze disturbed the courtyard, as it was protected on two sides by the university and a wing of friars' cells, and the night was particularly still. Even so, the air was cold, and Heinrich was glad he'd had the foresight to retrieve his cloak. An apology rose to Heinrich's lips, for coming while it was likely Luther had been attending evening exercises or maybe participating in their modest meal. But the friar lowered himself onto a bench and spoke before Heinrich did.

"What brings you here at this late hour, young Ritter?" asked Luther as he raised the hood of his habit to cover his head.

Rather than sort out his confused thoughts so that he might answer, Heinrich chose to deflect the question. "Why do you call me 'young Ritter'? Did you know my father?"

Luther raised his brows and chuckled a bit. "No, I never met your father, God rest his soul. But I see a bit of me in you, I suppose."

Heinrich did not understand, but said nothing.

"You are aware that I was on track to study law, yes?" Luther asked as he tucked his hands into his sleeves. Heinrich nodded. "And that my father was from a poor peasant's family until he managed to maneuver his way into the mining business. When he recognized my aptitude for learning, he decided to send me to school with the hope that I would become a barrister and raise our family further from the lowly status of peasants from which my father hailed. You remind me of me. A young man in his father's shadow, being promoted in life by the sweat of his father's brow. Friends of his would call me 'young Luther' on occasion, so I suppose that is how I came to call you that." Luther paused a bit, chuckling to himself. "Though it was *Luder* back then, and I fear I was not so kindly disposed toward my father as I am now; he was a harsh disciplinarian."

"I am honored that you see any resemblance between you and myself, sir." Previously, Heinrich had known vague details of Luther's background, but he was glad to hear it from the man's mouth, rather than whispered hearsay from other students.

Luther chuckled, then changed the subject. "Come, come, sir. You can't be lacking conversation at Diefenbach's house, with all those people and children underfoot. Why did you come to see me?"

Heinrich forced himself to meet the man's gaze, which was open and honest. It was not so gaunt and haunted as when he first sat in one of his lectures, but one could see clearly that Luther lived the stringent life of a friar: a life of poverty and humility. Still, the troubled crease to his brow that had been so prominent when Heinrich first saw him almost four years ago was now gone. It seemed that the study and teaching of the Holy Scriptures agreed with the man.

Knowing he could not avoid answering any longer, Heinrich struggled to find words to express the turmoil in his mind. "There's been . . . some . . . difficulty recently with some members of the household where I reside."

"Ah yes, the Diefenbachs. And am I to guess at the nature of the difficulty, or will you enlighten me?"

"Forgive me, Father Martin." Heinrich paused to gather his thoughts.

"Ought we move to a confessional booth?" quipped Luther.

Heinrich looked up into the friar's face that was brimming with mirth. "No, I just meant—"

"I know what you meant," Luther assured him. "You seem so lost, though, I'd hoped to lighten the mood."

"I see." Heinrich cleared his throat and plunged in, describing what had just taken place.

As he listened, Luther hummed periodically, rubbing his lower face and chin. Heinrich knew he couldn't have been hiding a smile. "I was wondering how long it would take for you to come to me with this."

"Father Martin?"

"I observe that there are two prongs to your problem," he began to explain. "Your affection for Marlein has been evident for quite some time, and it has been growing of late, has it not?"

Heinrich's face heated at the unexpected observation. "But . . . but how could you possibly know that?"

"You mention her often in our brief discussions after lectures. And when you attend Mass with the family, you are more solicitous of her welfare than anyone else's. Except, perhaps, your sister's."

Heinrich had no answer to Luther's observations. Instead, he pressed, "And what of the other prong that you mentioned?"

"You are still struggling with bearing others' burdens."

"Sïfrit was purposely goading me!" Heinrich all but cried. He wondered if Luther was even listening to him. "He was being too familiar with Marlein, and on more than one occasion, I've heard him—"

"What burden," interrupted Luther with a stern voice, "does Sïfrit bear?"

Heinrich felt as though the ground had dropped from beneath him, leaving him unsettled and unsure of what he'd been convinced was truth just a moment ago. Namely, that Sïfrit was in the wrong and all he needed to know was how to keep him from pestering Marlein and taunting him.

"We've already discussed this." He tried to keep the petulance out of his voice, he truly did. He was fairly sure he did.

"Yes," Luther spoke calmly and patiently, as if speaking to a child, "but I want you to tell me again. What is Sïfrit's burden?"

Heinrich sighed, finally admitting utter defeat. He could see that Luther was not going to tell him what he wanted to hear. "His burden is his conceit and resulting ignorance."

"Hm, that seems familiar."

Heinrich hung his head, feeling the weight of his own blindness. It took him a moment to place the sound, but after looking up at Luther's face, Heinrich saw that the friar was laughing at him. "What?"

"It seems the Law has done its work on you, young Ritter." This time, there was no laughter in Luther's voice, only quiet compassion.

"Yes, I suppose so." Heinrich heaved a breath. "I never considered myself a particularly prideful person, but my inability to see my own hand in a difficult situation is a clear indicator that I am more prideful than I'd care to admit."

"But confession of sin, which is a step beyond admitting it, is an important part in the life of a repentant Christian."

Heinrich nodded his agreement and asked, "Shall I confess now?"

"If you feel compelled to do so, I'll gladly hear your confession. However, after learning firsthand that it is not a sacrament of penance that saves us, but rather the sacrifice of Christ, I would personally recommend we further examine your situation first, that you may understand it and, in the future, bear sweeter fruit in keeping with repentance."

A small smile teased at Heinrich's lips, until he found himself unable to keep it at bay any longer. "Very well, then," he conceded, though the sincerity of his heart added weight to the tone of his voice, "examine away."

Luther smiled in response to Heinrich's unspoken admission of how difficult this conversation would likely be for him. He'd hoped an impassable expression would cover some of his uncertainty at such a careful self-examination as Luther was suggesting, but it seemed he had seen through the nervous smile.

"Each of us," began Luther, "has a struggle of his own. Sometimes, I believe, our struggle changes. But often, Satan uses the same thing to poke at us, time and again, year after year, the same fire on his flaming arrows. He finds a weakness in us and does all he can to claw at it and exploit it, to cause as much damage as possible."

Heinrich nodded, wondering what this had to do with his personal struggle.

"For a long time, my struggle centered on my perception of God. He never changes, but through His Word, He has been changing me, changing how I see Him. Not as a God of righteous, wrathful judgment—certainly, that is an aspect of who He is, but that is not all. His Word has shown me His loving, merciful nature."

Heinrich nodded as Luther was speaking, understanding what the friar was saying, but again, not how it pertained to his situation.

"Yes, Father Martin," he began, trying to express his confusion, "I am glad and happy to have learned that perhaps some of what the church has been teaching about the practice of penance and the work a sinner must do to cleanse himself before being allowed into the presence of God is not reflective of Holy Scripture. But I had never been particularly terror-stricken at the prospect as you were."

"And why is that, do you think?" The almost smile on Luther's face told Heinrich that they were likely reaching the crux of the matter.

Rather than blurt the first thing that came to mind, as a large part of him wanted to do, Heinrich allowed himself several moments of consideration before answering. Luther sat patiently on the bench, his eyes steadily moving from barren tree to the purple sky to the packed snow beneath their feet. Heinrich's thoughts ran through the heated conversation, if it could be called that, at the Diefenbach's house. He thought of his anger that had spiked immediately, his annoyance and frustration. It wasn't born of Sïfrit's actions that evening, or even of the man's propensity to pester Marlein. He could see, now that he was calm, that Sïfrit would never have acted on any of his suggestions, improper though they might be. He was like a loud clucking rooster. Perhaps intimidating and seemingly proud, and could certainly inflict some damage if he wanted, but would not wound mortally. No, Sïfrit had taken minor liberties, or implied them, and Heinrich had reacted out of wanting that for himself.

"I'm selfish, I believe," he breathed out on a ragged sigh. "I'd always thought I wanted to become a lawyer for my father, and now for his memory, and to provide for Brigita. But my discontent lately is born of more than worry for my sister's future. I've come to love Marlein, though likely in a more selfish way than I ought, and when Sïfrit stood so close to her, I was jealous."

"There is nothing wrong with a husband being jealous over his wife."

"She is not my wife," Heinrich pointed out, though he felt it was somewhat needless. "She never will be."

"Can you be sure?"

"She said as much tonight."

"You reacted badly," Luther reminded. "Is it not possible that she did, as well?"

Heinrich had not considered that she might have spoken without thinking. He could do little else than shrug his shoulders helplessly.

"Before you determine your course with Marlein, though, perhaps you ought to consider your course with the Lord."

"What do you mean?"

"You say that you love her, though not as you ought."

Heinrich's face flamed, but he nodded his agreement.

"Where can perfect love be found?"

"Nowhere but in God."

"Yes." Luther stood and began pacing a bit. "The more I study the Holy Scriptures, the more I see that He is love. Love that gives of Himself, love that comforts and soothes, love that seeks sinners for repentance, not chases them for condemnation."

Luther's face, as he spoke, had begun to emit such joy that Heinrich could not help but smile. Luther tirelessly sought to know God better, to understand the heart of the one who had given His most beloved Son as a sacrifice for the sins of all people. He could see that Luther felt keenly the wonder of his salvation.

Still, it was a bit amusing that Luther's focus was so very narrow. The man had started a fire that was quickly catching around the countryside as his Theses were translated and distributed in German. People were reading of God's love and mercy and the abuses of the church, and here he was, immersed in his studies.

"Thank you, Father," Heinrich said. "You've given me much to consider."

"The Word of God tends to do that, does it not, young Ritter?"

"Yes. In fact, your counsel to Matthäus Falk has been beneficial to me, as well as him."

"Oh? How is that?"

"We have been studying Scripture together lately," Heinrich explained, "and I believe it has been permeating his heart. His eyes no longer look so haunted, and he has been smiling a great deal more of late."

"I am heartened to hear it," Luther responded. "Now, I shall pray that it similarly permeates your heart, as you continue your studies."

"May I ask, Father Martin . . ." Heinrich began, but stopped. A whim had motivated his request, but he suddenly feared it was over-stepping.

"Ask what, young Ritter?" smiled Luther.

"Well, sir, we've gone over Galatians and now Hebrews several times. We plan to read each of them one more time, but I was wondering, though it is a bit early, if there is a possibility of obtaining another book for the summer recess?"

Luther grinned and said, "I'm sure I could find something for you by then. We have several months before summer."

Heinrich could not contain the wide smile that broke across his face. "Then my course is set. I shall continue to seek guidance from the Word of God."

"And forget about Marlein?"

Heinrich's exuberance was somewhat dampened by the reminder of the initial reason for his visit, but he set his shoulders as he answered. "I suppose it is not out of the realm of possibility, but I believe at this point, it would be best to simply befriend her as much as I am able, as I have been, and see what she allows in the way of furthering our relationship."

He was gratified to see Luther's smile, affirming that his decision was a good one. Holding out a hand, he shook with Luther and thanked him for his time and counsel. Not many minutes later saw him riding back to the Diefenbach house in the fading twilight.

# 31

Keterlyn had been drifting in and out of sleep all day. The glass-block window in her room was admitting the fading light of the day's end as the fog cleared from her mind. Voices—one of them Marlein's—coming from the other side of the bedroom door reached her ears, and when she heard the strong emotions behind it, she had an unusual urge to exert herself.

Slowly, so slowly that the voices had stopped and doors closed in the meantime, she dressed, smoothed back her hair, and pulled the white linen cloth over her head. She would come out for supper this evening and see if something was the matter with her daughter. Though she was forced to fight the heaviness in her limbs and the strong desire to bury herself beneath blankets again, she was glad that for once, she also desired to fight.

*** 

Sïfrit was walking toward Wittenberg when a horse and rider pounded past him in the fading light. Though he could not quite make out the features of the rider and the horse was dark and indistinguishable from a dozen others he'd seen in the area, he was reasonably certain that the rider was Heinrich. He was the only one he might see riding so quickly in the direction he was, coming from where he was.

Sïfrit stumbled in his haste to remove himself from the path of those thundering hooves.

"What a farce," he muttered to himself after regaining his feet. "I simply wanted to have a bit of fun, and Heinrich had to go and take me too seriously."

He huffed and scowled as he passed under *das Elstertor*. It wasn't as though he'd have pressed Marlein as his actions had implied. The university loomed ahead on the left, and Sïfrit couldn't hold back the scowl. He had never really regretted his inability to attend university—at least not until he met Heinrich after coming a year ago to begin his apprenticeship. Ritter had everything he could want, though. A shop he didn't want or need inherited from his father, a sister who could be married to improve his standing, and an education for a lucrative profession. And the true, if not unattainable, affection of a lovely woman.

"Marlein may say that she won't ever marry," he groused as he turned down the street for the tavern, "but I bet she'd leave in a heartbeat if he pulled his head from the academic hole he's had it in and asked for her hand."

The tavern's windows, thrown open to cool the crowded place, glowed welcomingly down the street. Sïfrit picked up his pace, eager for a stein of beer to drown the frustration brewing in him. Once Heinrich left in the summer, after he'd earned his degree, life would be so much more pleasant.

Sïfrit burst through the doors of the tavern, the raucous drinking song assaulting his ears as the bass and tenor voices rose in sloppy harmony. He scanned the room, finding only a few places open on the benches. Deciding against sitting with his usual crowd, he sauntered over to sit near the end of a table where two men bent low over their drinks, talking across the table between them.

"May I join you, good fellows?" he asked as he slid onto the bench beside the fair one without waiting their permission.

The other man raised a dark brow at him, but said nothing. When the barmaid, a buxom beauty with loose hair, came to bring him a stein, Sïfrit flipped her two coins. "I'll need another soon."

She nodded and settled back to wait. Sïfrit grasped the stein, tipped it back, and drained it down his throat. His belly felt warm and full, and he looked up at the barmaid. Her lips quirked into a grin, lifted her brows once at him, and then reached for the stein to go fill it again.

Sïfrit considered entering a flirtation with her when she returned, but his pride still ached from Marlein's outburst. If she was upset enough to rail at Heinrich as she had, her ire at him must be far greater. Rather than grin at the barmaid when she returned with his drink, he merely jerked his head in a brief nod. Draining half of this one, he turned and scanned the room again, hoping his usual set had not spied him. As he did, he couldn't help but overhear the conversation of his table mates.

"And he says it avails for all," said the dark-haired one to the other.

His table mate hummed, musing on his companion's words for a moment before he replied, "That would present a man with much more opportunity for . . . shall we say . . . *the enjoyments of the world*?"

Both laughed, and Sïfrit couldn't help but look over at them as one of them had swayed in his merriment, leaning momentarily on Sïfrit's arm.

When the dark-haired one returned Sïfrit's gaze, he also put a question to the young man. "Are you inclined to agree with us or to chastise us? Be warned, though, that we are in no mood for chastisement."

Sïfrit shrugged and raised his stein to his lips to take a long pull of his beer. "I am inclined to chastise no one. Agreement? Well, that remains to be seen."

The two men stared at him for a moment before breaking out in laughter again. Sïfrit felt his chest swell at their apparent acceptance of him. Heinrich could keep his silly little family and Marlein. He suspected he'd just stumbled upon two men who could introduce him to far greater enjoyments than any afforded by that family.

"Well, Gwerder," said the fair-haired man with a mode of pronouncing that sounded familiar to Sïfrit, though he couldn't place it, "I need to get back to the smithy's shop. He's been taking more orders than I can fill if I allow myself to remain here with the likes of you."

More laughter, and while Sïfrit didn't entirely understand the meaning behind their laughter, he appreciated the carefree tone of it. He wanted that for himself, and so he laughed along with them.

"Before I go, allow me to introduce myself to our new friend. I am Nikolaus Alscher, at your service, here on business over the winter from Braunschweig."

Sïfrit opened his mouth to reply that he knew someone from Braunschweig, but the other man spoke up before he had opportunity.

"And I am Willeic Gwerder; I'm sure you've heard my name," he said with a self-assurance that Sïfrit hoped someday to have. Gwerder was well-known in the city for his success in his craft and for his boldness in displaying the wealth he had accumulated for himself. Sïfrit hoped also to have the same wealth.

"I am Sïfrit Hahn," he replied with the intent to share where he was apprenticed, but Nikolaus spoke up first.

"Very good to meet you"—as he rose and stepped back over the bench—"but I am afraid I really must be off. I look forward to another discussion, Gwerder." He leveled a meaningful look in that man's direction. "You are welcome to join us, of course, Hahn, if you are inclined to the same sort of . . . conversation . . . as we are."

Sïfrit merely nodded, and both men watched as Nikolaus made his way from the tavern.

"He is here to reclaim something of his that thought herself too good to remain where she belonged."

Sïfrit raised a brow at him. "Really now." His mind went to Brigita arriving so unexpectedly, and from the same city.

Gwerder nodded. "But that is his tale to tell. I'll just say he seeks an advantageous marriage, and the lady seemed less than enthusiastic."

Given the state of Brigita's health and dress upon her arrival, and her brother's having not yet amassed enough wealth to make any marriage to his sister advantageous, he supposed the woman in question must be some other.

"But tell me, Hahn." Gwerder's smirk was condescending, but Sïfrit chose to ignore that in hopes of currying the man's favor. "What of you? You are apprenticed to Diefenbach, are you not?"

Sïfrit nodded and enthusiastically launched into an animated discussion of one of his favorite subjects—himself and his views on how Diefenbach ought to adjust the practice of his craft to improve his income. If he failed to notice the occasional slip in Gwerder's interest, or the way that the older man agreed a bit too readily with every assertion he made, the young man couldn't be blamed, for never before had he held so captive and agreeable an audience.

# 32

Marlein hurried across the field, her feet carrying her along the worn path they had followed so many times before. Stinging eyes and anxiety clouded Marlein's vision, but she didn't need to see beyond the place she set each foot. She neither stumbled nor fell, and her thoughts were free to torment her as much as they pleased.

Her outburst was entirely uncalled for—what an ungracious way to behave! Had her mother been present, she would have given her a stern dressing down. But her reaction was less to their squabbling than to Heinrich's silence. Sïfrit asked if he had a claim on her, and Heinrich had no reason to answer in the affirmative. She shouldn't have reacted as she did.

For the first time in her life, though, Marlein wished that she was free to allow such a claim.

*I'm not. I can't. I won't.*

But she wanted to.

"How can I rid myself of this?"

As she spoke, she noticed her breath puff in the cold air, lit by the lowering sun. The realization brought her to the stark reality of her numb fingers and cold, wet toes. It had not snowed for several days, but the field, which had not been disturbed, still sported a thick, cold blanket. Her shoes were sturdy but low, and with each step, snow fell in around her ankles, melting and seeping down to her toes.

She shivered.

Just ahead, over the trees at the edge of the small field, was a faint trail of smoke leading up into the pinkening sky. Marlein hurried toward Emnelda's tiny cottage.

Emnelda answered Marlein's knock, her eyes wide and fearful, and the door only allowing the merest sliver of the cabin to be seen over Emnelda's gray head. When she saw it was Marlein, though, she relaxed and opened the door all the way.

"Come in, child."

As she stepped into the cottage, Marlein wondered at the fear in Emnelda's eyes, but her own discomfort from the cold and her swirling emotions quickly pushed their way to the fore.

"I'm sorry for coming empty-handed, Emnelda," she began.

"When have I ever said I expect something from you when you come to visit me?" Emnelda said as she lowered the bar across her door. Marlein stood near the sputtering fire, shifting from one foot to the other and trying not to shiver. "Marlein, what is troubling you?"

"I've had a bit of an argument." Marlein suddenly wondered at her wisdom in coming here as she shivered in her shoes. Emnelda had an uncanny way of seeing someone's heart, and she wasn't certain she wished to be examined closely. "Of sorts."

"Take off your shoes and stockings," Emnelda instructed. "With whom was this argument of sorts?"

Marlein sighed and sat on the stool in obedience to the older woman. It might help to talk about it after all, though she was uncertain where to begin; she so seldom shared the entire depth of anything that was bothering her. And how were her feelings on the matter so inconstant? It was as though she could not make up her mind. Emnelda added a log to the fire before she took some wine and poured it into a kettle that was hanging above the hearth.

"I've a responsibility to my family," Marlein began, thinking that the heart of it might be the easiest place to begin.

Emnelda nodded.

"But I find myself beginning to long for . . . something else, something more." It was difficult to admit this, and Marlein kept her gaze on the flames that were dancing in delight and leaping to include another log into their merriment. If only her life were as simple in purpose as the fire. It burned and did nothing else. When there was more fuel, it burned brighter. When there was less, it rested and waited for fuel to be added.

Emnelda held out her hand expectantly, so Marlein passed her the soaked stockings and lined her shoes up beside the fire while Emnelda hung the stockings from the fireplace mantle.

"Nothing is improving. My *Mutter* can scarcely rouse herself from bed most days. My *Vater* works and is happy with the children, but I see how defeated he is that his *Ehefrau* is not thriving. I do all I can to help, but it is not enough. I am not enough." The last part was whispered as the reality of her insufficiency sank like a rock in Marlein's stomach, making her all the colder. She moved her feet a bit closer to the warmth emanating from the fire. "If I believed that I was helping my family, I would gladly stay with them for the rest of my life. But it seems that nothing is better."

"If things were better, you wouldn't need to stay." Emnelda reached for two cups made of stoneware. She took a rag to lift the kettle and poured the steaming wine into the mismatched cups.

"But they aren't better." She took the first cup from Emnelda's extended hand.

As Emnelda poured her own cup, her hand shook and some of the wine spilled on the hot stones nearest the hearth, popping and sizzling until it disappeared. "If I had younger hands, I wouldn't spill so."

Marlein believed she recognized the point Emnelda was making right away. "I know wishing for something that cannot be is foolishness."

"Whoever said that an improvement is impossible?"

"I am saying it." Marlein suddenly wanted to shout at the old woman, but didn't. Her voice sounded hollow even to her own ears. "Because I cannot help my mother. I never have been able to and likely never will."

"Oh, child," Emnelda breathed out, reaching for Marlein's cold hand and squeezing it.

Marlein stood, stepping away from the fire's warmth. The cold dirt floor chilled her feet that had been warming, but she didn't care. "I am not enough. I cannot ease my mother's burden. I cannot be enough of a *Mutter* to the little ones. Nearly every night, Herlinde cries for her *Mutti*. I can't support my *Vater* as I should."

Her chin trembled and her eyes stung. She closed them as her held breath burned her lungs, pleading ineffectually for release. Finally, it burst forth in a rasping cry. "I am not enough."

"No, my dear, you aren't."

# 33

Emnelda almost laughed at the shock on Marlein's face. The girl was so much more than she believed, but she was also correct. She wasn't enough, nor would she ever be on her own. With Christ in her, though, she would be a force for good in this world.

Marlein sank back onto the stool, and Emnelda pulled up an old chair, the bottom made of woven reeds; it was light enough that she could manage.

"Did I ever tell you that I used to be deeply in love with your grandfather?"

Marlein's face showed her confusion, more than previously, and Emnelda noted with satisfaction that the confusion had at least momentarily pushed away the despair that had been threatening.

"Oh, by the time your father came along, I had long since been released from that. But there was a time when he was my sun and moon."

"I . . . didn't know that." The girl's voice was quiet and tired.

"For years, I was haunted by the idea that I hadn't been enough to attract him, and in time, to attract anyone." Emnelda felt the long-forgotten stab in her heart of not being wanted. "I could not fight the grip that sense of unworthiness maintained on my heart. Maybe I didn't want to fight it. But I was trapped by this feeling, whether by my own choice or by my emotions. But one day, I was in the City Church, and the priest spoke of Christ's treasure of merit, of His sacrifice. I believe he went on to say some other things, but my mind was arrested there.

"If even salvation from sin, which so polluted us, so filled us, so infiltrated every thought and word and action—if even that was not too much for our God to deliver from, then why could He not also deliver me from this? And so, I prayed. And fasted. And recited every bit of Scripture I could recall, that I had memorized from the teachings of our priests. And do you know what happened? He was enough for me. It didn't happen immediately. But as I meditated on verses—I even asked my priest to share some with me when I'd dragged up every one I could recall—His Word made its way into my heart, pushing out those thoughts of not being enough. I did not need to be, for He was. He is."

She had been so lost in her memories that she'd nearly forgotten Marlein was there. The girl's ragged breath coaxed Emnelda from her thoughts, and she looked up at the younger woman's face. Her chin quivered, and her face was flushed a bright pink.

"And what should I do, Emnelda?" Marlein's voice shook, but grew stronger as she continued. "Ask Father Martin if I may study one of his books, like Heinrich and Matthäus do? I cannot read Latin!"

"No, child. But perhaps Heinrich can help you. He is a student of Father Martin's, is he not?"

"He is the cause of my heartache!" Desperation ripped through the poor girl's voice. "I cannot ask him to read to me!"

"Well, then, perhaps you can come to visit me, and I will tell you what I can remember. For today, though, I'll share this one. The apostle Paul wrote of a hardship he suffered, and that he asked God to take it away, several times. Do you know what God told him? In the twelfth chapter of the Second Letter to the Corinthians, he wrote that God said to him: 'My grace is sufficient for you, for My power is made perfect in weakness.'"

"What can that mean? God wants us to be weak and helpless?" She was confused; Emnelda could easily see it.

"I think it means," Emnelda did her best to explain, feeling as she did the importance of the words breaking through Marlein's confusion, for she had been in Marlein's place many years before, "that God wants to be our strength Himself. Because even when we aren't enough—and we never will be—*He* is enough. For all we need."

***

Marlein's head was full, and her chest felt hollow. What Emnelda said seemed true enough, and she claimed experience to further validate it. And yet, Marlein had questions. What was St. Paul's difficulty? Why would God not take it away? Had he not suffered enough for his sins? She pondered all those questions and more as she walked away from Emnelda's cottage.

"Heinrich would be able to answer," she whispered into the dusky air. The sun's rays fought to shine over the western horizon, lighting the world just enough that Marlein could see to reach her family's house. The darkness that descended when she thought of Heinrich, however, was another thing entirely.

She had no hope where he was concerned.

But perhaps she would be able to ask him about this. Just this. Because Marlein felt that if she unlocked the secret here, she would finally be released from such a foolish dream as her heart begged her to entertain.

The house was quiet when Marlein entered by the side door. She could hear whispers down by the stalls, and the gentle nickering of a horse or two. But no one was in the kitchen. The stillness added to her feeling of fatigue.

Her nose caught the strong aroma of their supper in the oven. She hurried to remove the pies from it, glad she arrived when she did; they'd have burned if left much longer. She then set out to find everyone. She wanted to sleep, but knew she could not until the children had been fed and sent to bed.

Marlein found her father, Matthäus, and the children with the horses.

"Supper is ready." She hoped her voice sounded even.

Matthäus looked uncomfortable as he stepped from the large stall that housed two horses. Marlein felt awful that she had allowed herself to react as she had in front of so many people.

"I apologize for my outburst, Matthäus."

Rather than answer, he seemed more surprised than anything. "Think nothing of it. Those two sort of forced you into it, I'd say."

"That is kind of you." Marlein wanted the attention off her. "Where are the Ritters?"

"I believe Brigita is in her room, and Heinrich left on Jäger soon after you did," Matthäus answered.

"I'll go and fetch Brigita, then."

Matthäus opened his mouth to speak, and Marlein waited. After a moment, though, his jaw snapped closed. Unsure of his strange behavior, Marlein moved back toward the room she shared with Brigita.

Opening the door, Marlein's eyes widened at the sight before her, before rushing through and shutting it quietly. Brigita had changed from her new dress and had struggled into the threadbare one that she'd worn when she arrived. She was hurriedly throwing things into an old sack that matched her dress.

"What are you doing?" Marlein finally found her voice.

Brigita finally looked up, tears and fear streaking her face, but she didn't seem startled. Exhausted resignation left no room for an emotion that demanded so much exertion.

CHAPTER

# 34

Brigita had scarcely been able to finish preparing supper. Her belly, which had seemed small enough before to keep hidden at least by her cloak, now got in her way. She went to retrieve bowls from behind the table and could barely fit between the bench and the wall. She dropped a cloth she'd been using to wipe down the table and, when she stood again, forgot to keep the cloak around her. She hunched down to check on the meat pies in the oven and could not bend as far as usual. And she felt Matthäus's eyes on her throughout her struggles.

No longer able to keep the trembling at bay, she mumbled something about forgetting to pull up the covers on her bed and nearly ran into the little room she shared with Marlein.

Never had she been more grateful for a room. Her room at her father's house had been a cubby in the back of the one room of their dwelling. Her bed at the Alschers' had been a mat on the floor near the fire. At the convent, a cell she shared with some of the novices. Here, she had a place to let her tears flow freely. And they did; for how could she stay now?

Her shame was in the light, for all to see.

She jerked at the borrowed dress she wore, painstakingly re-hemmed by the young woman who had no time for such tasks, who had been so very kind to her. Brigita could not stay and allow her shame to taint such a good, kind family.

The dress came off easily enough, but when she dug for the one she wore when leaving the convent, the one she also entered it wearing, she saw the tear she'd mended on the shoulder, where Nikolaus Alscher had wrenched it from her body. The memories, the feelings of helplessness, all came flooding back.

She'd allowed him to kiss her, but when his hands began to stray from the sides of her face, she'd attempted to pull back. He had been persistent, though, and by the time she realized his intent, his grip was too strong, his passion too ignited. She had allowed it and would forever carry that shame.

It ripped through her as she struggled to pull the dress over her body. The shoulders still fit, even though she had lost about a finger's width of space in repairing the tear. When she pulled at the skirt, though, to settle the dress into its proper place, it caught on her belly. She pulled and tugged, but it refused to cover her. Brigita sank onto the floor near the trunk, sobbing as silently as she could. For her shame, for the loss of her innocence, for the feeling lodged deep within her that all good was lost to her. Her tears ran down her face, mingling with the drips from her nose and her mouth, making her chin and neck slick with it. She sucked in large gasps of air, despising herself as she pressed her face to the cold, hard flagstone floor.

Time passed. She wasn't sure how much, but voices drifted from the table. She heard her name, as well as Marlein's and Heinrich's. With shuddering breaths, she wiped at her face with the lopsided hem of her old dress, and forced herself to her feet. She carefully loosened the lacing on the front of the dress, adjusting her chemise beneath as she wriggled and coaxed the dress to cover her. Finally, it was more or less in place and she tied the lacing, glad for its extra length. She had just grabbed the bag Sister Margreth gave her and was preparing to hide it under the bedding and pretend she was asleep until the entire household had settled, but the door opened.

Startled, she looked over at Marlein. Her face was weary, and her eyes red-rimmed. They widened, though, and Brigita knew the exact moment Marlein realized she was leaving. Her heart fell and she wanted to explain, but Marlein spoke first.

"You aren't leaving, are you? Brigita, you can't!"

She didn't trust her voice, but forced words out anyway. "Matthäus knows," she croaked, and although she didn't specify what he knew, understanding and alarm flooded Marlein's face immediately. "He saw, and his eyes followed it the whole afternoon. I can't stay."

"We knew they'd all find out eventually," Marlein reminded her in a voice that attempted to soothe.

Brigita just shook her head.

"Listen, dear," Marlein said, taking a few steps toward her. "We will talk to—"

"No!" The sharpness of her voice halted Marlein in her advance and shocked Brigita to some degree. "I can't ask everyone in this house to share in my shame. You may not plan to marry, but your sisters might. Your brother will need to take a wife to carry on the family line, and Matthäus and your parents and the children—"

"Wait." Marlein no longer looked uncertain, but rather like she'd just discovered a secret. "Why did you say Matthäus's name? Your circumstance is not his shame."

"What? I didn't. I—"

"No, you most certainly did." Marlein stepped close and reached for Brigita's hand. "You are fond of him, are you not?"

Brigita couldn't speak for the heat that overtook her face and parched her throat.

"He is fond of you, as well."

"Stop!" She couldn't bear to hear anything that would give her such futile optimism. "If things were different, if I had not traded my innocence, I might have reason to hope. But he is too good a man, too kind a father, too devoted a husband for the likes of me. I'll just slip away in the night. Tell Heinrich I love him and will send word once I am able. He will tell you where he goes after he finishes school, yes?"

"Brigita, I really don't think that this is the way to—"

"What other way is there?"

"Matthäus hasn't said anything." Brigita paused at that, and Marlein continued pressing her argument. "Won't you at least give the household the chance to decide? We can wait until the children have gone to bed. We will tell everyone right now that you are suffering from a headache, and you can just sit at the table. Here, put on your dress. Why wouldn't you have worn it anyway? This old thing barely ties! Really, I should cut it up for rags. Maybe the rags we'll need when your baby comes."

As she spoke, Marlein had retrieved the dress Brigita threw into the trunk and had begun unlacing the old dress. She stopped then, looking at Brigita and smiling gently.

"We'll at least talk to them?"

Brigita felt her eyes well once again, but with grateful tears this time, and she nodded.

"Very good." Marlein gave Brigita's shoulders a gentle squeeze before helping her ease off the dress. "For the rag bin?"

Still unable to speak around the emotion clogging her throat, Brigita nodded again.

"And really, Brigita," Marlein went on with a teasing tone, "would I have made such changes to these dresses that I grew too tall for, adding room to the waist and shortening the hem, if I didn't mean for you to keep them?"

It finally broke through Brigita's fog of sorrow that Marlein truly meant it when she said she would do all she could to help. She would stand by her side, defend Brigita to her family if need be, just as she had done with Heinrich. She would plead her cause.

"Thank you, Marlein. Truly." Brigita settled the newer, warmer dress over her unfamiliar frame. "Every time I think I've gotten used to this," and she patted her belly, "it seems to grow larger overnight."

Marlein chuckled with her, then turned and lifted the hem of her own dress. "I came in here to change my stockings, but forgot entirely when I saw how distressed you were."

"What happened to your stockings?" Brigita brushed at her hair, trying to tame the pieces escaping the strip of leather she'd used to secure it in the back.

Marlein padded over in bare feet on the cold floor. "When I flew out of here in such a tizzy, I didn't even consider that the snow was deep and my everyday shoes wouldn't keep the snow out."

"I can't imagine having two pairs of shoes."

"My *Vater* gave me a second pair last year, when we determined my feet had stopped growing." Marlein started tightening the lacing in the back of Brigita's dress. "I must go outside so much to care for things, he thought taller boots would be helpful in the winter and when the mud is abundant in the spring. I suppose they don't do much good sitting in the trunk while I'm out traipsing across the snowy field."

Brigita's laugh was genuine this time. While she tied her *Steuchlein* over her hair, Marlein turned to rummage in the trunk in their room.

"My stockings should dry by morning, but I'll have to wear these until then." She held up a pair of stockings scattered with several holes.

Before long, the two emerged from the room together, Marlein's arm looped through hers. Brigita's heart had never felt fuller. The children were all sitting around the table, Heinrich, Matthäus, Diefenbach, and even Keterlyn with them.

"Well, we certainly have a full table today, do we not?" chuckled

Diefenbach as everyone shifted and shuffled to make room for the two young ladies. Brigita squeezed in beside her brother while Marlein found a spot between Matthäus and her mother. After Diefenbach offered thanks for their food, Brigita began to eat.

She could hardly believe how quickly she gobbled up her pie. When Matthäus caught her eye across the table, she was shocked to see him smile and offer her the last quarter of his own pie. She wanted to refuse it, but her stomach rumbled then.

"Here, take it," he said. "I ate far too much at midday; the bread and cheese and apples were tastier than I'd expected, and I stuffed myself."

"If you're sure . . ."

As she ate, Brigita glanced over at her brother, only to find him staring across the table at Marlein. For her part, Marlein kept her eyes on her food. The one time she did look up to see Heinrich staring at her, she flushed and looked back down. With her earlier fear of discovery gone, Brigita found her curiosity piqued at the antics of her two favorite people.

After supper, which was a bit later than usual, the dishes were cleaned quickly and the children dispatched to bed. Marlein, still avoiding Heinrich's gaze, raised her voice just a bit to say, "Everyone, please. There is . . . a situation we must discuss."

A couple of brows were furrowed, but no one objected. The six of them sat around the table: Diefenbach at the head and his wife across from him, Matthäus on the bench to his right, and Heinrich and Brigita to his left.

"What situation, Marlein?" asked Diefenbach, once Marlein had passed around mugs of steaming wine and scooted onto the bench beside Matthäus.

"We all knew when Brigita first came to us that she did so under difficult circumstances." No one denied her words, and several eyes looked between Marlein and Brigita expectantly. "The full extent of those circumstances is about to come to light, and we must find the best way to aid her."

Everyone was quiet and looking directly at her. Brigita didn't know how she would ever find a way to speak, but then she felt a warm hand cover her own where it lay on her lap. She looked up to see her brother smile encouragingly. A glance across the table revealed Marlein's gentle smile and the slight nod of her head.

Reassured, Brigita began. "I've done . . . I did . . . something. When my—our—father died, some neighbors, the Alschers, offered to allow me to stay with them. I accepted, and cooked and cleaned for my keep." She was stumbling over her words, but was unable to stop. "One of their sons, Nikolaus, the second born, was a bit of a bother, but I avoided him when I could, ignored him when I couldn't, and otherwise just did my best to be polite, but not to encourage him."

No one spoke, and while an interruption might have completely scattered her courage, Brigita almost hoped for a distraction. None came, though, so she forged onward.

"One night, though, while I was cleaning up from supper after everyone else had retired to bed, I couldn't get away. I would have run then, if I could, but he had me cornered. At first, I thought he'd leave me alone if I stopped fighting and let him kiss me; he told me he loved me, after all. But he didn't stop. I fought then, but he was stronger."

"You didn't tell me," Heinrich whispered urgently, "that you did not consent."

"I did consent," she protested. "Nikolaus told me as much. When I started to cry, he told me that it was too late, that I had allowed kissing and . . . and some touching . . . and now it was too late to change my mind."

"It should never be too late," Matthäus muttered.

Brigita was confused. Both younger men looked angry, and even Diefenbach had a deep furrow in his brow, his bushy brows nearly meeting in the middle. Marlein's face was pale, and Keterlyn's held deep sorrow. Unsure what else to say, Brigita continued her tale.

"A-after, he went out. I-I think to a tavern. I went to bed. When I arose the next morning, Alscher's wife told me that I would have to leave within a month; they were unable to continue supporting me. She was generous in giving me so much time to find another position. That's when I wrote to you, Heinrich. Well, Nikolaus offered to write the letter, and I signed it."

"The letter didn't arrive for weeks," Heinrich interjected. "I wonder if Nikolaus failed to send it right away."

"Perhaps." Brigita drew another deep breath before continuing. "I believed that if I entered a convent, I might learn piety and make amends for my wickedness in not stopping Nikolaus from taking . . . from doing . . ."

"It's all right, dear," Keterlyn spoke up for the first time, her voice rough from disuse and perhaps emotion. "Tell us when you left for the convent."

"Oh yes. Well, Nikolaus approached me later that day and told me that if his mother learned what happened, she would throw me out on the street and write to the convent, and that they would not want a soiled girl in their midst. The next night, when he came to my pallet in the kitchen after everyone had gone to bed, I told him to leave me alone. He again overpowered me, and when he had finished, I left. I'd been afraid and had packed a small bag of food when he threatened to tell his mother. I arrived at the convent at nightfall the next day and begged them to take me in. I didn't confess all, but I told them I'd been mistreated, and they allowed me to stay." Brigita kept her hands in her lap, for they were trembling uncontrollably. She could barely keep her shoulders from shaking.

"What Nikolaus did was the worst kind of mistreatment," ground out Heinrich. "We can press charges, you know."

"But I allowed . . ." She trailed off as her brother's scowl darkened. "Well, I felt safe at the convent. The sisters were kind, and they allowed me to simply work for a while before taking any vows. I had been there just over a month when I started to suspect that I might be with child."

Brigita continued, describing her time at the convent and what she'd already told Marlein and Heinrich about Sister Margreth's help and, finally, her arrival in Wittenberg.

As she sat, slightly winded from the exertion of revisiting all the memories she'd previously worked to push away from her mind, a warm hand came to rest on her shoulder. She turned with difficulty on the bench, her growing belly hindering her movement. Keterlyn stood behind her, eyes shining and face streaked with wet tears.

"You poor dear. Don't worry about a thing. We will see to it that you are cared for."

"How can you pity me?" asked Brigita, looking down at her hands folded in her lap again.

Marlein gaped at her mother. The woman before her was more like the mother of her youth than of recent years.

"This is not a case of you provoking the man, or allowing him to seduce you," Marlein's father answered. "He overpowered you and took what you were not willing to give."

"But I've sinned!"

"Not in this case, Gita," Heinrich breathed, raising his hands to frame her face. "I'm mortified over what I said to you when I first learned you were carrying a child! It wasn't your sin. I've known Nikolaus for years and shouldn't have assumed he held himself to a higher standard than he does. I carry more responsibility for this than you do. I should not have allowed you to be taken in by the Alschers. I let my own sorrow and the pain of being in our old house keep me away, and I shouldn't have. Our father loved us as best he could, but he was a broken man after our mother died."

Glancing around the table through her own tears, Marlein saw that everyone's eyes were glassy, if not downright tearful. When she looked back to Brigita, she saw that her mother had seated herself beside the girl and had drawn her into an embrace. Her heart clenched with a painful joy to see her mother so alive.

"We are all broken," Keterlyn murmured while stroking Brigita's shoulder, "one way or another."

The emotion rose in Marlein's throat at her mother's brave admission. Swallowing the tears that threatened, she said, "What is to be done? We all want to protect Brigita, but what is the best way to go about it?"

No one spoke right away. Sniffles and cleared throats competed with the lowing of the cow in her stall just down the hall, and the occasional *pop* from the fire. Matthäus shifted several times and took a breath as if to speak twice, but never did.

"Brigita." It was Johann who spoke. "If you wish to stay here, birth your child here, you are welcome. If, however, you would prefer to be sequestered elsewhere, away from prying eyes, we will respect your wishes. But please know we are glad to have you with us."

"If I went somewhere else before anyone in Wittenberg knew, would it protect you all from a scandal? If I simply disappeared?" Brigita's knuckles were white as they lay clasped on top of the table. "I don't know that I can leave Heinrich again so soon. I'd miss him too much."

"Of course, you can't go far," Marlein answered. "I was at Emnelda's place today, and she mentioned that she wished she had a younger pair of hands. Perhaps she would be willing to let you be those hands? And when the time comes for the birth, you could not be in better hands than Emnelda's."

Hope blossomed around the table. Heinrich looked at his sister with raised brows. "Would you be comfortable there?"

"I believe so."

"And your time spent in the infirmary at the convent will make you very useful to her, I'm sure," Marlein added.

"That is settled, then," Diefenbach stated. "We will go tomorrow to speak with Emnelda."

Five of the six seated around the table made ready to stand.

"If I may," Matthäus blurted, his nervous voice staying everyone else's actions. He sat stiff and straight, hands gripping the edge of the table. "I have something else to add."

Everyone sat again, and Marlein couldn't help but feel a little alarmed at the paleness of his face.

"What will happen if someone does see her? Or if this Alscher character comes here?" No one spoke, but the concern on their faces was growing. "What if I married her?"

***

After Matthäus's question, everyone was silent, contemplative, and perhaps a bit shocked. On the surface, the offer seemed to solve a great deal of the difficulty of Brigita's situation. Heinrich couldn't help but wonder, though, if his sister would agree to it simply as a means of escape. At length, Diefenbach asked the question that was likely on everyone's minds. "Do you wish to marry him, Brigita?"

Heinrich felt her racing pulse as he held her hand in his own hands.

"I do not object to the idea," she said. "But what happens when the danger has passed? Matthäus, do you really want to be bound to me, and my child, for the rest of your life?"

The young man, for his part, appeared calm and unperturbed by her question. A smile quirked his lips as he said, "Truthfully, if this had happened even a couple of weeks ago, I'd have said no. After my Petrissa died, I thought I could never risk binding myself to someone again. But since I've begun reading Scripture with Heinrich, I believe that I can do anything the Lord asks of me."

"And He asks this of you?" questioned Brigita.

"It isn't quite as difficult as it might seem, for I have been attracted to you ever since I saw how you care for the children. While I recognize that this is very little time for a courtship, please know that I understand entirely the magnitude of pledging myself to you. I've told you a bit of my late wife, and the pain her death left in me. It has been healing, and because we would be marrying as a means of ensuring your protection initially, I believe it would be prudent for us to continue with the initial plan."

"So, we would marry," Brigita spoke slowly, as if trying to grasp the implications of his suggestion, "but not live as if we are married?"

"Yes."

"That would give them time to continue deepening their acquaintance." Keterlyn's tears had dried, and interest lit her face.

"Heinrich," Diefenbach said, "as her guardian, it falls to you to bless this union or not."

Heinrich's stomach twisted and his thoughts swirled. If he was not earning his law degree to provide for his sister, if someone else would be assuming that responsibility, then what was it for? He felt that the world was shifting around him. Still, because she was his sister and her security was his responsibility and foremost on his mind, he said, "If Brigita is amenable to the union, I will freely bless it. I've known Matthäus three years now and trust your judgment, Diefenbach, in taking him on as an apprentice. I have no objection."

# 36

Sïfrit had nearly floated to his room above the shop after talking far too long with Gwerder. The good mood from the previous evening disappeared the next morning as he battled a horrid headache and stumbled down the narrow, rickety stairs to the shop. He could not help scowling and wincing when he was assaulted by two things that always annoyed him the morning after indulging too much: bright sunlight streaming in through the back door that was propped open to help with the stench of the melting tallow, and Matthäus's whistling.

"Whatever can have you whistling so piercingly this early in the morning, Matthäus?" Sïfrit grumbled as he thumped down onto a stool to stir the tallow in the pot while Matthäus was busy braiding wicks.

Matthäus's already obnoxious grin only grew. "You should congratulate me, Sïfrit. I am to be married soon."

Sïfrit nearly fell off his stool. "What? How'd that develop?"

Matthäus ducked his head in some false show of modesty, Sïfrit was sure, and said, "We have been talking some—"

Here Sïfrit felt obliged to interrupt. "Talking? How does talking lead to marriage? Less talking, surely, would be more likely—"

Apparently Matthäus felt he had to interrupt Sïfrit at that point. "Talking can lead to marriage much more respectfully than other paths. Regardless, she has agreed to be my wife. She's had some . . .

difficulty in the past, though, so we do not plan on living as married people until she is comfortable with it."

"I've never heard anything so ridiculous—" Sïfrit started to say, but Matthäus was on his feet and towering over him before Sïfrit could get another word out.

"I'll not have you say anything disrespectful about Brigita."

The fire in Matthäus's eyes spoke more of his determination than the words of his mouth; Sïfrit didn't doubt him and so nodded wordlessly. Considering Matthäus's aggressive stance, Sïfrit wisely chose not to voice his surprise at the name of the man's bride.

"What we choose to do once we are husband and wife is our business, not yours."

Sïfrit nodded again, holding his breath even as Matthäus breathed deeply and rapidly. After the space of several of those disconcertingly intense breaths, Matthäus shook himself and retreated to his stool and his wick braiding.

"So, you will be married soon. Is that in a month or two, so that there is time for all the niceties women seem to want at their weddings?"

Matthäus leaned forward eagerly, and Sïfrit thought he'd never seen the reserved man so animated. "We discussed it with the Diefenbachs, and while they were eager to contribute whatever food we'd like for a wedding celebration, we decided that a quiet ceremony will be best." Matthäus's face grew stern as he continued, "And by 'quiet,' I mean that you can't tell anyone, Sïfrit. It is a secret for now. Perhaps we will have a celebration later. Heinrich also objected to the expense and suggested that if we wait until summer, he can save the small wage Diefenbach pays him to help around the shop to purchase the necessities."

"In a few weeks, then?"

Matthäus shook his head. "Sunday next. I'll have just enough time to obtain a special dispensation for the hasty marriage."

Sïfrit dropped the paddle with which he was stirring the tallow, cursing as he fished it from the hot, slimy, stinky substance.

"You mean to tell me," he said when he found his voice, "that you, the steady and quiet one, will be married. Sunday next. To Brigita Ritter."

"You have the whole of it."

"And I can tell no one."

"If you please."

Sïfrit grunted. Such politeness, but remembering the fire in the other man's eyes when he dared to express any negative reaction to the news, he had a second moment of wisdom in the space of a quarter-hour and begrudgingly nodded his acquiescence.

"Very well, I shall tell no one. But what will happen if anyone challenges the marriage later, due to the odd nature of the wedding?"

Matthäus returned his gaze for a moment, perhaps considering whether Sïfrit had a valid question or if he was merely taunting in a less-obvious manner. Sïfrit wanted to be offended, but could not find it in him, due in part to the usual course of their conversations—largely, him taunting Matthäus—and in part to his still-raging headache.

"There will be no doubt," Matthäus finally said slowly, "of our marriage being legitimate."

"Oh, so I suppose you don't merely talk, after all."

Matthäus's glare, still so unusual for his perpetually kind face, caused Sïfrit's heart to tremble ever so slightly.

"Her brother has given his assent, the wedding will be witnessed by the family and performed by Father Martin, and anything beyond that is no business of yours."

Sïfrit considered his answer and, supposing that the marriage likely was not important enough to be challenged, did not press the matter.

Several days later, when the couple was married, Sïfrit was still feeling bewildered, even without the obnoxious headache that had plagued him all that first day of finding out. Still, when he met Gwerder and Alscher at the tavern for beer and mutton later that evening, he refrained from mentioning the wedding. Why, he could not say, for he had never felt particularly loyal to Matthäus. Still, he did not see what good it would bring him to break Matthäus's confidence, however stupidly it was given. Sïfrit had no desire to test the validity of the threats in Matthäus's eyes to cross him regarding his new bride, Brigita.

***

The wedding occurred without fanfare. Before Mass the following Sunday, they met at the doors to the *Stadtkirche*, Brigita wearing the nicest gown she had that Marlein had made over for her. Father Martin met them all with a wide smile. He asked the party gathered if there were any impediments to the marriage, and when there were none, he spoke the rite of marriage and blessed their union before God. They all then proceeded into the church and attended Mass.

The next day, Matthäus remarked to Heinrich that his second wedding was much like his first, regarding the lack of celebration.

"Is that so?" Heinrich replied as he carried a trunk full of his sister's dresses that Marlein had helped her fashion from several old gowns of her own.

"Yes. Though the presence of my bride's family is a nice difference."

Heinrich smiled, understanding what all this man was taking on for the sake of his sister. He felt an uncomfortable gratitude at the protection Matthäus offered that Heinrich himself was unable to provide.

"It seems this is the last of it," Matthäus said as he hefted the handles of the cart into which they had piled the trunk, a chair, and a crate of candles. "Is Brigita already at Emnelda's cottage?"

"Yes. She, Marlein, and Keterlyn took the children and went this morning to help Emnelda prepare. I imagine they're sweeping and scrubbing the place clean."

"I remember when I first came here to work for Diefenbach how odd it seemed to me that this family is so involved in the lives of so many people. The tiny town I grew up in was a very solitary place. Each only concerned himself with his own."

"The Diefenbachs have suffered their share of tragedy, and I think it's taught them the value in supporting one another."

The two men continued conversing idly as they made their way across the snowy field and pulling the cart. Heinrich helped to push from behind a few times when the wheels got stuck or the ground was too uneven to allow easy passage.

"There you are!" called Marlein as they approached. She stood in the doorway to shake a large piece of heavy cloth, face flushed and strands of hair hanging from the sides of her hood. "We've been waiting for you and all but driving Emnelda batty with our incessant activity." She folded the fabric and carried it to one of two cubby beds in the wall.

"Brigita will use this bed," she said, indicating the one that she was spreading the coverlet over.

Heinrich and Matthäus got to work unloading the cart. Once everything was arranged and Brigita's bed made up, they shared the meal that Marlein had stewing over the fire.

"I'll be along to stock the woodpile at least twice a week," Matthäus offered.

"And I'll be bringing meat and cheese and bread whenever we have it," Marlein added.

Warmth spread in Heinrich's chest. Emnelda had been more than willing to host Brigita, even before any promise of assistance. These people truly cared for her. He hoped that her healing would soon begin.

"Well, now, everyone," Emnelda spoke up. "I surely thank you for everything—"

"Thank us? But you're the one taking me in," Brigita interrupted.

"Don't be ridiculous! I'm an old woman and have needed an assistant for years. I'm so grateful that you are here," she said to Brigita, clasping her hands warmly. Then turning to Heinrich and the others, she assured them, "I'll do my best to be good for her as I know she will be for me."

Keterlyn surged forward from her place on an old stool to embrace the woman. "Emnelda, you've been as a mother to me, and I've shown my gratitude so poorly. I will be visiting more now, as I should have done for years."

"Don't you fret over it, Keterlyn," Emnelda crooned so softly that Heinrich could barely hear her. "God has a way of working healing in His time, for all of us. I know that you have done what you were able."

Not long after, everyone said their goodbyes, leaving Emnelda and Brigita to settle into their new arrangement and rest for the evening.

Luther was eager for the coming disputation in Heidelberg. Finally! A chance to discuss with those who could effect change all that the study of Holy Scripture had revealed to him. That it is not following the Law that saves, as so many of his contemporaries would say (but of course he would not name names . . . yet!), but that the Law can only point out that God is just and good and righteous, and that people are not. But it is the Gospel to which the Law must drive a person, and the Gospel that saves. Yes, this was how he would frame his theses for the disputation, and surely from those sparks of truth, change would begin. God's grace could not be added to, nor did it need to be added to. It was enough!

Even so, he knew that attacking the selling of indulgences directly would not be a prudent way to start. Or so his colleagues counseled him. He planned to outline the faith as St. Augustine taught it, and pray that God would lead them to draw the same conclusions that Scripture had revealed to him. With Easter fast approaching, the university term in full swing, and the disputation at Heidelberg shortly after, he had plenty to keep himself occupied.

His quill flew across the paper, scratching and looping and dashing as his thoughts poured from his heart and mind. Too often, the blasted instrument leaked ink or smudged what he was writing, but he didn't have time to stop writing, for the thoughts flew faster than he could write as it was. Perhaps the next time young Ritter offered to cut his pen tips, he should accept.

A knock on the open door of the nearly empty lecture hall jarred him from his thoughts and his pen stabbed into the paper. Thank the good Lord that these were merely his notes, or he would be very cross indeed with the person who interrupted.

"Father Martin? Pardon me for intruding, but I wish to speak with you."

He turned to see the man standing behind him, though he knew the voice before he saw his student. "Young Ritter. I was just thinking of you. Here for more advice to wait?"

"No."

The silence stretched, so Luther asked, "And how are the newlyweds?"

"I mentioned when we spoke to you before the wedding that the circumstances surrounding her pregnancy are such that she holds no blame for its occurrence." Heinrich shifted on his feet as he spoke, seeming unable to find a comfortable posture. "Now, I fear that healing is a terribly slow process for her. I think she still blames herself, still feels the taint of a sin that is not hers."

Luther allowed himself time to consider before he answered. "I cannot claim to know the mysteries of a woman's mind, young Ritter, and even less so for one who has experienced such violence against her person. I do know, though, that God is a God of mercy, and His mercy extends in an unmistakable way to the downtrodden. We must trust in His mercy, and trust that He will bring healing to your sister."

"If you think so." Heinrich's voice betrayed his doubt.

"I do. Pray for her, speak words of comfort and mercy to her, assure her that while all have sinned, her sin lies not in this. And that Christ's blood suffices for it and for everything. You and Matthäus have been reading Scripture together, yes? Encourage him to read it to her. You can, as well. It is in His Word that we find hope and healing, and His Word alone."

"Why is it so easy to say that to someone else, and less so to absorb it in one's life?"

Luther chuckled.

Heinrich shifted uncomfortably a bit more, then blurted, "I think I am in the wrong school."

This surprised Luther, and he did not suppose after the last few months that much young Ritter said could surprise him. "What do you mean? You've nearly finished your studies."

"Yes, but . . ." Brow furrowed, the young man shifted, paced, and fidgeted with his hands before he crossed to the window ledge and sank defeatedly onto it. "Her struggles aside, my sister was married, by you, to a good man who can very well provide for her as soon as he finishes his apprenticeship, and she is cared for until then. I was studying law to provide for her. I am not needed for that now."

"Ah, I see." Luther steepled his hands, considering what the young man before him had just said. "Tell me, then, young Ritter, what it is you would do if you hadn't that responsibility from the beginning."

"I cannot say." His bowed head lifted, hope and annoyance and embarrassment fighting for dominance on his face. "But I can say that now, now that I am free, I think I should like very much to study theology."

Luther fought back a chuckle. He didn't wish to discourage the young man, should he think the laughter was derisive. But what irony!

"I have long thought that you would excel in such a course of study. However, as I knew your aim was the provision of your sister, and you'd never said anything of the sort to me, I did not suggest a change to you."

"I suppose it is too late now, anyway." Weariness belonging to a man much older than Heinrich weighed his words.

"You likely should finish your law degree," advised Luther, "as you are so close to it now."

"Yes." Heinrich shrugged. "Besides, I haven't the means of paying tuition."

"Ah. Well, young Ritter, I shall pray that God guides you in the way He would have you go. If He truly wants you to study theology, He will provide a way."

Heinrich's lips pressed themselves into a small smile before he nodded his head. "Yes. He will. More trusting in His mercy, yes?"

Luther believed Heinrich would do well studying theology. He showed great aptitude for it, after all, and was even teaching what he'd learned to Diefenbach's apprentice Matthäus. That man needed grace if ever anyone did. If what he heard from him in confession was any indication, guilt from his wife's death had plagued him for years. But Luther trusted that God's Holy Scripture was working in his heart, as it was in his own. Matthäus had been smiling more, and when greeting Luther after masses, now looked him in the eye. It was over a month since he first did, soon after his wedding to Brigita, and Luther found his heart encouraged by the sign of God's Word, living and active in this man's life.

"Before you go," Luther said as Heinrich stood, "have you the time to trim my pens? I can never seem to bring myself to stop writing long enough to do it."

The young man smiled, then laughed. "Of course."

Heinrich finished the first pen quickly and handed it to Luther. He immediately dipped it in the inkpot and positioned it to write. Before he did, though, Luther was still a moment, watching Heinrich's movements on the next pen and contemplating.

God's Holy Scriptures, active, working, transforming lives.

Excellent, truly excellent to witness.

Suddenly, he bent to his paper, scratching furiously with his pen.

\*\*\*

Matthäus arrived at the small cottage just as the sun began its descent in the sky; Diefenbach had allowed him to leave early today to run an errand. Brigita let him in, as Emnelda was crouched over the large pot hanging close to the fire, stirring and occasionally adding a pinch of this and a dusting of that. He did his best not to stare, but it seemed Brigita's belly had grown almost twice as large since their wedding. He supposed if she wished to keep her secret, she would not be able to leave the cottage much past Easter.

She was uncomfortable, if her inability to meet his eyes was any indication; whether the discomfort stemmed from his presence or from something else entirely, he couldn't say. Matthäus knew that her past haunted her, even as his own haunted him. Just yesterday, though, Heinrich had counseled him to perhaps try reading some of the Book of Galatians to her. Brigita needed healing, and while he wished he could help her, he knew that only God's Word would be able to speak to her heart, as it had to his.

"Good afternoon."

She nodded in return.

"I, uh, I have something . . . a gift, of sorts." Interest sparked on her face, and Emnelda peered over her shoulder to watch as he stepped outside to retrieve the small cradle he had fashioned. Lyngstrom, in the shop beside Diefenbach's, had assisted him in finding a quality piece of wood and allowed him the use of several of his tools. It was not a splendid piece, but sturdy and a good size for a new baby.

"Matthäus . . ." Brigita breathed. He looked up to see a tear drip from her watery eyes, her lips pressed together and her chin trembling.

"I thought you might need it for the baby." He despised how bashful he felt, but was gratified to see the smile that spread across her lips.

"Th-thank you," she whispered.

He returned her smile, a bit awkwardly, and gently clasped her upper arm for a moment. "Where would you like me to put it?"

When she indicated the corner nearest her bed, he carefully placed it there. Stepping back toward her, he asked, "Have you a moment to sit and read with me?"

"I never had much opportunity to learn."

"Neither did I," he replied, "but your brother has been teaching me. I've copied some things, and I can show you the letters that make the words, and how the phrases are formed."

She glanced over at Emnelda, who nodded before shooting him a secret grin after Brigita had turned back to face him.

"Very well, then. If we sit by this window, there should be light enough to see."

Matthäus pulled the two seats that Emnelda was not using over to the window before retrieving the paper he had tucked into the cradle. Heinrich had provided it after the two men discussed sharing words of Scripture with Brigita. When he turned back toward the window, she was perched on the stool, her back arched and her legs somewhat sprawled to accommodate her baby. He couldn't help the smile that overtook him.

"I know I look ridiculous, and I'll thank you to keep quiet about it." Mock haughtiness drew her shoulders back and her mouth curled downward into a sneer.

"I see Marlein's firmness of speech has left an impression on you," he teased gently, causing her to dissolve into a brief fit of giggles.

"I would be very happy to show any resemblance to her," Brigita finally said. "She is a fine woman."

"Yes, but I believe that you are a fine woman, as well."

Brigita's face flushed at the apparently unexpected admission from him. "You do?"

Careful to meet her gaze in hopes of communicating his sincerity, Matthäus asked, "Would I have married you if I didn't?"

She didn't answer, so he let the matter drop and instead held the paper out to her. "Do you recognize any of those words? Or letters?"

"I know my letters," she said as she studied the paper. "I see the word *Christ*."

"Very good! Anything else?"

"Well, *I* and *live*. Oh, and *no*. I'm not sure what it is saying, though."

"Let me read it to you," he offered. Rather than taking back the piece of paper, he pointed to each word as he read. "'I have been crucified with Christ. It is no longer I who live, but Christ who lives in me.'"

Silence filled the cottage, save the occasional scrape of wood against iron as Emnelda continued to stir her pot. "This word is *crucified*?" Brigita asked eventually.

Matthäus nodded.

"In German or Latin?" she asked curiously.

"German."

Brigita's voice was hushed when she asked, "Are we allowed to have Scripture in such a common language?"

"Heinrich told me that Father Martin said that God wants His people to know His Word," he assured her. "That even the translation from the original Hebrew and Greek into Latin was an attempt to put it into the language of the people. But most people don't read Latin now."

Silence.

Matthäus waited, remembering how he had needed time to turn the words of the Scripture verse over in his mind when he first heard them.

"So, Christ is in me?" Brigita's voice was doubtful.

"He is."

"But I'm—"

"Baptized into Him? Yes."

"Filthy." It was whispered.

He wanted to shout indignantly, but forced himself to match her whisper. "You are not."

"I feel it." The pain flowed through her words to pierce his heart.

"It isn't the same," he said, his voice embarrassingly hoarse, "but I thought the singe from the fire that took my first wife would never leave my soul."

"Did it eventually?"

"It's lessened."

"How?"

"Knowing that Christ lives in me."

"I feel"—he could scarcely hear her as she breathed out the words—"that my body disgraces Him."

"No, child." It was Emnelda who spoke this time, from over in her corner; Matthäus didn't know how she'd heard her words. "His Spirit brings honor to your body. Redemption."

No one spoke. Brigita stared at the paper, occasionally tracing the letters Matthäus had carefully copied. Matthäus sat quietly, praying and hoping. Eventually, Emnelda rose and retrieved some small stoneware bottles and began ladling the liquid from her pot into them. It was late when Matthäus left the cottage, his heart warm and full.

# 38

Easter came and went. The celebration of Christ's resurrection held a great deal more poignancy this year than years past, as its all-availing nature fully permeated Heinrich's heart. He prayed those around him in the sanctuary found similar significance in the celebration.

A few days later, the joy of the resurrection was still inspiring a jaunty stride and ready smile on his lips. Additionally, it seemed spring was finally there to stay. Winter, with its short days and cloudy skies, had been pushed from the land by sunshine and a great expanse of blue overhead. He breathed deeply as he exited the university building, having just sat through his last lecture of the day. He still was unsure whether he would find a way to pursue a degree in theology after this term, but he was unconcerned for the present. God's mercies were literally springing new every morning, and the soil, budding leaves, and warmth for the first time in a long time made the air sweet.

Making his way toward the shops, he noticed a crowd of about twenty or so men gathered and murmuring among themselves. Angry tones and furrowed brows came to his ears and eyes as he drew nearer, and when he heard Emnelda's name, fear thrust itself into his veins in an icy deluge, driving away his enjoyment of the sunshine. The mob suddenly took off toward the outskirts of town, to the west, in the direction of the Diefenbach house and Emnelda's cottage.

Heinrich didn't hesitate to take off after them, cutting through the forest. He stumbled on roots and undergrowth, but managed to keep his feet as he pushed onward. His breaths came with difficulty, and he found himself wishing that he ran more often.

He broke through the tree line, just thirty paces or so from the cottage. But the mob was already there. As he drew up behind them, two men emerged from the cabin, dragging out first Emnelda and then Brigita. He saw Marlein follow of her own free will, fear and anger written all over her face. She was saying something to the men, but he was too far away and the mob too noisy for him to hear. They began shouting accusations, Willeic Gwerder leading them.

"She despises me! She enchanted one of those bees of hers to sting my son with a poisonous spell."

"I heard that she dances with Satan every Saturday night!" cried another.

"See the girl with her?" hollered still another. "Emnelda conspired with a devil to cause her to conceive!"

Heinrich managed to push into the back of the group and could hear Marlein's voice calling over the crowd that they were all being ridiculous, and Emnelda's feeble attempts to tell Gwerder that her refusal to end the pregnancy of his mistress was no cause to blame her for the death of his wife's son. No one else seemed to hear Emnelda's or Marlein's words, though, and the crowd pressed closer still. He looked again to Brigita, whose face was ashen and tear-streaked. He couldn't imagine what memories flooded her at being so manhandled.

He could rush to the cottage and try to protect the women, but what was he against so many men? If he could find Father Martin, he would be able to help; the man commanded a crowd easily, and because he spoke strongly against witchcraft, the crowd would listen to him defend Emnelda. Heinrich knew Luther saw her devoutness, for he visited her regularly and prayed for her.

## CHAPTER 38

Even that, though, would take more time than Emnelda, and now Brigita, had. Feeling his only hope for aid lay in the Diefenbach house, he turned and sprinted across the field.

***

Marlein stood in the doorway, behind the men who were holding her friends in place. Fear for them coursed through her, racing against relief that the men had left her be. For now. She apparently was well-respected enough to be ignored in this mob trial. The dutiful daughter who disdained marriage to care for her ailing mother.

When she noticed Heinrich in the crowd, relief overtook the fear momentarily, but she immediately noticed that he was alone. Just before he'd taken off across the field, he'd locked eyes with her, and she felt he was trying to tell her something, but she couldn't decipher it. Her heart sank as she watched him disappear, even as she knew he was seeking help.

She wished she could call after him, to warn him that no one was at the house who could help. It was only her *Mutter*.

# 39

The side door burst open, startling Keterlyn enough that she stabbed her finger with her needle. She stared at the welling drop on her fingertip, deep red and shiny and fascinating.

Heinrich was speaking, and her attention was finally snagged at the words "Marlein, Brigita, and Emnelda." She forced herself to hear his words.

There was a group of men about to accuse Emnelda of witchcraft, if they hadn't already. He was asking if anyone else was home, and she finally looked up, taking in his frantic face.

"They could be in danger."

While Diefenbach had taken the children to the shop to help put the candles in crates, Marlein had taken advantage of the free time to visit Emnelda and Brigita.

"Is there anyone else here?"

There was no one else in the house, save Keterlyn.

"No, Heinrich. I'm alone."

Both were silent, fear shooting between their glances and thickening the air until it was nearly suffocating. For Keterlyn, though, the pressure inside her chest was worse than the silent exchange with Heinrich. Both she and Heinrich may fruitlessly wish for different circumstances, but it was her heart prodding her to action that was truly causing her discomfort.

For the first time in years, she *wanted* to do something more than drown in despair. There were times when she felt closer to her old self, but they were so seldom, and she had no control over when the gloom might momentarily lift. But now, she wanted to fight the gloom, to move away from it. Keterlyn stood from her place near the fire's warmth. She wanted to march from her house over to the cottage, through the crowd, and embrace her dear old friend, her strong, capable daughter, and the young, frightened girl who would soon be blessed with a child of her own.

But therein lay the problem: if she went, Keterlyn would be forced to face the darkness within her.

To defend Emnelda, she would have to share that it was only the woman's care and love that prevented Keterlyn from taking her own life after her latest baby was lost. Four after Marlein's birth, then the three girls and boy survived, and now she mourned the loss of a fifth. Almost as many babies dead as alive.

She stumbled backward and would have tumbled into the open hearth, had Heinrich not lunged forward and grasped her arm, steadying her.

"Are you unwell?"

She couldn't answer, not truly, so she simply shook her head.

"Kete . . ." He stopped to clear his throat of the emotion that had suddenly clogged it. "Keterlyn. I . . . I have not been a friend to you, and for that I am sorry. We are to bear one another's burdens and I . . . I've more . . . resented you for your burdens than wanted to take them onto myself. I love your daughter, but she would never marry me because of her love for you and desire to help."

"That girl bears everyone else's burdens and holds her own too close."

"She and the others have a terrible burden now," he reminded, his voice cautious and his hand squeezing her shoulder gently.

"I will go with you." To her own ears, her voice sounded weak, so she made another attempt. "I will go with you."

"Are you certain?"

Rather than answer—because no, she was not certain at all—Keterlyn marched decisively toward the side door, which was swinging on its hinge from when he had burst into the room. At the threshold, she hesitated.

A firm, warm hand tentatively touched her own, increasing pressure until her palm was pressed firmly into Heinrich's.

"I'll be there, too, with you." He leaned close before whispering, "Bearing your burdens."

Lips pressed between her teeth to hide their trembling, Keterlyn nodded. They stepped from the house together.

\*\*\*

Heinrich, still holding Keterlyn's hand, approached the crowd. It was a paltry defense against the small mass of men, but he hoped and prayed that God would aid his cause. He politely but firmly made his way through the crowd, pulling Keterlyn along in his wake. Marlein smiled briefly when she saw him approach, but it drooped as the grumbling grew louder.

Looking back at Keterlyn, Heinrich saw that her face was ashen, mouth moving with no sound. It appeared that she would not be able to address the crowd as he'd hoped. Drawing on all his experiences debating with other students at the university, he turned to face the crowd.

CHAPTER
# 40

"Good people of Wittenberg," Heinrich began.

"Now, Ritter," interrupted Klaus, the basket weaver with two young children, "you are respected about our city on account of your devotion to the Diefenbach family, even with the apparent state of your sister's associations. I suggest you stand down if you do not wish to suffer our bad opinion."

"Thank you for your consideration, Klaus," Heinrich began, "but tell me. Did you hear Father Martin's homily on Sunday? He spoke of God's grace and mercy poured out in Christ for all the world, and His Spirit poured out on all Christians. I ask you, how can you treat a fellow Christian in such a manner?"

"She consorts with the devil!" called someone from the back of the small crowd.

There was a general murmur of consensus, stirring up and causing the crowd to shift and even surge forward.

"She charmed her bees to kill that boy!"

Heinrich followed the eyes of many in the crowd to look at Gwerder. He was a wealthy fellow, dressed in velvet and furs, a leader in their community and a known adulterer. It was his face that struck fear in Heinrich's heart. A self-satisfied smile appeared for a moment before being hidden by a grimace of feigned pain. Heinrich wondered what had transpired to so raise his ire against Emnelda, to bring these false accusations to her door. For they must be false; the Diefenbachs lived in closer association to Emnelda than anyone. If she was practicing witchcraft, they would know.

"She never forgave Gwerder's father for encouraging his friend to marry Keterlyn's mother instead of her."

This was news to Heinrich, but a glance at Emnelda's face showed only sorrow, and no animosity at all. He didn't understand how these men could level such accusations.

"Emnelda," he said, forcing his voice above the murmuring of the gathered men, "you have been accused of consorting with the devil. Is this true?"

"It is not."

"Are you then a Christian?"

"I am."

"What of her not attending Mass?" asked a man by the name of Sommer.

"My joints ache so that I can only walk twenty or so paces before I have to rest. Father Martin or another of the priests in the city comes to say Mass over me at least twice a month."

"And my family brings her in a cart when she is able," Marlein piped up.

"How often do you attend Mass, Sommer?" another called out. This was followed by some laughter, which faded in discomfort as they all realized there was a more serious issue at hand.

"What . . . what of the bees?" Klaus finally asked. His voice was decidedly less confident than it was the last time he spoke. "You've been working with them for years with no ill effects."

The calm patience on Emnelda's face belied the severity of the situation as she asked the man holding her arms if she might be released to roll up her sleeves. When she did so, there was a scattering of sting marks and small welts on her forearms.

"One of the hives split the other day, and I was helping them settle into a new hive, and this is the thanks they give me for my efforts. As you can see, I've been stung plenty of times."

"What of Keterlyn Diefenbach? Did you not curse her?"

Silence. Like a clap of thunder, it was ominous and tense.

Heinrich opened his mouth to speak, but a light pressure reminded him that he still held Keterlyn's hand in his. Pale and trembling, she nodded her head at him before releasing his hand and stepping over to wrap her arms around Emnelda's frail shoulders.

"No." Her voice was raspy, weighed down with emotion. She cleared her throat and continued. "She did not. She helped me."

Emnelda leaned her head against Keterlyn's, grasping her arms with gnarled hands. "Keterlyn, you don't have to."

But she was already shaking her head. "Yes, I do," she whispered. Aloud, for all to hear, she declared, "She saved my life."

A murmur went through the crowd like wind through a field of barley.

"I don't know why God allowed so many of my babies to die, but it was not at the hand of this woman. I was so lost, in so dark a place, that I despaired even of life. But He sent her to find me, bind up my wounds, and hold my hand while I cried. I confessed that I did not want to live. She held me tighter while she said that she knew I didn't. But she reminded me of my family, and their need for me. I have not been able to be the mother I should, but God has been healing me.

"After Emnelda found me, and saved me—"

"It was God, not I," interjected Emnelda.

"I avoided her because of my shame." Keterlyn released Emnelda's shoulders and reached down to hold onto her hand. "But now I see that such avoidance has not helped me, and it may very well harm her. Emnelda, I am deeply sorry. Will you forgive me?"

"Of course, child." Tears streamed down Emnelda's face, mirroring those on Keterlyn's.

"I have been so lost, so caught in the mire of my sorrow, but I can't stay there. We can't blame others for our misfortune when it isn't their doing. We are all broken. I know that more than most."

The silence remained for a time, punctuated by an occasional ragged breath, as Keterlyn and Emnelda held one another and wept silently. Marlein stepped forward and gently stroked both women's hair and shoulders. When Brigita attempted to join them, the man holding her arms called out, "And this girl? If she's living here, she isn't living with a husband. What are we to assume?"

"I am the father of the child!" called a loud voice that Heinrich had not heard since he was home last. Those nearest Nikolaus Alscher stepped back from him, making it easy for Heinrich to find the rake who had inflicted so much pain and harm on his sister. "I am prepared to marry her, after discussing a dowry with her brother."

Rage flared in Heinrich's chest. Heart thundering and the sound of rushing water stifling his senses, he could see nothing but his sister's tear-streaked face and broken posture as she confessed what had been done to her before the Diefenbachs, Matthäus, and him.

Several people had begun to speak at once—gasps of surprise, questions as to their relationship, and even some unnecessary speculation. But a gruff voice from the back of the crowd sounded over them all.

"She is *my* wife." Heinrich had never heard Matthäus speak so loudly, so confidently. "What happened to her is no more your concern than it is her fault. We were married in the winter, to secure her good name."

The murmuring was not quelled, but every accusation had been refuted. No one seemed interested in hearing more of Gwerder's blustering. Emnelda's reputation, Brigita's reputation—both were intact. Heinrich and Matthäus guided the ladies back into the cottage, and Marlein poured some weak wine into a pot to warm over the fire as everyone settled into seats with careful relief. Peeking through the door, Heinrich saw that the crowd was dispersing slowly in groups of two and three, discussing what had occurred. Klaus and Sommer both glanced at the house and met Heinrich's eye. Both shot him remorseful grimaces.

But not one word of apology was spoken.

# 41

Nikolaus was displeased. More than displeased, he was angry. Incensed. Infuriated. There were no words sufficient to describe how cheated he felt. He'd worked for such a long time at the smithy, bided his time and planned a way to compromise her. If he'd known all along that she was pregnant, he could have forced her into marriage before winter set in. He wasn't certain the child was his, but the timing seemed about right, and she hadn't acted afterward like a woman who would run out and immediately find another lover. But no, in the time since he took her those months ago, and possibly impregnated her, she had married. His child would be raised by another man. And worse than that, the shop that should have been his would belong to that ridiculously hulking man.

Had she seduced him soon after and convinced him the child was his? He couldn't possibly know she was pregnant by another man and still be willing to marry her. Could he? What had been his exact words?

*What happened to her is no more your concern than it is her fault.*

Perhaps he did know. One thing was clear to Nikolaus, though: he could not stay in Wittenberg. After claiming publicly to have sired a married woman's child, none of the connections he'd made in the city looked at him with welcome anymore. Instead, they shot him poorly concealed looks of disgust and contempt.

He ducked his head and hurried toward the city; he would clear out the cramped room he rented and leave for Braunschweig at first light.

A hand on his arm made him leap a good foot in the air, heart racing and fists raised to defend himself.

"Whoa-ho, man!" laughed Heinrich, enjoying his reaction far more than Nikolaus liked. "A little jumpy, are you?"

"Ritter." Nikolaus was in no mood to deal with the man who thought he was too good to continue in trade, but had to go and receive an education.

"You are returning to Braunschweig, yes?" The words were formed like a question, with the inflection of a question. But Nikolaus didn't miss the command behind them.

"Of course." He glanced over Heinrich's shoulder, then had to look up to sneer at that hulking brute's face, who'd claimed to have married the wench. "There's nothing for me here."

Surprisingly, the giant's face remained impassive, rather than growing murderous as Nikolaus expected.

"In that case," Heinrich drew Nikolaus's attention back to him, "I have a business proposition for you."

"And what is that?" he asked.

"I want to sell my shop."

"And?" He stared at Heinrich for a heartbeat. "You can't think that I have that sort of money."

"No, but just like there's nothing for you here in Wittenberg, I find that there's nothing for me in Braunschweig. I don't want the shop anymore."

Nikolaus sighed heavily. "And what do you want me to do about it?"

"Find a buyer." The calm confidence in Heinrich's voice was a far cry from the anger and hostility he'd expected when the man first approached him. It was unsettling. "I've written here how much I want for the place and everything in it." Heinrich extended his hand, a piece of paper in it.

"You don't want any of the trinkets?" Nikolaus studied the sum and saw that it was considerable, but certainly a fair price. The shop was in good repair, sturdy and spacious enough, and in a prime location in the city. He looked back up at Heinrich.

"No," Heinrich said as he shook his head, "I do not. You can have any surplus you are able to get for it."

Nikolaus pondered Heinrich's words for a moment. He could ask his father to buy the shop. Coin was hard to come by, even with the growth in the economy of crafted goods and the expansion of the merchant class in recent years. Still, if he could manage to acquire the amount on that paper, the shop could be his without the need to be shackled by a tiny scrap of a wife he'd thought would be necessary to obtain the building. Even if she had filled out some carrying a child and was more pleasing to his eye than when she lived with his family.

"I'll see what I can do," Nikolaus said, careful to allow just enough disdain into his voice to avoid Heinrich learning how pleased he was with this turn of events.

"I expect to hear from you within a week."

A week was a short time, but he knew that Heinrich's expectation was reasonable, with the appeal of the shop's assets. He offered his hand as a pledge to report back within a week. After forcing himself to meet Heinrich's eyes as they shook, he glanced over at the giant. Emboldened by the neutrality on his face, he asked haughtily, "Pleased with your acquisition? Seems to me that I got the better end of it."

The other man's face turned deep red, almost purple, and he shouldered in front of Heinrich, who stepped back with something almost like a smirk on his face.

"Listen to me, and listen carefully." The man's voice was low, gravelly, and dangerous. Chills shot down Nikolaus's spine, and he wished he'd kept his mouth shut. "When you leave Wittenberg, no later than tomorrow, you will never return. I don't want my wife upset by the sight of your slimy self. If you do return, it had better not be for a year, and you had certainly better be coming in repentance and sorrow for what you did to her."

"She wanted—"

"No. She did not." The voice was new; Sïfrit had joined them. For a moment, Nikolaus had hoped for an ally, but soon saw the ugly scowl on the young imp's face and realized he'd been the one to speak.

"Sïfrit Hahn," he scoffed "I see you've decided on a less . . . jovial pair of companions."

All three men were looking at him, stone-faced, and he decided to cut his losses. "I will hire a courier to carry my report to you within a week, Ritter."

"Very good. If I do not hear from you, I will assume you were unable to find a buyer and I will come to Braunschweig myself to dispatch the property."

Nikolaus nodded to communicate that he understood, then turned and promptly tripped on a branch lying on the ground behind him. He wanted to scream his rage for all to hear, but instead righted himself and stomped away.

***

"Emnelda and Brigita simply can't stay in that cottage, so far from anyone, by themselves." Sïfrit had not spoken the words, but he agreed with them wholeheartedly.

Keterlyn had spoken what was on everyone's mind, almost before the adults had settled around the hearth at the house, just hours after the near riot at Emnelda's cottage. The fire was burning low, warm wine was passed around, and the children had been bundled off to bed. Sïfrit felt that most likely, everyone in the room shared the conviction with which she spoke. He'd always figured she was just a slothful woman, content to lie abed while her daughter did the work.

Perhaps that was part of why he enjoyed flirting with Marlein—the clear fact that she could never marry while her mother shirked her duties and the children were too young to keep the household running. Marlein was a prisoner. No commitment from either would ever be necessary, despite how much he flirted or how much she would like to leave. But he wasn't sure she wanted to leave, as she never gave any indication that his flirtations were welcome.

Still, it humored him to see her grow flustered.

Now, though, he was ashamed of his thoughts. Several around the room murmured their consensus, drawing Sïfrit from his musings. He was glad he'd broken ties with Gwerder, if he kept company with men like that Nikolaus Alscher. He'd been heading in a bad direction, worse even than what he'd believed about Keterlyn.

He felt as though his eyes had been opened after years of blindness.

She wasn't slothful, but rather fighting demons he had never considered. And Brigita! The girl was pretty, and perhaps that had been more a curse than a blessing in her case. Sure, he flirted even when it wasn't necessarily wanted, but he thought back to the times he'd leaned close to her to make some remark or other and she'd stiffened. The instances he had complimented her and she'd appeared almost frightened. The innocent touches to her arm or wrist, and her face blanched as she turned away from him.

He was sunk to a new level of worm.

And Matthäus, whom he'd mocked for being unable to read, had been able to read Brigita's fears and hesitation and offered her kindness, patience, space, and compassion. He felt as though his world had shifted, and nothing that had been familiar remained.

"I—" Sïfrit's voice was rough and nearly cracked. He cleared his throat before making another attempt. "I agree."

He clenched his jaw, feeling foolish for speaking once all eyes in the room were fastened on him. In a matter of seconds, though, eyes blinked or lowered, and the focus went to Diefenbach, who had stood from his fur-covered chair and cleared his throat.

"I agree, as well. Things cannot remain as they are. The cottage has only two beds, though. I suppose a pallet may suffice for a time, if Heinrich or even Matthäus—"

"Oh, I don't know about that," objected Matthäus. "I doubt she'd be comfortable."

"You are her husband," Johann reminded him.

"That is true, Diefenbach," Matthäus conceded. "But it is not a usual marriage, and I do not wish to impose upon her."

Matthäus shot a sideways glance at the girl as he spoke. As far as Sïfrit was concerned, that was Matthäus's only fault, ridiculously good man that he was. Honest, kind, patient, and altogether too careful.

"I . . . I think I would feel comfortable with Matthäus sleeping on a pallet in the cottage." Brigita spoke slowly, careful as Matthäus. "But what about Maria?"

"Well, she could stay with us, in the girls' room," offered Marlein. "If there isn't room for her there."

"Or she could sleep on the pallet with me," Matthäus added.

"Or in the bed with me." Brigita laughed a little. "I suppose there is no difficulty in that regard."

"It seems that all involved agree; I will walk with Brigita back to the cottage and discuss it with Emnelda." Johann looked over to Heinrich. "If that is acceptable with you."

"Of course, but perhaps it is her husband you should ask." His smile was a bit wry.

Everyone laughed, likely relieved to have something dispel the tension the earlier commotion had left in joints and limbs and heads. Sïfrit knew he was not feeling himself, and none of it had even directly involved him.

He stood with the others, feeling an urge to speak with Brigita, to apologize for any offense or discomfort he might have caused. But she was standing near the side door of the house with Matthäus, discussing something. He instead withdrew, exiting through the front door, and turned toward his small room above the shop.

It suddenly seemed a very lonely prospect.

# 42

Johann drew his wife into a tender embrace.

"They are settled safely, Kette."

She nodded into his shoulder. He had just returned from accompanying Matthäus to the cottage, and Emnelda had been more than happy to receive another tenant into the small space.

"It hasn't been this full since my *Mutti* and *Vati* were still living." She had chuckled in delight. In a more serious tone, a couple of breaths later she had added, "I think having Falk here will be a blessing. I feared for my life earlier today, but more than that, I feared for poor Brigita. Her time will soon come, and unpleasant excitement could easily make it more difficult for her, if not deadly."

Now, back in his home with his wife, Johann felt weariness like he'd not experienced in a while.

He buried his face in the side of her neck and sighed deeply, something he hadn't done in years. "Today could have ended so badly, Kette." As he breathed in, the scent of her calmed him, soothing his aching heart.

She nodded against the side of his head. "I know. I almost couldn't go, but Heinrich helped me."

"Is that so?"

"Yes." She withdrew a bit, took his hand in hers, and led him to his chair. After gently pushing him to sit, she perched on his lap.

"We haven't sat like this in ages, my dear," he commented. Noticing her weight on his lap was considerably less than he remembered, Johann asked sternly, "Have you been eating, *Ehefrau*?"

She had the good grace to look chagrined as she answered, "You know more than anyone the answer to that. I can say, though, that I have hope for perhaps the first time since . . . since the first was taken from us."

"Hope for another child?"

She just shrugged at that. "Whether we are given one or not, I have hope that life can be good again. Hope that someday, I will heal."

"It gives me great happiness and relief to hear that."

"Well, I can't credit myself with it. Remember when I said that Heinrich helped me?"

"Yes."

"Well, he helped with more than getting me to go to the cottage."

Just then, Heinrich opened his door and stepped from his room. "Sorry to interrupt," he began awkwardly, staring at his booted feet, "but I needed to speak with you both and wasn't sure when another opportunity would come."

"Of course, Heinrich." Johann grinned as Keterlyn rose from her place with him to go sit on the bench near the wall. "What's on your mind?"

"I've spoken to . . . an associate . . . about selling my shop." He fidgeted with the sleeves of his shirt for a moment before rushing on. "Years ago, my father had bought it outright, reasoning it was less of an expense in the long run than paying to lease a shop. I plan to use the funds from the sale to support myself in pursuing a second degree. With Brigita married, I no longer need to support anyone but myself.

I already spoke to Matthäus, and kind man that he is, he insisted that he needed no dowry for her, as he'd never planned on marrying this quickly and has no immediate need of it. I did decide, despite what he said, to lay aside a portion to assist in setting up a shop for him when he is ready."

Johann listened carefully, wondering why he needed to speak to them privately about this.

"Of course, the funds may not entirely cover my expenses, so I wanted to know whether you'd consider hiring me, to work in the evenings and weekends of course, for odd jobs. I do a fair job at trimming candles and can muck a stall or mow a field as well as Steffan."

"Likely better, given the strength that age has not yet stolen from you," commented Johann. "Yes, I'd be happy to hire you, if needed. That doesn't answer, though, why you needed to speak privately with us."

"Well, given that Brigita and Matthäus are becoming more comfortable with one another, and that Emnelda is having so much more difficulty living by herself, I thought you might invite her to come live here soon." He paused as Johann exchanged a raised-brow glance with Keterlyn, but continued when neither spoke. "I know that I have been staying in your son's room, and it would make most sense for her to sleep there. Might I suggest I take Matthäus's room above the shop? I could rise early before morning prayers at the university to light the fires or assist Sïfrit in whatever needs doing."

Johann considered silently for a moment. Heinrich had been very helpful as part of their household and seemed to fit well and comfortably into it. Now, he was asking to change the arrangements.

He must have taken longer than he thought to consider the request, for Heinrich added uncomfortably, "Unless you plan to take on another apprentice, now that Matthäus has completed his time with you? I could let a room in the city; there must be houses not yet filled with students."

"No, I do not plan on taking another apprentice. On our walk, I asked Matthäus if he would be interested in joining me as a partner." Heinrich's smile told of his appreciation for the gesture. "He is a good worker, more skilled than any apprentice I've ever had. And we've grown quite fond of him and Maria, as well as your dear sister. We would like to keep them around a bit longer, and when my Johann returns, I believe he and Matthäus will get on just fine. If not, Matthäus is free to strike out on his own."

Heinrich nodded. "He returns in a year?"

"Yes, and none too soon. I am ready to let go of some of the responsibilities; these bones of mine are not as young as they once were. You see, age *has* stolen much of my strength."

"You are quite determined to leave us then, Heinrich?" asked Keterlyn. Johann had almost forgotten her presence, so quiet had she been throughout the exchange, from where she sat on the bench.

"Only for a time," he answered immediately. "I hope to, possibly, join the family again in a much more permanent fashion."

"Marlein?" Her voice was hushed.

"I want to study theology, and I don't believe that God is calling me to enter a monastery, but I can't exclude that possibility. Regardless, I think it best if I wasn't under the same roof as her for a time."

"Are you asking for her hand?" Johann wanted to be sure he understood.

"Not yet. I suppose more declaring my . . . hopeful intentions." Heinrich's grin held a touch of self-deprecation. "I never really expected to be at a point where it would be possible, but after today, seeing that more than I'd imagined in life is so very tenuous . . . I figured that perhaps it is best not to allow opportunities to pass."

"And studying theology and perhaps courting Marlein are two of those opportunities?"

"Courting her would be . . . wonderful. If it seems that God allows, I will gladly pursue her. And theology . . . the pull is too strong to deny. I have been studying with Matthäus almost daily the three books I have of Scripture, and doing so with a man learned in what the Word of God contains . . . I cannot think of anything I desire more. Even Marlein, if you'll forgive me for saying so."

"There is nothing to forgive, Heinrich," Keterlyn said right away. She rose and approached to take his hand. "I would be beyond honored to call you a son someday, but never apologize for desiring to follow the Lord more than desiring the person you love. For a time, I misplaced my love, and it led to years of heartache for me."

Johann's throat was suddenly suspiciously swollen and he coughed roughly to clear it.

"I lost sight of a good deal during the dark years following the loss of my children. As I lay abed these last few months, though, I often heard you and Matthäus discussing together as you studied. The bench you used is between your door and mine, and it was difficult not to hear."

"I am sorry if we disturbed you."

"You did at first, but never apologize. I had lost hope, but it found me through the words the two of you spoke."

Heinrich offered a small smile, sincerity shining in his eyes. "I am heartened to hear it."

"For so long, I supposed that my poor babies, lost either before they were given the chance to be born or before they could perform penance for the sins they had committed . . . I worried about them in purgatory, without me to comfort them. And I felt that God wanted nothing to do with me. I could not keep nearly half of my babies; they left me.

"But as I listened to the two of you read aloud these past weeks . . . that God is mercy and love. And you read passages that said He is. It

... it was as though you were speaking to me, that those words were for me. It is just now breaking through that perhaps I was not as broken as I'd supposed, for He held me together and . . . and might, someday, even use my brokenness to help others."

Johann's throat was swollen again. And his eyes burned and even watered terribly. He gritted his teeth against it, trying discreetly to clear his throat and swallow the threatening tears.

"Keterlyn, this is precisely why I want to study theology." Heinrich's voice was filled with conviction and peace. "There is so much to learn! I had a misunderstanding of what God expected of us, but in Father Martin's lectures, I have seen that He expects nothing but grateful service. Not penance, though that is certainly good exercise for one's soul. Not disdain for those struggling, but support and help. Not empty repetition of words we don't know, but engaged study of His Word in Holy Scriptures."

# 43

Heinrich was running late. Unfortunate, considering the decision he'd come to regarding his education and future, but it couldn't be helped. After yesterday's stressful afternoon, long evening, and late night, he had overslept and barely had time to say good morning to Marlein or anyone else around the gruel he was shoveling before he hurried toward the university. As soon as he was moved into the room above the Diefenbach shop, he wouldn't have to travel as far in the mornings. Neither would he see Marlein so often, but considering the state of his feelings toward her, he had to admit that it was for the best.

As Heinrich approached *das Elstertor*, he saw someone leaning against the wall nearby. Drawing nearer, he recognized the red-blond hair of Sïfrit beneath his flat hat.

"Heinrich!" called the young man as he approached. "I'd hoped to run into you."

"Is that why you're waiting here?"

"Yes." He chuckled, looking down and jerking his hat from his head. Could he be . . . self-conscious? "I, uh, I wanted to know—"

"Listen, Sïfrit, I'm happy to give you the seven minutes I have until lecture begins, but I must walk quickly, or I'll be late. Otherwise, I can come to the shop after, if you think it will take longer." Heinrich said the last portion as he strode past him.

"No! That's fine."

Heinrich heard Sïfrit jogging; then he was abreast of him and try-ing again to speak.

"I wanted to ask about . . . about Brigita." He faltered when Hein-rich turned and quirked a brow at him. "Uh, I mean, have you known all along what . . . what happened to her?"

"I've known since just before Advent."

"Oh."

"And Matthäus?"

"Just after the Epiphany. He learned of it just before their wedding."

"Even though . . . I'm assuming from what he said at the cottage yesterday that the child isn't his?"

"No, but he will be a father to him. Her. Whichever it is."

"I see."

They were silent and approaching the courtyard. "Was that all, Sï-frit?"

"Well, no. But the rest can wait." They'd stopped, and Sïfrit bounced on the balls of his feet a few times. "Actually, no. I wanted you to know that I appreciate what you did for them. The women, that is. I mean, I respect it. I think I've been concerned with . . . unimportant things for quite some time, but am now beginning to realize that is no way to live. I thought that you should know."

Heinrich finally understood what he was trying to do. "Sïfrit, I ac-cept your apology. And I beg your pardon for my short temper with you in the past."

The younger man's face cracked into a smile. "Thank you, Hein-rich. That's very good of you, considering what it looked like I was trying to do with your sister and with Marlein. I think . . . Well, I'm not sure what I was thinking, but I'd like to talk more with you, another time."

"Of course. I should go now, but we will have plenty of time to talk later," Heinrich finished as he turned and tossed the rest over his shoulder, "seeing as we will be roommates soon."

"What's that?" he heard Sïfrit call after him.

"I'll tell you about it this afternoon!"

\*\*\*

Marlein had a warmth in her heart that had nothing to do with the oven into which she was sliding the special wedding *Springerle*. Because Brigita and Matthäus had married quietly, Keterlyn and Marlein decided they needed a celebration. It would take place in June, more than a month away—plenty of time for the *Springerle* to be ready and the flavor to develop fully. Marlein's heart was warm because her mother had been in the kitchen with her every day since the frightening experience outside Emnelda's cottage just a week ago.

"Shall we go to the market for some bread after these finish baking?" Keterlyn asked after Marlein had straightened her posture and pushed the hair from her face.

"That sounds lovely. While we wait, I wanted to finish the hem on the dress for Brigita."

She had found a lovely rose fabric to make a dress for Brigita. She thought the girl—woman, really—should have something new to wear at the celebration of her wedding. The baby would be born by then, and Marlein was making it accordingly.

"I have some plain linen in my room. Does she need a new chemise?"

"Most likely." Marlein smiled at her mother, so glad for a reason to do so.

Keterlyn returned the smile. "I'll start on that while you work."

After she fetched it and ripped along the fabric's weave to make several rectangles that could be stitched and gathered to fit Brigita's frame, the women sewed quietly for several moments. When the smell of the biscuits reached their noses, Keterlyn spoke.

"It is good to be out of my room and around these sounds and smells again."

"It is good to have you here with me," Marlein answered, reaching to clasp her mother's arm for a moment.

"I am feeling well now, daughter," she cautioned, "but I am afraid it will not last."

Sadness washed over Marlein, cold and dark. "How long until you stop coming out here with me? With us, I mean. With us."

Keterlyn reached to gently grasp her daughter's shoulder. "I can't say how long until it becomes hard to come out. But I will. I must. You must help me, though. If I am not out by sunrise, come in to make me get up. Your father is kind and honorable and good, but he can't bring himself to be firm with me. I will need it." She swallowed, then drew in a great breath of air. "Will you do that for me, Marlein? Will you help me remember the blessings I do have, rather than ignore them in my sorrow?"

Marlein's eyes were full and her heart overflowing. "Of course, *Mutti*."

"You are a good girl, Marlein." Keterlyn sewed a few stitches before looking up with a sly smile. "And perhaps, in very little time, you will be a good wife."

"Oh, I won't—"

"Don't be so sure. I dreaded thinking of it, but I am learning to look forward to the day. I will be more healed by then, and I think that when Brigita and Matthäus are ready to live alone under the same roof, with his daughter, Maria, we will invite Emnelda to come live with us. There is no doubt I will have good friends after you are gone."

"I'm not even sure who I would marry."

"Don't be foolish, girl." The words would have been harsh, if not for the light laughter behind them. "Did you know it was your Heinrich who has helped me the most?"

Marlein almost felt sad that someone who was a stranger until a few years ago had helped her mother more than anyone in their family had been able to. Then she realized that perhaps it didn't matter where the help came from; did not the Lord work in ways beyond her understanding?

Aloud, she only said, "He is not *my* Heinrich."

"I have seen and heard you two together. He clearly sees himself as yours."

"I do *not*—"

The side door burst open, and Marlein's words fell silent. "Marlein!" cried Aldessa. She had been at the cottage with Maria and the other Diefenbach children to learn from Emnelda what plants were good to eat and which would cause illness. "Emnelda said to fetch you. Brigita's baby is coming!"

The women hurried to store their sewing, grabbed baskets with rags and broth, and followed Aldessa across the field back to the cottage.

Inside, the windows were all thrown open, allowing sunlight to stream through, flooding the place with light. The children were working in a corner, plucking leaves from the branches and placing them in a basket. Emnelda hobbled along, supporting Brigita as she paced the floor. Tendrils of hair damp with sweat clung to the sides of her flushed face, looking more brown than blonde.

"Emnelda," Keterlyn said, "I'll walk with her. Why don't you prepare whatever poultices or tinctures we might need. Marlein, can you take the children with you and tell the men at the shop that she is laboring?"

Marlein nodded, secretly relieved she wouldn't be there. She had assisted with one of her mother's births, and the experience was not one she wished to repeat very soon. Still, before she bundled the children along, she stepped up to Brigita after the current rush had faded and gave her a quick embrace.

"You are in good hands. I will petition the Lord on your behalf, and be sure that Matthäus and Heinrich are ready to come and see you whenever you send for them."

Brigita nodded, but said nothing as she began panting again, another rush overtaking her.

Marlein hurried the children outside.

"What is wrong with Brigita?" asked Leonetta.

"Is she hurting?" Maria added.

"Hurt?" echoed Fridolin. The young boy had just recently begun talking.

"Nothing is wrong, children; she is preparing to give birth. Do you remember when the cow had her calf last year? How she paced and paced before it came?"

Aldessa tugged on her skirt and asked, "Will they have to pull the baby out like Steffan pulled out the calf?"

"We will pray not." Marlein picked up her pace. "Come, let's go and take a meal to the men, and tell them the news."

"News," cooed Fridolin.

They stopped at the house to fetch some cheese and the last of the dried apples, then proceeded to walk into Wittenberg. Aldessa carried Fridolin on her back when he got too tired to walk, and Marlein allowed Maria to carry the basket. They swung around by the university on the chance Heinrich was finished with his lecture, but he was not in sight. The *Markt* was their next destination, to purchase bread. After that, they proceeded to the shop.

Inside, the sweet smell of melting beeswax met their noses, and Marlein was glad it was not a tallow day.

After Maria had handed Diefenbach the basket, Marlein said, "Please be ready to come when we send word. Brigita is laboring, and we expect the baby to be here before tomorrow morning."

Matthäus stood from his stool where he was braiding wicks. "Already?"

"Ready!" gurgled Fridolin.

"Emnelda did not seem concerned, so neither should we be."

He nodded, sinking back onto the stool.

"I suppose after all this unpleasantness, you and she will take the children and try to start over somewhere?" asked Sïfrit.

"Where!" cried Fridolin.

With a fond smile at the tot, Matthäus shrugged. "I don't know what the future will hold, but I'm certain that God will provide for us in some manner or another."

Sïfrit didn't answer, and Marlein wondered at his new quietness. He was always one to have the last word in the past.

"I should get the children home and feed them. Fridolin will be needing his nap soon."

"No nap!" pouted Fridolin.

Everyone chuckled.

"He's an outspoken little thing since learning to speak, isn't he?" chuckled Diefenbach.

## CHAPTER
# 44

Brigita's baby girl was born that evening, after supper had passed and the children were tucked securely into bed. Keterlyn came at dusk to tell everyone that Brigita had safely delivered. She adored her tiny daughter and was eager for everyone to meet her. Diefenbach said that he could wait until the morrow and so waited at the house with his wife and the slumbering children as Heinrich, Matthäus, and Marlein set out with lanterns. Sïfrit seemed to hesitate when Matthäus invited him along, but eventually said that he should get back to the shop.

Heinrich offered Marlein his arm as they walked, and she was grateful, as the ground was uneven and the lantern's light somewhat dim. She hadn't had a chance to clean the glass recently.

"Do you know what she will be named?"

"I was just about to ask you the same thing!" Heinrich laughed. "I suppose we shall find out soon enough. Matthäus, do you know?"

The other man pressed his lips together, hiding a small smile. "I'll let Brigita tell you."

Heinrich chuckled at his friend. "Will you be taking the child to the church tomorrow?"

"Yes." Matthäus grinned bashfully. "Never imagined I'd have opportunity to bring another little one to be baptized."

They continued walking happily until they reached the cottage door and were admitted by Emnelda. Her face was weary but happy, and Brigita's weary but brilliant. Matthäus approached first, stooping to kiss Brigita's forehead where she lay in the cubby bed in the wall. She held the infant in her arms, the smile never leaving her face.

"This little one may have been born from a dark time in my life, but my happiness could not be greater than in this moment."

"I am happy to be her father, if you wish it." Marlein noticed that Matthäus had left his hand resting on Brigita's, where it held the tiny bundle. His face radiated joy and peace, quite unlike most of what Marlein had witnessed in him.

"I do."

Heinrich came closer then, pulling Marlein along.

"What will you call this little one?" he asked. "Marlein and I realized we had no idea what it might be."

"She will be baptized as Lucia," whispered Brigita.

"An Italian name?"

"St. Lucia's day was back in December, but it means *light*, and since about December, God has been shining the light of His Word into every part of our lives," Matthäus explained. "It's the light that has awakened us to His grace and mercy . . . for us both."

Brigita yawned then, her hand slipping from Matthäus's and flying up to cover her mouth. "I am sorry! I think maybe I need to rest."

"Well, dear," interjected Emnelda, "you haven't eaten in hours, and you've just performed one of the most strenuous tasks a woman ever will."

Both men in the room looked a bit uncomfortable, but chuckled good-naturedly when the women laughed together.

"Here, Brigita," Marlein said, reaching into her basket and pulling a cloth-wrapped piece of bread and some salted meat. "Eat to restore your strength; then you can sleep."

Brigita accepted the food, breaking off some for Emnelda before she devoured the rest. "Heavens! I think I've never been so hungry, even when I went without for a few days on my journey to Wittenberg."

"Might we offer our thanks to God?" spoke up Emnelda. "Heinrich, why don't you pray."

Heinrich looked startled to Marlein, but he recovered well as he cleared his throat and murmured, "Let us pray, then. O Lord, our God, who has delivered countless infants from their mother's wombs, we thank You for this safe delivery. Grant that Brigita recovers well, and that her child grows and thrives. Be a comfort, O Lord, to those mourning the loss of a child, and bless all parents with love and good discipline for their children. For the sake of Your servant, Christ, we ask this. Amen."

The cottage fell silent for a few moments. Marlein could scarcely believe how much had changed in just a few short months. There were moments of immeasurable pain, but to see how God was moving in their lives, to see that He was a God of love who was living and active in the lives of His people—it was a blessing beyond anything she had ever expected could be.

The tiny cry of a baby broke the silence.

"Someone else is hungry!" chuckled Emnelda. "It's hard work to be born too, you know."

"We should leave you, Brigita," Heinrich said. "Matthäus, I assume you will come for Maria on the morrow?"

"Yes. Thank you, Marlein, for keeping her."

"'Tis no trouble."

Heinrich came near and bent to smooth some of the hairs back from her face, dropping a kiss on her forehead as he did so. "You did well, sister."

"Thank you, brother." In a rare moment of mischievous mirth, she added for his ears alone, "I hope that soon you will be welcoming your own little one."

His face was so alarmed she almost burst out laughing. "What can you mean, saying that?"

"Only that if I'm right, you'll be married very soon."

"No, I won't be."

She was certain Keterlyn was doing better. Didn't that mean that soon Marlein would not be needed as much?

Heinrich leaned in and whispered in her ear. As she listened to his words, her happiness and her smile grew, expanding until they almost hurt.

"Oh, Heinrich, that is wonderful news. You run along now. It is late. We'll be fine here."

She smiled widely at Marlein as she came to give her a hug.

"I am glad you and Lucia are well, Brigita," her dear friend said.

Her face was hurting from smiling so much, yet she could not maintain even a neutral expression. "Thank you. Good night, Marlein."

***

"Are you sure you shouldn't go get Maria now?" Brigita asked after Matthäus had followed them to the door and barred it behind their guests. "I've grown accustomed to having her sleep with me."

What she meant was that she felt more comfortable with the little girl there, to act as a barrier between her and Matthäus. She trusted him entirely, but being in a group with him was not the same as being alone with him, after Emnelda went to bed.

"We are married, Brigita," he reminded her, "so there would be nothing wrong in it. And I will sleep on the floor, as I have these many nights before."

With a tired nod, she acceded.

Over the past weeks, she had found his presence to be comforting—first with his visits and then when he began sleeping on the floor near the hearth—but she still felt oddly unsettled around him.

It was finally beginning to sink in that she was not to blame for what Nikolaus did to her, but shame still haunted her at odd times. When Matthäus held her hand as he had earlier. When she observed his pleasant form. When she saw Diefenbach and his wife speaking closely, in low tones. And sometimes even in the middle of doing a chore like cleaning a dish or sweeping out the hearth, suddenly she could feel his hands on her skin and his breath on her face and she wanted to run to the stream and scrub herself clean.

But when Matthäus was near, even though he knew the truth, he looked at her with kindness, with compassion, maybe even with love, and she felt whole again. Those moments had increased in frequency since their marriage, and she hoped for a time in the future that she would find only comfort in his presence.

"Are you sure you want—"

"Yes, of course. Maria is safe and sound asleep at the Diefenbachs', and I want to be near you; I have slept here every night since . . . well, since that day."

Feeling her face warm, she said with all the courage she could muster, "Then, Matthäus, I'd also like for you to stay."

Matthäus moved to a corner to ready himself for bed. Emnelda hobbled about, doing the same. Taking advantage of a moment alone, Brigita braced herself before pulling open her chemise and bringing her fussing baby's mouth to her breast. After a few moments of discomfort, Lucia found a comfortable pattern and Brigita relaxed. She was glad Emnelda and Keterlyn had helped her teach the baby to suckle before everyone arrived; Lucia had not taken to it as easily as she had expected. Matthäus, for his part, was standing near the fireplace, staring into the white-hot wood as it burned.

"Thank you for giving me a moment, Matthäus, but she's feeding well now, and I'm covered."

He turned with a sheepish smile and said, "I hadn't thought I was that obvious."

Brigita took a deep breath to steady her nerves and banish the shame that tried to creep up on her. "Would you like to share the bed? There is room for you, and it would be more comfortable than the floor."

He seemed to hesitate a moment before asking, "Are you certain?"

She smiled at the irony of his question and used his own words to answer him. "We are married, so there would be nothing wrong in it."

He smiled then, broad and bright and beautiful. The bed was about the same size as the one she had shared with Marlein, but Matthäus was larger than her friend. Much larger. As he climbed into the bed, over her feet, she giggled at the way the straw tick mattress shifted.

"Sorry."

She just smiled over her shoulder at him as he settled carefully beneath the covers behind her. They were both quiet for a time, and she listened to his breathing grow slower. Emnelda must have gone to bed, for the two candles that were lit had been extinguished and the cottage was silent.

"Matthäus?" she whispered. "Are you asleep?"

"No, I'm awake still."

"Are you . . . is this . . . sad for you?"

"Is what?"

"Having a wife again. After . . . Petrissa."

"Oh." He was quiet for so long a time that she wondered if he'd fallen asleep. When he did speak, his voice was gruff. "A little. We were so young, and so sure of what life held for us. So very much in love."

"I know you miss her very much." Brigita knew he'd only married her to protect her, and perhaps a little for his daughter to have a mother. That his wedding her was something of a sacrifice, for her good. She couldn't help but hope, though, that someday he might love her just a little. But she didn't say any of that to him.

"I do miss her. But I also have come to a place where I think I'm starting to heal. I was never so distraught with grief as Keterlyn, but there were days that it was all I could do to rouse myself from bed in the morning. Caring for Maria was nearly impossible some days."

"You won't need to care for her alone anymore," Brigita reminded him. "Once I recover, that is."

She felt the vibrations from his chuckle, as well as a puff of his breath on the back of her head. "Take your time. Petrissa stayed in bed for nearly an entire week after delivering Maria."

"Thank you. I am very sleepy right now."

"Understandably."

Just as she began to speak, a yawn overtook her, cranking open her mouth and popping her jaw.

"You should sleep," he chuckled again. "You'll never recover without rest."

"I think Lucia has fallen asleep. Let me put her in the cradle and—"

"I will," Matthäus interrupted. She wanted to protest, but he was already climbing over her legs and from the bed. "You rest."

"Yes, sir." She smiled as he took the infant carefully and gingerly, cradling the tiny bundle in one arm while using the other hand to pull the heavy cradle flush against the wall of the bed. He kissed the baby's soft cheek beside her slightly parted lips.

"Sleep well, little one." He got back in the bed and stretched out beside Brigita, whispering to her, "Sleep well, my slightly larger little one."

"I know I am small, but I'm more than *slightly larger* than a baby."

"But you're still little."

Brigita chuckled. "Compared to you." She snuggled under the blanket, tired and sore and incredibly at peace. She knew she didn't deserve it, but God had seen fit to see her through this ordeal and even bless her with a tiny little family. She wasn't sure what would come next, but with the light of God's Word guiding her, she knew she could face it.

# 45

Heinrich nudged Marlein's shoulder as they walked slowly back to the house. She glanced over at him in the light of the lantern he carried, a question in her eyes.

"I can scarce believe that Brigita is a mother."

"Is that so?" She tucked her hands beneath her apron, a habit she had that made him smile. As if she had to hide her hands if they weren't being industrious.

"Brigita has always been a sweet, cheerful girl," he admitted, "but she never showed any inclination toward, well, *that.*"

"She has grown much since you left home, hasn't she?" Compassion softened her voice.

"Too much."

Marlein's laugh, so spontaneous and carefree, blew away the angst he felt concerning the sudden and complete maturing of his sister. Not only had she endured such a violent crime against her, but she was healing and even beginning to flourish in the aftermath of it. The way her face glowed as she gazed at her baby, and the shy happiness when Matthäus clasped her shoulder affectionately—those things made him hope that she would, someday, recapture a portion of the girl she once was. The woman she could become.

"Do you not think she will thrive in this marriage?" Marlein's voice was thoughtful.

"I do. She has a kind husband, who has also suffered in his life. I believe that together they will encourage each other to heal."

Marlein smiled at him, saying nothing. He noticed how frequent her smiles were this evening.

"You seem to be very happy right now."

"Certainly, I am!" She laughed as she spoke, shaking her head disbelievingly at him. "My good friend, your sister, has successfully delivered her child, and both are healthy. How could I not be happy?"

"How is your mother?" he asked. "She likely can't help but remember her own losses in such a time as this."

"We spoke of it earlier today." Marlein was quiet for a time. When she continued, her voice was hushed but buzzing with the urgency of her conviction. "She is fighting, Heinrich. For the first time, she wants to fight the melancholy."

"Then she is not much affected by this birth?" he asked with a sideways glance.

"Not in the way that we might have expected. She seems to have risen to the challenge of helping and offering support to Brigita."

They fell quiet for a time, enjoying the cool air and the sounds of frogs and crickets, come back to life after the winter's cold.

Heinrich began drumming the fingers of his free hand against the side of his leg as they walked. He was trying to think of how to broach the subject on his mind. They were nearing the house, passing the fence surrounding the garden area.

"Did I tell you," he said rather abruptly, "that Nikolaus Alscher sent word that his father will buy the shop from me?"

"No, you hadn't." Her steps slowed to match his.

"I found out yesterday." He swallowed, his nerves suddenly a bundle of discomfort in the pit of his stomach. "He agreed to pay installments over the next few years."

"Will you draw up the contracts when you receive your law doctorate?"

He laughed a bit at the irony of it. "Perhaps, but I've decided not to practice law."

"No?" She stopped walking in her surprise.

They were just beside the woodshed, and Heinrich balanced the lantern on a relatively even log.

"No." Taking a moment, he looked down at his booted feet to collect his thoughts. Suddenly feeling awkward, though he had rehearsed this conversation in his mind so many times, he cleared his throat and swallowed the nervous knot lodged there. Gathering his courage, he lifted his head and stared straight into her eyes. "I, uh . . . I actually plan to return to classes in the fall. I want to study under Father Martin, to earn a doctorate in theology, and the funds that Alscher is sending will finance that."

"Is that so?" She looked down for a beat, and her shoulders shook in a gentle laugh. "I feel very dull with my words tonight."

"Well, I'm not being very direct with what I want to ask you, so it stands to reason that your responses would be rather . . . uncertain. I'm sure you are wondering why I would bother sharing all this with you now, when we are without an audience."

Her eyes reflected the lantern's shining light and her cheeks were flushed, though he wasn't certain if that was from the cool night air or from the same reason that his heart was pounding in his chest.

Her voice was a whisper when she breathed, "You wanted to ask me something?"

"I did. I mean, I do." He huffed out a breath of air. "I'm going to be moving into Matthäus's old room above the shop."

Marlein jerked back, just a bit, and her brow puckered in confusion. "You are? I thought you were comfortable with my family."

He realized he hadn't explained why, and closed his eyes in frustration. "I'm sorry, I didn't explain."

"And you wanted to ask me something," she quipped, some of her easy humor returning.

"I do." He contemplated simply blurting out the question: *Will you* . . . But to be fair to both of them, she needed to hear everything, from the beginning. "I've been thinking for some time about the possibility of studying theology further. The lectures I attended as extra classes have been fascinating."

"Yes, you've mentioned that."

He nodded, excitement at the topic urging him to reach and clasp one of her hands. "Yes, but until recently, it's just been wanting to and talking about it. Now, it's happening."

"Because of the sale of your father's shop?"

He nodded eagerly. "I know he wanted me to go into law, but I believe that had he learned what I have about God and His mercy, he would not have been so worried and distraught at my mother's passing."

Marlein nodded, showing her interest, even though she didn't comment.

"And studying Scripture with Matthäus these past months has been so fascinating and rewarding. To witness faith take hold of his heart, open his eyes, and heal his wounds . . . I can't even express the fulfillment I find in that."

"You wish to be a priest?" She was smiling, but it was stiff and trembled at the corners. He'd have missed the trembling, had he not been standing so close to her—until she pulled her hand from his and took a step back from him.

"I don't think so," he answered thoughtfully, wanting to be as truthful as he could and hoping to give her space by answering her question thoroughly. "Perhaps just for the sake of learning. I could always go back to law, but maybe I will teach theology someday. I want to show others what I have learned. This brings me to the question, Marlein, that I wanted to ask you."

"Yes?"

"As you know, the plan has been for Emnelda to move into your parents' house, and for Brigita and Matthäus to live in the cottage. As soon as arrangements can be made, I plan to move to Matthäus's old room above your father's shop."

"That is not a question," she pointed out testily. "And you've already told me that." He realized she saw it as her parents had at first, that he was removing himself from their lives.

"I've bumbled this, haven't I?" He reached for her hand again, frustrated that his trembled slightly when he felt the cool skin of her left hand. "Marlein, I . . . I came to respect you very soon after we met. You are loyal to your family and love them with a love that I sometimes envy. Soon after, I saw how hard you worked for them all. Cooking and washing and giving to others. It inspires more kindness in me, and has generated a . . . deepening of my feelings for you."

Her eyes were wide and had welled up.

"I love you," she whispered. "I have for longer than I wanted to admit. It wasn't until recently that I began to hope that there might be a day when I would not be needed at home. It will not be for some time, but there is reason to hope that my mother is beginning to heal."

"I will be in school still for several years, so even if she were entirely free of her melancholy tomorrow, I am afraid I would not be ready to pursue a marriage yet." He reached up with his free hand to touch the side of her face. "And you did not allow me to finish my declaration before you made your own." He leaned close, allowing his forehead to rest on hers, and his nose brushed against hers as he whispered, "I love you too."

## EPILOGUE

Luther wearily replaced his quill in the pot, the prelude to a sigh expanding his chest. If the feelings swimming around within him were anything like the apostle John's when he penned the last of the Book of Revelation, he suddenly had a greater appreciation of the man's entire collection of writings. But Luther knew he was no saint, nor were his written words directly inspired by the Lord God.

Even so, he hoped that He had at least guided his pen, even just a little.

The Heidelberg Disputation had been a victory in that everyone had agreed with each point he made in his disputation, even those regarding the Law and the Gospel, which the current teachings abysmally misapplied. Still, Luther could not help but wonder if more might have understood the magnitude of what lay ahead for those convinced of the truth laid out in Holy Scripture. That indulgences were no more than a conniving on the Pope's part to extort coin from poor peasants too ignorant of Scripture to know better. That Holy Scripture was the only source from which man may find the Law and the Gospel, not anything a man claimed he received directly from God apart from that Scripture. That God was a God of love and mercy and grace, as well as a God of justice and righteousness. That righteousness was given to man when he was found to be in Christ, the only name by which he may be saved.

There was still a long road ahead of them. And just now, he had merely finished writing an explanation of his Theses firmer in its wording than anything else he had said or written. They were just scratching the surface of what remained to be done.

But God would guide him. Of this he was certain. For no endeavor toward the truth would not be blessed by the God who is truth.

## AUTHOR'S NOTE

It was with much prayer, deliberation, and even tears that this novel came to be. It was sparked at a Reformation celebration at my church and kindled over the next several months as I read as many books on the history of the Reformation as I could from my history professor husband's library. I spoke with him and with my pastor at different times, as well as with my writing buddy Heidi. When it came time to write, the plot began forming and the characters revealed themselves to me, and the complexities surprised me.

Not only did I strive for historical accuracy, I also strove to be true to life. My intent when I set out to write this novel was a lighthearted romance that showed the light of God's Word dawning on people lost in darkness. What the characters gave me was a bit messier. I considered cutting those parts out—the loss and deep-seated heartache that resulted—but the fact is that life is messy. Shared suffering can move casual acquaintances into a deeper relationship, seeming villains might have suffered unspeakably, and sometimes the most cheerful people we know are holding a world of hurt. So, I left the mess.

As is so often the case in life, it was through the messes in the story that God's working began to show through. His ultimate care for us—sending Christ to pay the price for our sin—did not end with His death and resurrection. These are certainly pivotal moments in history and in the life of the Christian Church, but they are also the moments through which flow His continued care.

He has always been with us in the mess, brothers and sisters.

## ACKNOWLEDGMENTS

There cannot be thanks enough given to those who have helped me with the writing of this book.

Thank you to those who gave of their time and energy: my husband, Karl, and children Chazz, Magdalena, August, and George, who put up with me being glued to the computer for hours on end.

Thank you to those who loaned me books and other resources that helped me gain a full picture of what life was like five hundred years ago: Pastor White, Julie, and Vickie.

Thank you to the amazing editors and staff at Concordia Publishing House, who worked to make this book the best that it can be, Peggy, Jamie, and Emily; as well as Tammy, who designed the book and came up with the map; Holli, the book's marketer; Elizabeth and Lindsey, who help me publicize *A Flame in the Dark* and secured the endorsements; and Sara, Hannah, Pam, Aaron, Laura, and many others, who worked behind the scenes to get this story into print and tell others about it.

Thank you to my wonderful readers, both past and future, and especially my early readers who gave such helpful feedback and suggestions: Gary, Lindsay, Kristin, and Heidi.

Thanksgiving always to God, who saved me and gave me the desire to share His love in Christ in fictional stories that carry eternal truth.

Soli Deo Gloria.

Adult Fic BAUG          200
Baughman, Sarah
Flame In The Dark, A : A Novel About
Luther's Reformation